WORRY BEADS

WORRY BEADS

A NOVEL BY

KAY SLOAN

LOUISIANA STATE UNIVERSITY PRESS BATON ROUGE AND LONDON

1991

Manufactured in the United States of America
First printing

00 99 98 97 96 95 94 93 92 91 5 4 3 2 1

Designer: Amanda McDonald Key
Typeface: Palatino
Typesetter: Graphic Composition, Inc.
Printer and binder: Thomson-Shore, Inc.

Library of Congress Cataloging-in-Publication Data

Sloan, Kay.
Worry beads : a novel / by Kay Sloan.
p. cm.
ISBN 0-8071-1636-X (cloth)
I. Title.
PS3569.L544W67 1991
813'.54—dc20 90-22655
CIP

The author offers grateful acknowledgment to the editors of the publications in which three chapters of this book originally appeared in a slightly different form: *Oxford Magazine,* "Holiday Screening" (Spring/Summer, 1989), "A Private History" (Spring, 1987); *Southern Review,* "The Hermitite" (Autumn, 1990).

Publication of this book has been supported by a grant from the National Endowment for the Arts in Washington, D.C., a federal agency.

The paper in this book meets the guidelines for permanence and durability of the Committee on Production Guidelines for Book Longevity of the Council on Library Resources. ♾

For my family, especially David

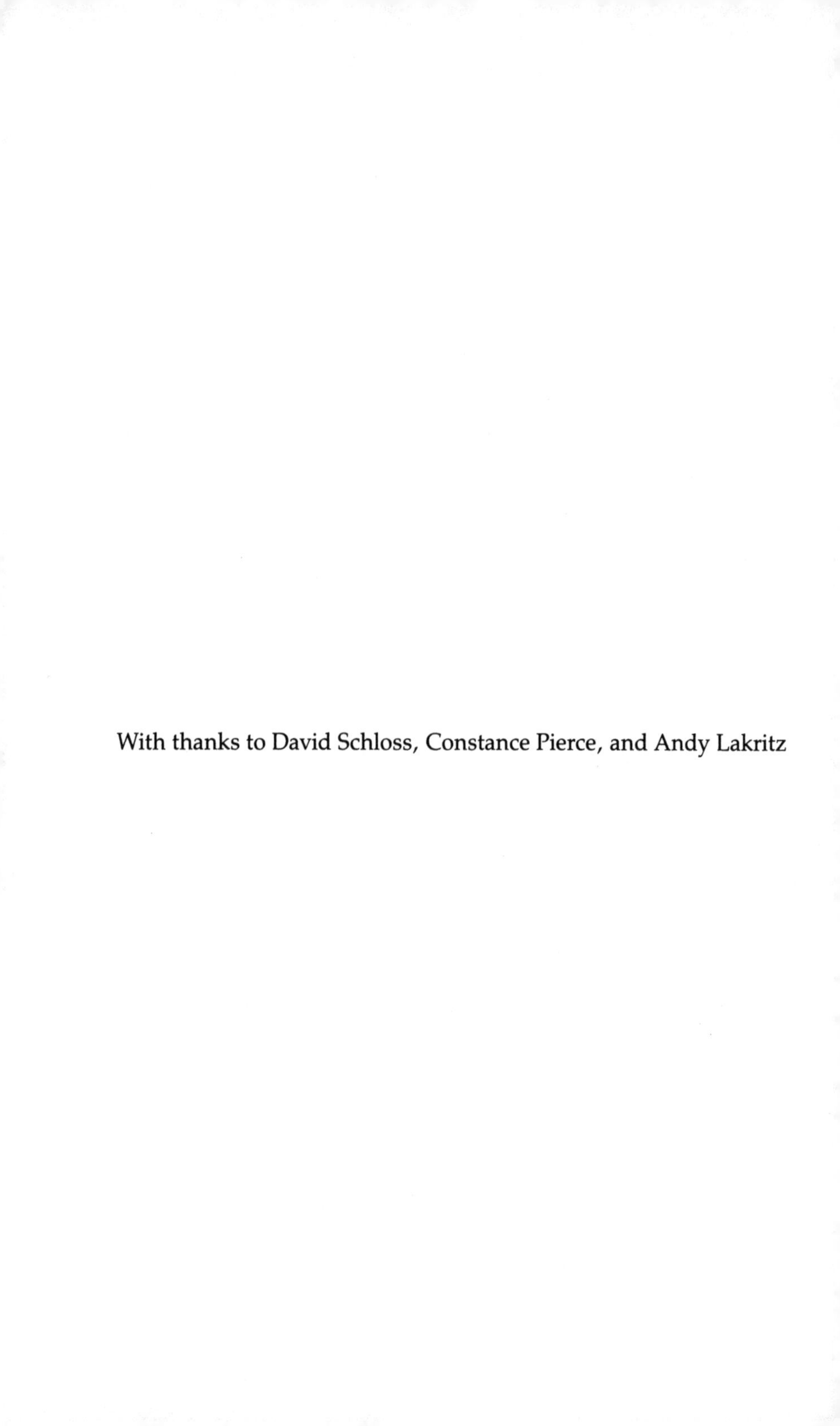

With thanks to David Schloss, Constance Pierce, and Andy Lakritz

CONTENTS

We are persuaded that a thread runs through all things: all worlds are strung on it, as beads: and men, and events, and life, come to us only because of that thread: they pass and repass, only that we may know the direction and continuity of that line.

—Ralph Waldo Emerson, *Montaigne; or, The Skeptic*

WORRY BEADS

ONE

REUNION
1986

Above the rolling hills east of Libertyburg, Mississippi, the July sun bears down on a small park buzzing with noise and activity. Volleyball games, puffs of barbecue smoke, and a parking lot full of variously colored car plates mark a large family reunion. From a rusted pole, an American flag stirs in an occasional breeze, nearly hiding the banner beneath it that reads Welcome: Bloomer Family Reunion 1986.

A green Chevrolet cruises down the gravel lanes among the parked cars, sending dust billowing behind it. In the front seat, Sheridan and Jacob Stern wear nervous frowns, though they have different worries on their minds. Sheridan grips the steering wheel tightly, glancing alternately at the people grouped together in knots in the park and at the dense lines of parked cars.

"Would you look at this?" she asks, surveying the next row of dusty car hoods. "I come all the way from California to a family reunion for the first time in five years and—what do I get?—not one parking space left."

"Try not to take it too personally," mutters Jacob. He is fumbling through a canvas knapsack that he has spread on the floor between his knees, pulling out a ragged road map, a pair of binoculars, and a bag of aging grapes. With a sigh, he replaces the items, and ties the canvas flap shut.

"Well, I left the camera in L.A. all right," he sighs. "Jeez. What a start . . ."

"No camera and no place to park: let's go back to California." She glances at him quickly, looking for the ironic smile she knows will be nudging at one corner of his mouth. Satisfied, she continues, "Sometimes I don't know who I am when I come here anyway." She shoves the gear stick from third back to second and runs one slender hand through her long hair.

"You're still Sheridan Bloomer Stern." Jacob cups his hand behind her neck and smooths out a strand of her hair that has gotten caught down the collar of her shirt. "The best actress to come out of Libertyburg, Mississippi."

She throws back her head and laughs, a sound that lilts above the crunch of the gravel beneath the car's wheels. "At least I'm famous here in Libertyburg. But"—she waves a hand at the crowds—"*there* are your most memorable characters. Not me."

As if the blue sky is a vast circus tent, celebrations buzz on the green stretch of Libertyburg Park. On a dusty square divided by a volleyball net, twelve players argue over which team will have the seventh member, an adolescent boy who stands patiently waiting for the adults' decision, his arms folded across his thin chest. Closer to the parking lot, another cluster of people in bright tee shirts, plaid shorts, and cutoff blue jeans hover around a picnic table, their hands filled with paper plates, plastic cups of beer, and

Coca-Cola bottles. Near them, a handful of variously sized children scream their way down a tall sliding board. A circle of five young girls hold hands and dance in a ring, chanting a song that ends their game abruptly with "All fall down!" The high, faint words reach Sheridan and Jacob in snatches. Above them, the white clouds of a summer afternoon shift and rearrange themselves, refusing to remain long in a single shape, like designs in a slowly turned kaleidoscope.

"Who are all these people, anyway?" asks Jacob. "I don't recognize anyone. Are you sure this is the right park?" He rolls down the window and sticks out his head, squinting.

"There's Mama," Sheridan says, pointing to the picnic table. A plump woman with close-cropped gray hair stands removing the plastic lids and aluminum foil from the many containers there, arranging the spoons and knives, and stooping to check the supply of soft drinks and ice bags. "We should have gotten here earlier," Sheridan adds guiltily. "We slept too late."

"Come off it. Winnie would be just as busy if you'd been there helping her all morning. Besides, your Aunt Virginia just walked up—looks like she's carrying one of those sinful strawberry cakes she's so good at making." Jacob licks his lips. "God, would you look at all that food. And a whole keg of beer."

Sheridan squints down the dusty road ahead of them and adjusts her sunglasses on her nose. "That's Uncle Chester over there. And there's Smitty with him. Poor ole guy. Look how stiff his hind legs are getting."

Weaving his way among the station wagons, the many sedans, and the occasional sports car, Chester Bloomer bears a small spiral note pad in one hand and a pencil in the other. A terrier follows him, sniffing occasionally at a discarded potato-chip bag or candy wrapper. It rests on its haunches when Chester stops behind a silver Volvo. He props one foot on the fender, licks his fingertip to turn a page of his note pad, and begins to scribble there.

"What's he doing out here in the parking lot?" asks Jacob. "Looking to rip off some hubcaps?"

"Not hardly," Sheridan laughs. "He's counting how many states are here on the license tags." She smiles at the distant figure of her uncle.

Hunched over and balancing himself on one long leg, Chester reminds her of an old photograph of her father, a picture taken long before he died over twenty years ago, his life taken by his own hand. In it, her father, Fred, stands in a similar position, angular and awkward, bent over a large trout that he is dressing after the catch, while Chester, his older brother, grins triumphantly at the camera. It is one of the few photographs of her father that she has, and she has always wished that she could enter it, somehow, and ask him to raise his head, to glance at the camera before the shutter snaps the image that will capture him for the years.

"Hey, Uncle Chester! How many states are here?" She presses her foot on the brake and leans both arms out the window.

"Sheridan!" He tucks his note pad beneath one arm and strolls over, his new deck shoes stirring the dust behind him. "Why, that's you and Jacob here in this big old Chevrolet. I've been watching for you two . . . I wondered who in the world that could be with Louisiana plates."

She waves her arm and thumps the side of the car. "Oh, it's rented. We picked it up in New Orleans. Rent-a-Wreck. Like it?"

"As long as it got y'all here, that's what matters." He glances skeptically at the car and then ducks down to peer into the window across Sheridan. He adjusts the brim of his baseball cap in a greeting. "Jacob?" he says. "How you doing? Now y'all just get yourselves parked and come on over to the spread Virginia and Winnie put together. Over there . . ." He points to the far end of the lot. "There's a spot big enough for you. See you at the picnic table. I've got something special to show you, soon as I finish out here." He winks at them and tucks his pencil behind his ear.

Sheridan pulls off slowly, watching Chester in her rearview mirror as he stands and watches them for a minute, his head cocked to one side, a smile on his lips, as if he is remembering something pleasant or amusing. Seeing that image of her uncle makes her suddenly glad that she is here at the reunion, glad that she and Jacob drove in to stay with her mother, Winnie, the night before.

It was not until the last minute that Sheridan had even decided to come. She and Jacob had been on a trip to New Orleans, sent there by the company Jacob works for in Los Angeles editing industrial films. On occasion, he finds the money to make his own experimental films in his spare time. By coincidence, the nineteenth Bloomer family reunion had been scheduled for the weekend they were due to fly back to Los Angeles, and after several persuasive phone calls from Winnie, they had agreed to rent a car and drive up for the festivities.

"It'll be madness," she had promised Jacob in a bar on the rooftop of the old Jax Brewery in New Orleans' French Quarter. A half-moon had risen over the Mississippi River, making yellow ripples in the wake left by a barge. "Mama'll spend Saturday night teaching us how to can tomatoes, Grandma Bloomer'll try to convert you to the Baptist church again, we'll get a numerology reading or a tarot consultation from Aunt Virginia, and Uncle Chester . . . well, you remember his jokes."

But Jacob was looking forward to it. "Hey, I haven't seen some of your family since our wedding. Think about it: your cousins, it's been ages since I saw Amanda and Ruby Ann. I always liked them, you know, and ten years is a long time."

She raked salt from the rim of her margarita with the tip of her finger, and licked it off. Lapsing into silence, she settled back into her chair to watch the barge moving slowly down into the Gulf, and idly began twisting the emerald ring on her finger, a gift from her Aunt Virginia when she first left home years ago.

It all had to do, she decided, with things Jacob might never understand, a New Yorker trying to be part of a southern family. In the first years of their marriage, he had tried, she knew, to learn the language of her family, the generational codes and the acquired mannerisms of his newly acquired relatives. But in the last several years, she herself had wondered how well she knew her own family. The longer she lived in California, the more returning to Libertyburg became like going through a looking glass for her, so that she didn't know who Sheridan Bloomer Stern was anymore. She had looked in backstage mirrors at her face and seen a thousand moods, recognized the emotions of the hundreds of characters that she had played, usually on obscure stages in southern California. Yet, despite all those rehearsals, she still seemed to feel her way half-blindly off that stage and back into Sheridan—becoming like those other faces on the neon-lit streets below her now in New Orleans, sitting in those countless smoky bars, or strolling beneath the trees of that park that was Jackson Square, all those people still feeling their way along the dark corridors that wind between birth and death, touching faces with fumbling hands, searching for the script, the way out, the way in.

Coming back to Libertyburg always made her feel somehow lost, despite her family's love, despite all their attempts to help her and her mother in the long years after her father's suicide.

And that was it, after all, wasn't it? It all came back to the suicide, she told herself, seeing not the Mississippi River anymore but the memory of herself at sixteen in 1965 and . . . well, it all had to do with things Jacob couldn't possibly understand. Not, at any rate, the way it made her feel, the deep hollowness she glimpsed when she returned.

Now, in the park at the outskirts of Libertyburg, the strains of Bruce Springsteen's "Born in the U.S.A." come faintly across the grassy fields where a ghetto blaster has been placed in the outfield beyond the softball diamond. Chester Bloomer greets both Sheridan and Jacob with beers that froth with deep heads left by the spray of the keg. From the table behind him, he gathers up two plates of barbecued chicken and coleslaw and passes the food to them. Then he holds out another canister and shakes it gently, as if it too contains food. Sheridan starts to reach in for a handful of nuts or a potato chip, and then sees that it contains tangled coils of movie film.

"Oh," she laughs. "I thought it was something to eat." She eases past Chester and makes her way over to her mother, who is presiding over the potato salads and cream pies and casseroles that keep arriving in a steady stream at a large picnic table.

"No," Chester says in a low voice to Jacob. "It's the home movies I took years ago." He continues to hold out the canister of old movies, as if they too might be edible, another dish cooked up by Virginia from myriad ingredients, some exotic, some ordinary. "I just found these a couple of days ago," he continues, gazing at the film almost reverently. "I was looking for my fishing equipment up in the attic, pried open my old bait box and—what do you know!—there they were!"

"You don't say," replies Jacob, politely surveying the scraps of loose film. "In your bait box, huh?"

"Virginia used to kid me when I'd get out the movie camera. I was 'shooting the family,' she'd say."

Jacob grins. "What kind of weapon did you use?"

"Started out with an old Bell and Howell from the thirties—I mean, that son of a bitch was *heavy!* Then I got a portable camera. Turned out some darn good pictures." His eyebrows rise, as he cautiously searches Jacob. "You're a filmmaker, son . . ."

"An editor, I usually just edit them, that's all," Jacob corrects him. He bites into a drumstick and jabs a plastic fork into his slaw.

Chester shrugs and scratches the back of his neck. "Well, it's all a mystery to me, anyway, this filmmaking business. Once upon a time, I thought I could make 'em myself." He lifts out a tattered strand of celluloid, squints at it, and drops it back into the tin. "What in the world can I do about this? I promised Virginia I'd show these old things at the reunion next year. You know, we thought we'd lost my movies a few years ago, but now . . . well, hell, I tried to run this through my old projector, but you should've seen the mess. Couldn't even thread the darn thing."

Fumbling at the collar of his polo shirt, Chester looks at Jacob out of the corner of his eye. "You must have some fancy equipment out there in California. Maybe we could surprise Virginia with it next spring, if you could fix this up. I'm afraid she's counting on being able to see them. 'Of course they can be fixed up,' she says. 'Don't you worry.'" Chester shrugs again. "Think you could work on it, son? Would it take up too much of your time?"

Jacob gently stretches the celluloid between his fingers. "It shrinks, you know. That's what happens to this old stuff." He holds the strip up to the sun and peers into one frame. "Who is this? Is that Sheridan?"

Chester leans over and hands him the rectangular magnifying glass that his ninety-two-year-old mother uses for reading the Bible-study booklets that she mail-orders from a television preacher in Los Angeles.

"Sheridan's in the middle, on the bicycle," Chester says, leaning over Jacob's shoulder to look at the film, "and that's Ruby Ann on the porch of the playhouse. There's somebody across the lawn that you can barely see even with Mama's magnifier—you see that shape, there? I think that must be Amanda, standing off to the side, acting like she was getting too old to be in my movies. She was a spunky teenager, too big for her britches sometimes. Must've been our old house in Libertyburg, '57 or so."

A smile curls at Jacob's mouth, and he glances up affectionately at Sheridan, who stands talking to Virginia. Even with her back turned, Sheridan seems dramatic, waving and gesturing as Virginia flashes her deck of tarot cards. Virginia points a finger at one of the brightly decorated cards, as if she is telling Sheridan that her future lies there, somewhere in the colors and the design.

Jacob shades his eyes and leans closer to see the film better. "Look at that halter she's wearing. If she were five years older, it'd be a halting halter."

"Sheridan? Hell, son, you shoulda seen the girls in their majorette costumes. That wife of yours twirled a downright mean baton in the Shriner parades. She'd strut down Main Street just like she owned every shop on it. She'd push that chin of hers even higher in the air when she passed Ed Jolly's hardware store, you know, where her dad worked. And her only twelve or so. Just a kid. I took a lotta movies of those kids. I remember one of Sheridan flinging that baton of hers so high it was gone in the sun and then—boom!—there it was again, back in her little hands. Spinning just like an airplane propeller. And another year—whoo boy!—it slipped from her hands and she threw it right into Ed Jolly's store window. That was her dad's boss. You shoulda seen the look on Fred's face . . . I'll be darned if he didn't even look *pleased* with her, for breaking Ed Jolly's window. There wasn't a thing she could do wrong, that daughter of his. That's in here somewhere, if it's not ruined."

Chester shakes the canister, rattling the coils of film inside. He stares down at it, watching the ragged celluloid move as if it has nothing to do with the motion of his hand.

"A majorette? Yeah? She never told me that." Jacob smiles as if he is watching his own mental movies. "In Shriner parades, huh?"

"You bet. She was darn good." Chester tucks the canister under his arm to strike a match for his cigarette. "But you know, son, it's a funny thing. I can't remember if I ever took a movie of my own brother, Fred." He looks at Jacob with a cautious glance, waving the flaming match to extinction. "Of Sheridan's dad, you know. We don't talk about him much, but . . . well, you know all about that, about what happened and all." Chester's voice becomes confidential and matter-of-fact.

"Yes, of course," Jacob murmurs. He holds a forkful of coleslaw awkwardly at his mouth, wondering briefly if biting into it will appear unsympathetic.

"What I'd give to see movies of him. Of course Virginia'd love to see Amanda and Ruby Ann when they were just little ones—and Sheridan, sure, sure—"—he nods his head quickly, not to exclude his niece—"but what I'd give to see Fred again . . ."

As if she has heard her father's name spoken, Sheridan calls over to Jacob and Chester. She is still talking with Virginia, who is rummaging now through a paper sack, in search of more plastic forks. "Hey, you guys! Aunt Virginia's seen my future." She grins. "Movie work, she says. I'll have a part in a movie soon, maybe something made for television."

Before either Jacob or Chester can answer, Virginia strolls up to ask Chester to carve the pork roast on the picnic table. She has found an extension cord for the electric knife, and she holds it out to him.

Chester grinds out the cigarette he has just lit. As Virginia walks off, he leans over to Jacob.

"It'll be a surprise for her," he whispers.

"And a surprise for Sheridan," nods Jacob, as Chester hands him the canister, the movies coiled there as if they are withdrawing from history, shrinking from scrutiny.

TWO

WORRY BEADS
1942

In the late spring of 1942, Virginia Bloomer sits in the backyard of the boardinghouse where she lives in an upstairs room with her new husband, Chester. They moved to the Mississippi Delta after their wedding in Millsdale, down south on the Blue Moon River. Now, as the long afternoon shadows stretch across Virginia's face, she shells butter beans from the garden with the two older women who run the kitchen. They are sisters, one widowed in the 1918 flu epidemic, the other never-married. They chatter across her. Virginia, lonely and homesick out in the Delta flatlands, always joins them as they prepare for the evening meals.

She has hidden a new palmistry book, her deck of Egyptian tarot cards, and her Ouija board, tucking them all away under the mattress as if Chester were at home to scold her for them. "What do you want to play around with that stuff for?" he had asked when they first arrived in the mail. "That's just a bunch of silly hoo-doo."

Now the things belong there, she has come to feel, in their secret hiding place. Even when Chester is out of town, she still stores them away beneath the mattress.

Tonight Chester is somewhere between Kosciusko and Winona, on his way to the next small town that the Ace Farm Supply Company sends him to. He always returns with some memento for her from his travels, a porcelain thimble from Itta Bena, a pair of silk stockings from Ruleville, or, once, a set of watercolors and an easel all the way from Tishomingo—those exotic-sounding places that Virginia tries to imagine when she folds the laundry, tends her garden, or wakes to an empty bed. Several weeks ago, she mailed in an entry to the "Happiest Moment of My Life" column in *True Romances,* about how Chester had surprised her with the paint set. She embellished her story with how she had decorated the house with her own handmade paintings. Chester tells her it is still too soon to hear if she's won the twenty-five-dollar first prize.

She has set up the easel at their bedroom window, though the painting on it is not a scene of the bird feeder outside or the garden below. Instead, she has been copying the most colorful tarot card, adding to the picture her own ideas of what the Wheel of Fortune should look like. In it, a king and queen sit in the highest seat on a silver Ferris wheel, the queen's purple gown billowing out into the turning spokes, threatening to catch in them as they descend. She has wanted to make the king look like Chester, but his face is too narrow and his nose too long. In his hand, though, he bears a black easel much like the one Chester carried to her, the one on which the watercolor is clipped. Instead of painting the queen's face as a resemblance of her own, Virginia has painted her from a model on the latest cover of *True Romances;* her long yellow hair swells out behind her in an invisible breeze, making Virginia herself feel glamorous.

Though Virginia does not know it yet, on Friday Chester will bring home a gift more exotic than any other—a Bell and Howell movie camera that he traveled to Memphis to buy at an army-surplus store. He will say the camera is for her. Virginia will smile at that, especially since his birthday is coming up soon.

Right here is the future, Chester will say, thumping the camera with his hand. The way of the future. And all their memories? Right here, too. Now that they are parents, they will need those memories. Time speeds along, he will say, you never know where the years go, as if he is selling her the idea of the camera. And he will thump it, slap its black metal again.

Now Virginia looks over proudly at a small blue quilt where Amanda May, their daughter, sleeps. It will be over ten years before their next child, another daughter, is born. Then, she and Chester will own a split-level ranch house in Libertyburg, a town near the Mississippi Gulf Coast. She will be president of the coffee club there. Chester's younger brother, Fred, a new army private, writes them now that he may never come back to "Hicksville, U.S.A." ("You oughtta see this Pacific Ocean, Chester, hell, if there were a million Blue Moon Rivers, they still couldn't match this . . . ," his scrawl slants across the thin paper in one of those first letters.) But after the war, he will return to Mississippi, bringing Virginia a string of ceramic beads glazed indigo. Virginia will hold them up, puzzled. They are too small for a necklace, too large for a bracelet. "It's a game," Fred will grin. "Picked 'em up on Crete. You fiddle with them," he will add, taking the beads from her and slapping them against his palm so that they clink together musically. "See? The Greeks call them worry beads." He will hand them back. "You get worried? Then you play with these."

"Like a rosary," Virginia will muse, sliding the smooth beads along their thread.

"If you say so," Fred will laugh. "A rosary for wishes—one for every bead."

After a second decade has passed, in 1965, Fred will have died, a suicide, leaving behind his wife, Winnie, and their daughter, Sheridan. And no note.

No note, that is, to his wife. Instead, he will mail a brief letter to Virginia, his brother's wife. The note will be sealed inside a typed envelope with no return address, and the mailman will deliver it the day after his funeral. It will consist of a list, three sentences, one beneath the next, in Fred's scrawled handwriting.

"1. I love you.

"2. I love Winnie and Chester."

Then, with his pen beginning to run out of ink so that the words become desperate etchings into the paper, he will continue, as if in the list lay some measure of reason and rationality,

"3. But I hate myself. There's no way out. *Burn this.*"

The last words will be underlined, visible even though there is no ink in the deep grooves on the paper.

Virginia will hide the letter in a zippered pocket in her purse until she is alone long enough to make a tiny bonfire of the paper in Chester's barbecue pit on the patio. In 1965, wrinkles of fatigue and worry will have begun to curl gently around Virginia's eyes like the fine lines in the road map Chester uses now, in 1942, to navigate his brown Chevrolet down muddy roads marked by telephone poles.

But Virginia is twenty-two, and she smiles when she thinks of her husband's twenty-fourth birthday in a week. She plans to bake him a strawberry cake from the fresh berries in the yard where she is sitting. It is not the dessert that would please him most, but she knows that she can't compete with her mother-in-law's famous pound cake, with its dozen eggs, its pound of both butter and sugar. And its mysterious ingredient, the spice or foreign extract that remains unnamed. Even her own mother's cake recipes can't compare to it, but Virginia feels a pang of disloyalty at the thought.

On the two kitchen chairs beside her, her companions chatter about the empty whiskey bottle that the mailman found on Reverend Broussard's front porch the weekend before.

"It was Mrs. Broussard herself, don't you know it?" says one sister, circling her ear with one finger and rolling her eyes. "Why sure. Ever since she went down to New Orleans to have that female surgery back in February, the poor thing's been in so much pain she can't even come to prayer meeting anymore."

"Why, she's hardly out of the house before noon," clucks the older sister.

"You never know how things'll turn out when it comes to an ovarian cyst," sighs the other. "The knife slipped on Mavis Lafferty, you know—got her right through the colon."

"You never know how often the doctor'll come to visit, either," winks her sister. "Especially with that good New Orleans whiskey to kill an ache or two." She gathers another handful of beans from the tub at her feet and smacks her lips. "Well. A sip must be good for the pain, anyway," she adds. "Lord knows how that pain . . ."

Now it is their own "female problems" they compare, and the way Virginia's tarot deck seemed to promise relief from them when she spread the cards two nights ago.

"Now, maybe if we can just get that Ouija board to moving again, who knows what we might find out . . . poor Mrs. Broussard. Who's going to help her if nobody knows for sure what's ailing her?" The sisters glance over at Virginia.

Virginia, though, is no longer listening to them. She has been watching Amanda May napping, the way her little face closes in sleep. But Virginia's eyes slide away from her daughter and focus on a memory. She remembers the dances Chester took her to before they married . . . he is such a good dancer! Then it is her older brother, Harold Moody, that she nudges from some mental corner. He is wearing a pilot's uniform, waving to his parents and sisters from a bus that rolls away from the Millsdale depot. His plane will be shot down that summer, but now he is still safe.

The sun emerges from a pink cloud in the west and makes her squint. She shifts her wooden chair and catches a glimpse of the widow who lives on the farm down the road. She is beginning her evening walk. Two puppies, teased by a butterfly, trail behind the long black skirt she always wears.

In the oak tree shading Virginia's chair, a breeze carrying the taste of honeysuckle ruffles the new green leaves. It is that kind of evening, that time of spring, rumored with indecision and memory.

She shifts again, suddenly sad. What has she gotten into, she wonders. What is she doing with a baby—or even married at all? Sometimes she studies the lines in her palm and wonders what futures might have been there. In those moments, it seems as if her life has already been spelled out for her even though she holds other, unled lives right there in her own two hands. Just the other day, the last tarot card she dealt out for herself was the World. Now, what did that mean? she wonders, remembering the blue-and-green globe on the card, the two slender hands that held it. A trip to Memphis? To the Peabody Hotel, with its duck pond in the lobby? She begins to think of the most foreign place she can imagine, somewhere with camels and bright tents and sheiks who look the way Rudolph Valentino did in the very first movie she remembers seeing.

Chester seems foreign sometimes, too, but in a different way. When he drives into the gravel driveway in his muddy car, even the sound seems like an intrusion, or the feel of his rough chin scraping her face in a kiss, a stranger's kiss. His footsteps rattle the set of four china dishes she has propped in the cabinet in their room. Even his voice—he will yank off his boots and complain about the men he works with, about "that lazy Buddy Lee" or about "crazy ole Rudy Murphy, you won't believe what that nut did today"—seems to shake the room. And she misses the quiet, *her* quiet, the solitude that she knows Amanda May, too, will shatter when she stirs from her sleep in the predawn hours when the room is still dark. Often, after she has fed Amanda, she sits at her easel and paints until the sun rises, enjoying the stillness of the hour. It is a solitude that Chester does not even realize exists.

Sometimes she goes to sleep at night wanting her own mother to come kiss her good-night and pull the covers up under her chin. How silly, she scolds herself as she smooths the sheets before climbing into bed. She, a grown married woman, wanting her mother.

It is hard to stay in close touch with her family, isolated down on the farm a few miles out from Millsdale on the Blue Moon River. Once when Virginia was small, her father made a bedtime story of a legend about the river's name. Once on a blue-moon night—the second full moon in a single month, he explained, something rare—the river had overflowed its banks while a defeated Indian tribe chanted war songs against the white settlers, letting the swirling waters rise about them until the entire tribe drowned. And so the river had won its name, and on every blue-moon night, he promised, if Virginia would just listen hard enough, the rhythmic sounds of chants would come rising from the river banks, ghosts still claiming this very farm as theirs, reminding good white Christians that the past could come flooding up just like the Blue Moon River did when the rains were hard.

She smiles now at the memory of how the story had frightened her, and how her bewildered father had had to comfort her with reassurances that it all happened a "long, long time ago." ("Telling her that wild story!" her mother had scolded him. "Why, you'll scare the child to death!")

Virginia wishes that she could talk to her father now, but the house is far from a telephone. Letters cannot convey the sound of her father playing the piano, his boots pumping the pedals, his Irish red hair curling in defiance of the Baptist hymns her mother loves. And her mother, stern faced, toe tapping, as she sings the old favorites he plays. "How sweet the sound, that saved a wretch like me. . . ," she can almost hear her mother's trilling voice. Or the laughter of her two younger sisters, gossiping as they awkwardly roll their hair on rag curlers while. . .

One of the women who run the boardinghouse is talking to her. The narcissus . . . something about the flower garden she planted months ago, just after she and Chester moved in. Yes, their smell is wonderful, she nods. No, she is only lucky with plants. No one taught her about flowers, she explains, embarrassed to confess that they were a luxury on the farm, time taken away from potatoes or the henhouse or buckets of milk.

She smiles down shyly at the tub of beans in her lap as her fingers ripple through the pods. The tin pan fills quickly with shelled beans, each pod emptied like a string of worry beads, the thread discarded.

THREE

FRED HOME SAFE 1945

Draped outside every shop window on Libertyburg's Main Street, American flags hang down against the brick walls and white-washed shingles. A large Confederate flag hangs beside a smaller American one from a window above Jolly's Hardware Store. It is Ed Jolly's announcement to all his white customers—and to any Negro would-be customers—that he is patriotic to more than the national cause.

A rare warm breeze stirs the flags into undulating waves and cools the sweaty faces of the crowds in the street waiting for the parade. The buildings themselves seem to be waving with the wind, cheering the surrender of Germany.

It is July 4, 1945. The sounds of the Libertyburg High School band bellow through the street, the trombones swelling up toward the town square, nudged by grunting tubas and a bass drum.

Swallowed up in the crowd is Virginia, standing to the rear of the spectators in front of the H. & L. Green Five and Dime store. A bright red pinafore is tied over the white linen dress she bought for Easter Sunday—she has told Chester she will be wearing red so he can spot her easily in the crowd. But it seems the entire crowd wears red, white, and blue.

She fans herself with a folded newspaper, blowing the pink azalea that is pinned above one of her ears. Amanda straddles her right hip. She barely feels the weight of her bouncing daughter; she is too busy beaming at the crowds, nodding and waving to her new neighbors. She and Chester have just moved from the Delta to the Mississippi coast, since Chester has been promoted from salesman to district manager at Ace Farm Supply. Already she has made more friends in five months than she did in three years in the country. And now the war in Europe is over!

Making her way through the crowd is Mrs. Pucharski, the director of the church nursery where Virginia deposits a pouting Amanda during Sunday services at Forest Park Baptist Church. The old woman puts her fingers beneath her chin and waves to Amanda, who is sucking on a tiny American flag clutched in her right hand and looking suspiciously at Mrs. Pucharski's playful wave.

"Y'all come see me, you hear?" Mrs. Pucharski pauses as she passes Virginia. "Come see me while my peaches are still ripe and I'll send you home with a whole bushel to can." Just as the old woman slips back into the crowd, Amanda happily jerks her flag through the air and salutes her teacher's retreating back.

In the next block, in front of the Mississippi Security Bank building, Chester pushes his straw hat up on his head, showing the hairline that is already beginning to recede. He searches for the red pinafore that Virginia said she'd be wearing, and he is trying to look nonchalant with the tripod for his movie camera braced under one armpit. Today Chester is anything but nonchalant, though. Fred will be marching in the parade in his army uniform, and Chester has imagined this day for a long time. He wants it exactly as he has pictured it for nearly two years: Virginia by his side, holding Amanda, and him behind the whirring camera, looking through the lens at Fred in his uniform, at Fred home safe again.

The tubas and bass drum swell their gray sounds thunderlike in the distance, reminding Chester of the tornado clouds that threatened Libertyburg last March, only two weeks after he and Virginia rented their duplex. The clouds landed long enough to rip away a revival tent that the Church of God had pitched on the edge of town. Though Chester does not consider himself superstitious, it hadn't seemed like a good omen at the time. Today is a happy occasion, he reminds himself. But somehow these deep sounds the band is making don't seem happy.

"You looking for your wife, Mr. Bloomer?" It is Stanley, the kid who delivers the Libertyburg *Sun-Herald* every morning. "She's right over yonder, sir." He points toward the crowd in front of the H. & L. Green store. "I just saw her there with your little girl. What you doin with the crutch, Mr. Bloomer?" Now Stanley points to the folded tripod. "Hurt your foot?"

"It's not a crutch." Chester holds it out and stamps both his feet. "It's a tripod for this movie camera here." He points to the bulky camera sitting on the sidewalk.

"Gee whiz, Mr. Bloomer, you make movies?" Stanley's eyes are round blue circles.

Peeking through the crowd where Stanley pointed is a splash of red that looks to Chester as if it might be Virginia's pinafore, and he makes his way toward it, nodding a brief answer to Stanley's question. Mr. Lovelace, the head deacon of Forest Park Baptist Church, is standing in his path, and before Chester can avoid it, he stands face to face with him. His brotherly smile always makes

Chester nervous. It makes him think Mr. Lovelace knows something he doesn't know.

Chester rests the tripod on the ground and lifts his hat briefly. "Looking for my wife, Mr. Lovelace. This is a happy moment, isn't it? Yessir. All our men back home, isn't that a blessing . . ." Before Mr. Lovelace can try to shake his hand, Chester has moved on, weighted with the camera in one hand and the tripod in the other.

The smell of sweat lingers in unexpected places in the crowd like an aroma of overripe cheese. To Chester, it is a faceless crowd. It makes him feel as though he has moved to a foreign country. There are so many people here he doesn't know yet. The company calls Libertyburg a small town, but Chester still doesn't even know the names of the downtown shopowners. He misses the Delta, misses the cotton fields and knowing everybody by their first names. Virginia seems to like it here in Libertyburg, though, and that makes him happy. Sometimes when he comes home from work she'll start in telling him about her day, who it was she went shopping with, or who dropped in to visit, or where the coffee club met. She'll start in, he thinks with a nudging irritation, before he can even tell her about his own day. Rudy Murphy says the same thing about his wife, Lucille, and that makes Chester even more glad that Rudy transferred down here, too. It is good to have a buddy when you can't even talk to your wife at the end of a long day.

This is life in the city, he thinks. Why, you can hardly find your own wife in a crowd on Main Street.

As Chester walks by, a breeze lifts the corners of the solitary Confederate flag hanging above Jolly's Hardware Store. He glances up just in time to see the flag flutter loose from one nail as he moves past, waving at him as if it agrees with him about all these strangers crowding the street.

"Well, this is life in the city," he says to Virginia, surprising her with his arm around her shoulder.

She jumps and then laughs. "Here, have a flag." She sets a squirming Amanda down and pushes a small flag through the buttonhole in Chester's lapel. It sags precariously, so she bends the stick a bit to secure it. Then she pats the flag and feels Chester's strong chest beneath his thin linen jacket. She pats it an extra time and lets her hand linger there, eyeing the inviting tuft of hair curling at the open neck of his shirt.

"Now stay," she commands the flag, shaking her index finger at it, and then reaches up to kiss Chester's cheek.

He fidgets under her fussing and finally shoves his hands in his pockets, trying to be patient. When Virginia turns back to the parade with Amanda, he bends down to set up the tripod and the movie camera. According to the sounds of the drum rolls, the high-school band is nearing, and not long behind, he figures, will be the soldiers that Libertyburg sent to war. Fred is among them, though it had taken some persuading to get him to come down from Millsdale and march in the Fourth of July parade.

"Why, hell, Chester, I don't know those town folks," Fred had said over the telephone. "And they sure as hell don't know Fred Bloomer. I'd be just another schmo in a uniform to them."

Chester had argued until he was "blue in the face," he complained to Virginia. But a week later, Fred called back, agreeing to come. Chester suspected it had more to do with his brother wanting to escape the way their mother showed him off to her friends—her brave young son, he could just hear her voice—than with wanting to march in the parade. But Chester is happy just to have Fred staying with him here in Libertyburg, no matter what the reason.

Chester worries about whether his brother is enjoying this celebration, this happy time. He has been worried by the change in his brother—all to be expected, of course, after the fighting he's just seen in Germany. Best of all, Chester thinks, must have been watching that little town in Luxembourg celebrate the way they beat the Germans. Fred won't tell him much about it, though. He just clams up whenever anybody asks him, so that now Chester refuses to let his curiosity get away with him and push his brother for information.

But—hell!—he'd have liked to have been there, himself, Chester thinks, been a hero like that. He was needed here, though, he reminds himself. Amanda arrived just in time to keep him out of the armed services and in what he calls the farm-supply services instead. That is what he will tell his grandchildren, he has decided, since he will never fight in any wars, never be able to pull a purple heart or a war medal from his bureau drawer and impress his young children. Or grandchildren . . .

Fred, though, doesn't even seem proud of the medal he won. He seems distant to Chester, not even happy that the war is over, he thinks. Fred seems sad all the time now, the way even when he was a kid, Chester remembers, he'd go off for hours by himself, not saying a word to anybody, and come back looking sullen and dark. "Freddy's got a rain cloud over his head again," his mother would say. "Just let him be."

For Pete's sake! Chester thinks. Seems like having a war medal would snap him out of it this time . . . Maybe the parade will make him glad to be home. And if he can fix Fred up with that cute little number at the office, a receptionist named Winnie Franklin, why, who knows what could happen? Winnie is shy, Chester can tell by the way she ducks her head and blushes when he teases her, but she has a swell figure, and dimples in her cheeks to boot.

It'll be just the four of them, Chester tells himself, out dancing at the Green Lizard Lounge, that hot new nightclub Rudy Murphy's been telling him about. Winnie Franklin will be just the thing to make Fred feel welcome back here at home. And a job—that will help more than anything, of course. Chester has already checked on openings at the phone company, and the gas company too. There are at least a few jobs for the vets here in Libertyburg, so he hopes that Fred won't have to return to Millsdale and work a plow again, like Virginia's brother, Harold, is having to do on his family's farm.

"What're you thinking about? You look awfully glum. Is something wrong with the camera?" Virginia has set Amanda down again and she shakes out her right arm, stiff from the weight of her daughter.

"Oh, just hoping the parade's a good one, I guess," he says, adjusting the knobs on the camera. He raises his head when the sound of the tubas suddenly increases in volume, as if the band just turned a corner. "Sounds like they're right down at the square, doesn't it?" He stretches his neck to see above the crowd and then glances down at Virginia. "There's that cute little Winnie Franklin, the one I was telling you about, up there at the curb. C'mon, let's go get us a place next to her."

From the curb, the view of the street decked in its red, white, and blue banners brings tears to Virginia's eyes. A sound like applause ripples through the spectators down the block, and then the sound makes its way toward them. Virginia thinks of a row of dominoes that slowly tumbles and catches the crowd up in the motion.

The sound of the clarinets sails through the air, almost indistinguishable from the crowd's sudden cheers. Chester hunches behind his camera, swinging the lens across the rows of young marching musicians, then panning up to the buildings, paneled with flags, and finally back down to Virginia and Amanda.

He refocuses quickly, captured by the look on Virginia's face. He has never seen her look quite like this. Her eyes are even bluer than usual, and their glisten of moisture almost seems to reflect the clear sky overhead. Her entire face listens. The nearest he has seen her look like this was once in church, one Sunday morning over three years ago, the day she later told him they were going to be parents.

Virginia is listening to the band and the cheers of the crowd, but it is more than sound that she hears. The band is an eclectic cacophony of noise and movement, blending its missteps and its disharmonious toots and blasts into a single joyous spirit. The motion and sound swell together until the entire crowd is absorbed into the parade, a simultaneous wave of celebration that sweeps through the streets and over the curb onto the sidewalks. They are no longer high-school students or shopowners or salesmen or housewives but the same roaring rhythm to which Virginia listens with her entire face.

Amanda straddles her hip again, her chubby knees wrinkling the red pinafore, both her arms hugging Virginia's neck. She is wide-eyed as she points to the parade, calling, "Where is Unca Fred? Is that Unca Fred there?" But Virginia cannot speak anymore. She is thinking of her brother on the family farm now, beginning to walk without a limp. She wishes that Harold were here, part of the rhythm of this soaring parade.

From behind the noise of the brass horns comes another wave, another tumble of dominoes. It is the crowd greeting a group of men in army uniforms. The green rows of uniforms march crisply behind the straggly lines of the high-school band like a reassurance, a frightening reassurance, perhaps, that they may be needed again.

Chester has turned his camera back to the street, searching for Fred through the lens. One head rises above the others, the army hat at a jaunty, almost irreverent angle.

"That's him!" He rises from the camera and beams at Virginia. He quickly nudges Winnie with his elbow and points. "That's my brother Fred, there, that tall fellow in the back row."

"Gee, he looks like Gregory Peck." Winnie's cheeks dimple and she grinds the toe of her saddle oxford against the sidewalk. "Did y'all see him with Greer Garson in *The Valley of Decision?* Golly, he looks just like Gregory Peck did in that movie."

But neither Virginia nor Chester is listening to her. Chester is doing the best he can to focus the lens closely on Fred, and Virginia is waving her arm at him.

"Look over here, Fred! Here we are! Gee, you look swell!" Virginia's voice has come back, and now she aims her words over the noise of the crowd. "Hey, Fred! Give us a salute!"

Fred glances over and lifts his right arm to make a crisp salute at Virginia. Just as he snaps his hand to his forehead, a quick wind loosens Ed Jolly's Confederate flag from the last thin nail that has held it to the second-floor windowsill. It flaps down through the wind like some giant extinct bird, seeking the highest place to roost.

All that Chester sees through the lens is the figure of his brother suddenly struggling to free himself from a red, white, and blue cloth. Fred thrashes beneath it and finally bats the flag away from his head. There is a desperate, hunted look in his eyes.

"Don't let it touch the ground! The flag shouldn't ever touch the ground!" It is Ed Jolly, running out to the pavement, trying to rescue his flag from the perils, the sacrilege, of asphalt.

Fred glares at him while the parade marches on. "You just better burn your damn flag, then." He kicks at the crumpled cloth. "It's touching the ground, all right."

Quivering so that the word escapes his mouth as a hiss, Ed Jolly blusters out, "Blasphemy!" Even the bald spot on top of his head has pinkened with rage.

From the sidewalk, Amanda is singing out, "It's Unca Fred! There's Unca Fred!"

But a crowd swells into the street, obscuring the view of the fists that have begun to swing. Chester leaves his camera running and dashes out into the street, shoving aside Mr. Lovelace on his way. He hauls Ed Jolly away from his brother and stands between the two glaring men, his arms outstretched, his feet planted apart like two legs of a tripod. His hands are shaking.

"Now, settle down, boys. Settle down." Chester's head turns quickly from Fred to Ed Jolly.

Fred relaxes his fists and shakes his head at Ed Jolly, who is dabbing at the blood in the corner of his mouth with his handkerchief.

"Look, mister." Fred extends his own handkerchief. "Your flag landed on my head, for chrissake. How did I know what it was?" He stretches his mouth into a grin. "Hell, it couldda been a Kraut parachute, for all I knew."

The two of them move to the sidewalk, talking, shaking their heads.

Chester has let his arms drop to his sides. " 'It's okay, folks," he says to the crowd. "Let's get on with the parade."

On the curb, Virginia and Winnie stand on tiptoe to see

through the sudden crowd, their hands over their mouths. Winnie's other hand is pressed to the front of her pink organdy blouse. "Good gracious," she breathes. "He looked just like Gregory Peck in *The Valley of Decision.*"

FOUR

HAPPY MOMENTS 1951

The Mississippi Delta is flat, and there is no valley or mountain here, not even a small hill. Sometimes Virginia longs for a mountain or even an ocean, although she has only seen the ocean, seen those crashing whitecaps and infinite blue horizons, in movies playing at the Betworthy Bijou downtown. They make her think about the warmth of a tropical island, one of those paradises with women in grass skirts and dark-skinned men with strong, bare chests.

In the winter of 1944, the Delta is both cold and flat. Frozen cotton fields grow gray against a grayer sky. A light coating of snow transforms the cotton rows into low mounds rippling together like a sculpture of whitecapped waves. There is not even a promise of April.

Over the bulky radio in the living room come reports of the fighting with Japan in the Marshall Islands, and the new bombings of Germany. Edward R. Murrow says that the bombs are now being dropped "around the clock." At the sound of his voice, shivers keep rippling across Virginia's skin, even beneath the sweater she wears indoors. She is hardly ever warm anymore. There could not be enough heat in the entire world, it seems, to keep her warm, especially on these long nights when Chester is away.

At least her older brother, Harold, is safe now, returned home from the air force with injuries to his leg that are severe enough to let him remain home, but sufficiently healed that he can tend the soybean crop on the family farm in Millsdale. But Chester's younger brother, Fred, is still camped in Diekirch, a tiny snowbound village in Luxembourg. He has sent a photograph of himself playing Santa Claus to the children of Diekirch, and he looked oddly content to Virginia, though she did not mention that to Chester. Above the outsized white beard, there was a satisfaction in his eyes, a sparkle that she had not often seen there. Chester took the photograph down to Kosciusko, to have it framed at the camera shop ("No cheap five-and-dime picture frame for this!" he said), and now it sits on the coffee table, so that he can talk about Fred when their occasional visitors notice it.

When she is not listening to the latest reports on the war, Virginia eases her mind by working the "movie crossword" in back issues of *True Confessions,* patiently filling in the answers to "Merle Oberon's co-star in *A Song to Remember*" or "First name of hi-de-ho band leader." She passes the last two weeks of February by listening to "As Time Goes By" over and over on the record player Chester gave her at Christmas. She even hums the song to Amanda, to lull her to sleep in her crib. The move that it's from, *Casablanca,* hasn't come yet to the Betworthy Bijou, and the manager can't promise her when he'll be able to book it. Instead, *Coastal Command* is playing there. Virginia has seen it three times already, taking

Amanda with her to escape the urgency of radio voices and the chilly house. Its scenes of the ocean have her thinking about white-skinned women in green grass skirts, wearing gardenias in their hair. She has even begun a watercolor painting of an island scene, though Chester had thought it odd that bronze-chested men should be dancing with such pale-skinned ladies.

After the war has ended, and long after the winter of '44 has surrendered to soft April breezes, those fantasies of tropical islands linger in a corner of Virginia's mind. They linger, unremembered, as a wish to escape not Delta winters or Libertyburg or her marriage to a man who sometimes moves through the house like a stranger but to escape Virginia Moody Bloomer—or, rather, to escape who she is supposed to be.

Seven years later, in Libertyburg, Virginia is wearing a grass skirt to a beach party thrown by Chester's office crowd. She spends a week weaving together the waist of that skirt (how thick should a grass skirt be?), and then adjusting the length (how short would ladies have worn them in Hawaii?). With Amanda's help, she flips through Chester's old issues of *National Geographic* to find the answers, but there are no ladies in grass skirts in those pages, though she could have sworn she'd seen one or two. Amanda, at least, has a stack of elephants and tigers she has cut out. Finally, Virginia decides those questions of fullness and length, her mind forced to commitment by the square on the calendar's page.

It is Saturday morning, August 18, 1951. It is the day of Chester's office party at the beach. The hem will remain, then, an incautious one inch below her knee—so that the full curve of her calf shows. The skirt's thickness will be as it was when she adjusted it for the last time on Friday, removing a few clumps of grass from the elastic at the waist so that her knees will more easily penetrate the skirt when she walks. On this Saturday morning, she practices strutting in the skirt before the mirror on her closet door, swaying her hips just enough that she can feel the grass brushing the backs of her knees.

Though Virginia does not remember her fantasies about tropical islands during the Delta winter of 1944, the legacy of that February remains in the inspiration for tonight's costume. And now she is thoroughly enjoying the attention that Chester is giving her, in her grass skirt, in the summer of 1951.

Chester aims his brand-new home-movie camera at his wife, trying to catch her shimmying in her costume. An article in one of Virginia's latest *Parents' Magazine*s persuaded Chester to buy one of these portable cameras to replace his bulky old army equipment.

"Catch and Keep Your Happiest Moments," the article encouraged its readers. Chester decided it was good, solid advice. Now he stands in the backyard in his Bermuda shorts and Hawaiian shirt, a fat cigar between the fingers of his right hand. He is peering through the lens of his new camera, trying to catch one of those moments.

He is not entirely sure that he approves of the movement Virginia is making beneath the strings of plastic grass, but he pretends that it is okay. After all, his brother Fred is there, and Fred's wife, Winnie, too, wearing a long dress that sweeps her ankles. Now if only Virginia were wearing something as dignified . . . But he dismisses the thought quickly, since this is one of those happy moments he bought the camera for. Isn't there a beach party in store for them tonight?

He smiles from behind the camera and waves a hand at his sister-in-law, who is watching from the side. "Winnie, you get in the picture there too. Right there beside Virginia. Don't be shy. Sure wish this was that new color film I've been hearing about. That pretty dress of yours would look real nice in Technicolor. All that pretty purple and red . . . why, you're a downright glamourpuss." Chester peers into the lens of his camera while Winnie joins Virginia and awkwardly puts her hand on her sister-in-law's bare shoulder.

Fred watches, leaning against a banana tree in his brother's backyard, an old box camera gripped in one hand. He is staring at Chester, not his wife or his sister-in-law. Or, more accurately, he is examining Chester's new movie camera, wishing he had one of his own. And why the hell doesn't he? The question rises in his mind and wrinkles his forehead. He works just as hard as his brother does, he knows that much. He even works on the weekends sometimes. And he is just as devoted to his family, to Winnie and his little daughter Sheridan—a handful, at nearly two. But he doesn't have a movie camera to record her—only this cheap old Kodak, he thinks, glancing down at the camera. Who knew if the picture he's just snapped of Winnie and Virginia would turn out halfway decent? The salary he earns at Ed Jolly's hardware store just doesn't allow for splurges like a better camera, much less a movie camera. It's enough to make Fred wonder what a man's worth, anyway, when his paycheck won't even allow for some things his wife tells him are necessities—things like new striped window awnings for the house or a fancy washing machine Winnie saw advertised on Virginia and Chester's television set.

As if a pulse beats there, the muscles on either side of Fred's jaw work rhythmically. He watches his older brother, trying to be pleased that at least Chester is happy, in a good mood today, as he focuses the movie camera on their wives. But what is Virginia doing, anyway, dancing around in that grass skirt, her shoulders naked?

Fred turns to them, and his frown fades to a warm, appreciative gaze at Virginia as she dances, her slender bare feet gliding across the grass, making her red toenails look like rubies in a green carpet. Her arms and hips undulate in a rhythm that he can practically hear. If only Winnie were just a little less shy, a little livelier once in a while. Seems like she worries so much these days, she hardly laughs at his jokes anymore. And why is she wearing that long, baggy dress, like a sharecropper's wife in a flour sack? In the flash of his mind's eye, he sees her concentrating over the fabric at her sewing machine in the bedroom, and he feels a guilty pang. She's a good wife, he reminds himself, trying to appreciate the purple dress she has sewn for herself—a muumuu, she calls it. Why does Chester let Virginia parade around in some whore's costume, anyway? he wonders, suddenly angry. Even if she does have legs like Betty Grable's . . .

He looks at Winnie and a small shiver of pity touches him, from some unknown source. Maybe it is the bulge her stomach makes beneath one of the purple flowers on her dress; she still hasn't lost the weight she gained when she was pregnant with Sheridan. Or perhaps it is pity for himself that he feels, for the way life has stuck him in a town where the streets themselves seem to lead nowhere, and in a job that gives him no more than barely enough to pay the bills. Ed Jolly never has fancy parties like this for the people who work for him in the hardware store.

The only time his wife gets to go to an office party is when his big brother . . . Fred twists a tiny green banana from the branch by his head and hurls it at the fence, like a baseball, as hard as he can. At the resulting smack, the frown in his eyes eases into a satisfied glint.

"You tryin to be Stan Musial? C'mon, Fred. You get in the picture." Chester is waving his arm at Fred, making a flapping motion while he squints into the camera.

Virginia is swaying, bumping her hip against Winnie's, her arm around her, so that Winnie can find no escape. She waves at Fred with her other arm. "Yeah, c'mon, Fred. Get in here. Let Chester shoot the whole family."

Fred shakes his head. "Oh, I dunno. That's for you gals. You're the ones we'll want to see in the movies."

"Chester, you let Fred take the camera and you get in here then." Virginia prances eagerly and points at her husband.

Now Chester strides quickly into the movie, grinning at the camera held now by his brother, stretching his arms around both Virginia and Winnie, pulling them close. The three of them stand there, smiling at the camera, then at each other until their smiles turn stiff. Virginia swishes her skirt with her free hand.

Winnie looks down at the ground as if she is searching for something in the grass with the toe of her pump. She squints up into the camera, shading her eyes with one hand. "What do you want us to do now, Fred?"

From behind the camera comes silence, and Fred raises one arm in a shrug of disgust. "I don't know. I'm no movie director."

In the quiet that follows, Chester puts his hands behind his head and tries to move his stomach the way he has seen Jackie Gleason do on "The Honeymooners." He suddenly sweeps Virginia in his arms and does a quick jitterbug with her, a way of defiantly telling the camera that his wife's grass skirt—and her bare legs—are just fine with him. Laughing with delight, Virginia leans back in his arms and holds on to her skirt, suddenly afraid that the elastic in the waist will not hold.

Winnie stands awkwardly to one side, smiling at them as Virginia nearly spins into her, her grass skirt flying around her legs. She shades her eyes again and looks at Fred, hunched a little under the weight of the camera, under the weight of its responsibility. The Hawaiian shirt she made him for the party rides up over his back to expose the pale skin there. It's too short, she chides herself. After all that time she spent at the sewing machine, it's too short. She should have bought another half yard of fabric. Why did she scrimp like that? And she feels an unexpected touch of pity. Perhaps it is self-pity.

She slides out of the range of the camera, backing slowly away, as if she will blur the picture, ruin it for Chester and Virginia if she moves too fast.

FIVE

WEATHER VANE 1951

It is Christmas, 1951. Virginia and Winnie sit side by side on what Winnie calls her divan, the blue brocade sofa that she and Fred bought on sale from a furniture warehouse last spring. In a corner, before the double windows, stands a partly decorated cedar pine, its bottom branches sagging slightly under the weight of the flashing red and green bulbs. The top half of the tree shrinks against the windows as if embarrassed at being taken out of the woods and put on display. On its topmost branch is perched the tarnished silver-plated star that has been there every Christmas since Winnie and Fred married five years ago. It was a gift from Winnie's mother in South Carolina, an inexpensive ornament that she had bought in the thirties, and she had wanted to pass it down to Winnie. Though the thin silver plating has long since dimmed, Winnie refuses to listen to Fred's suggestions of replacing it.

Beneath the tree are stacked the presents Winnie has bought for Fred and Sheridan, wrapped in silver and red. Most of Sheridan's gifts, though, will be brought by Santa Claus. Those—a rocking horse, a Tiny Tears doll, and a huge teddy bear—are hidden in the attic. On the spindle of the record player that Fred gave Winnie for her last birthday, her twenty-sixth, is perched a stack of Christmas records waiting to drop onto the turntable. Bing Crosby's *White Christmas* album descends with a jerk, and his voice begins to croon "Jingle Bells."

Virginia and Winnie are stringing cranberries and popcorn on thread, holding their needles expertly, targeting the center of the kernels and berries. The chains that will decorate the tree when they are finished circle now in loops on the floor, forming red-and-white pools beside their feet. Winnie moves a string of popcorn from her lap, arranges it beside her, and scans the room quickly for her daughter.

"Where's Sheridan?" She pushes the needle into the arm of the sofa and rises, pushing aside the pool of popcorn and berries with the side of her shoe. "She was crawling around behind the tree a minute ago."

"Oh, she's probably in the kitchen with Chester and Fred. She's a lively one, isn't she? Honest to goodness, I don't know how you keep up with her, Winnie. She's more of a handful than Amanda ever was." Virginia shakes her head and slides the berries down on the thread she is holding so that they form a single unbroken row.

Winnie blushes. "Well, Amanda's old enough by now that you'd forget what she was like when she was a little bitty thing." She nods at Virginia's stomach, gently swollen beneath her maternity dress. "Wait till that one's one. You'll remember. Sheridan's just energetic. She's already trying to say whole sentences. Fred says she's a genius; we just have to put up with more from kids like that."

Virginia jabs her needle at a kernel of popcorn so hard that she breaks it, scattering pieces that bounce from her ballooning stomach and into the crease between the sofa cushions, where they will be found and eaten, stale, by Sheridan next summer. "Oh, Fred sure loves his little girl, doesn't he? That's a sweet thing to say."

The steel taps on Winnie's high heels click against the wood floor when she rises, quickly, to hide the new flush of anger on her face. She likes to wear the highest heels she can easily walk in, to bring her head up even with Fred's shoulder. Now they rap against the floor with a sound like the popping of toy guns.

She ignores Virginia's remark and looks at the kitchen door, raising her voice. "Fred, is Sheridan in there with y'all?"

And then she sits down again, abruptly. Chester, stooped behind his whirring movie camera, has come into the room. She smiles nervously and plucks her needle from the sofa arm, to pose for Chester's camera and the memories it will create for the family. Then she remembers Sheridan, frowns at Chester, and rises again.

"Aw, c'mon, Winnie," Chester wheedles. "Get back there on the couch. You're out of the picture now." Waving Winnie back into the range of his picture, he squats and aims upward to keep her in focus.

Winnie's first impulse is to obey. She sits briefly, has a second thought, and rises again, so that she seems to curtsy or genuflect to the camera. "Sorry, Chester. I've got to find Sheridan. Is she back there in the kitchen with Fred?"

Chester crouches back against the Christmas tree so he can pan over to Winnie. He follows her as she hurries across the living room to the kitchen, her high heels tapping the authority of her decision. The swinging door flaps behind her, releasing the sound and the smell of popcorn exploding in the skillet Fred is tending on the stove.

In a minute, she returns with Sheridan straddling her hip and nestles into the sofa, smiling at the whirring camera. She places her daughter beside her, and then scoots her closer to her, making sure they are both in the picture. Chester squats on his heels, refocusing the lens so that he can get a close-up of his wife and sister-in-law. Then he aims at Sheridan, who begins to grab at the string of cranberries Virginia is threading.

"No, honey." Virginia tries to loosen her niece's tight, chubby fist from the cranberries. "Don't do that. I don't want you to break the thread." She looks expectantly at Winnie, waiting for her to reprimand Sheridan.

Instead, Winnie is smiling at the camera, listening now to Bing Crosby's romantic version of "White Christmas." She wishes that Fred would come in and get in the picture. He seems to be hiding back there in the kitchen, delivering one bowl of popcorn and immediately starting up yet another batch, hardly speaking to anybody in between. Why can't he relax and join them? After all, she is thinking, it is Christmas. A time to remember, to celebrate.

Sheridan breaks a handful of berries from Virginia's thread, gurgles happily, and shoves it into her mouth. A couple of the berries roll down into her lap, and then to the floor.

"No!" Virginia shakes a finger at Sheridan and then frowns at Winnie. She pulls Sheridan's arm away from her mouth. "Winnie, she's got a whole bunch of berries in her mouth. She might get choked on one."

The rebuke in Virginia's voice turns Winnie away from the camera. She bends down toward Sheridan and fishes in her mouth with her index finger, holding the back of Sheridan's head so she can't squirm away. Bits of red cranberry skins are already stuck to a string of saliva hanging from Sheridan's chin.

"Good, good. Oh, that's a nice one. Smile at Uncle Chester." Chester, still squatting, moves in with a ducklike motion toward the sofa. But Sheridan is starting to kick the sofa and cry. The string of saliva and cranberries has dribbled down the Mickey Mouse face on the front of her romper, and now her tears begin to roll down her cheeks.

"Oh now, Chester, don't take a movie of this. Nobody'll want to see this." Winnie turns so that her back partially shields Sheridan from the camera. She presses a napkin into a drop of saliva that has fallen onto the sofa, trying to blot it out of the new brocade.

"That's right, Chester. You'll encourage the child. Hush, hush, there." Virginia has turned to Sheridan with a tissue, mopping at her chin with quick, efficient strokes, so that Sheridan's wail becomes a protesting siren.

"Cheer her up, honey," Chester tells his wife, the camera still whirring.

"Oh heavens, Chester," Virginia scowls, then remembers that she is still in the camera's range. She smiles down at Sheridan, putting her own rouged cheek next to the chubby cheek still partly filled with cranberries. She gives the camera a flirtatious smile and tickles her niece's stomach, a gesture that makes Sheridan squirm harder to get down.

The kitchen door swings open abruptly and bangs against the wall. Fred backs through the door into the living room, both hands holding bowls peaked with white-and-gold popcorn kernels.

"We sure need that popcorn, Fred. That's good timing," says Virginia, dropping her hand from Sheridan's stomach.

Then Fred turns and sees the camera, directed now at him. He angrily waves a bowl of popcorn toward the lens, as if he could turn the camera off with the motion. "Cut that out now," he growls.

Sheridan sees her father and wiggles out of Winnie's hands. Winnie sets her on the floor, holding her beneath her arms until she is steady on her feet.

Virginia beams. "Get her with her daddy, Chester." She waves both hands at Sheridan's little back. "Go on, honey. Go to your daddy."

Still squatting, Chester turns on his heels, balances by sticking one leg out, and follows his niece with his camera.

Sheridan toddles confidently toward her father's long legs. Her shoe soles slap softly against the floor, and Fred recognizes the sound for a split second before he sees her in the path of his next step. He redirects his movement so abruptly that his precarious balance of popcorn and anger tips into confusion.

As if in slow motion, Fred's leg swings to the left to avoid Sheridan. His body swerves in a long ripple while his foot finds a place to land.

The bowl of popcorn in Fred's left hand slips to the floor and shatters into ceramic fragments. Popcorn kernels scatter across the living-room floor.

Then it is stop action.

"Dammit, see what that damn camera made me do?" Fred sets the other bowl down heavily on the floor and falls to his hands and knees to retrieve the bits of broken bowl. Winnie rushes over to sweep a wailing Sheridan off the floor, rescuing her from the debris of popcorn and pottery shards. Sheridan's feet knock against each other in their white lace-up shoes, and she lets out an even louder wail when Winnie places her on the sofa.

"Hush, sweetie pie. It's okay. You're not hurt." Winnie lifts Sheridan into her lap and strokes her wispy hair back from her forehead. With a paper Christmas napkin, she tries to wipe the tears that are streaming down her cheeks. But she is more worried about Fred than about Sheridan.

As Winnie holds Sheridan on her lap and watches her husband scramble for the loose popcorn and broken pottery, the image of a weather vane atop the barn on the Bloomer family farm in Millsdale pops into her mind. Her mental picture of a rusted metal rooster dissolves then into Fred: Fred sent spinning uncontrollably by the climate around him. Only the week before, he was so depressed by the prospect of buying Christmas gifts that he asked Ed Jolly for an advance on his January paycheck. He went out the same day and blew most of it on a big rocking horse for Sheridan and surprises for Winnie. In a giddy mood, he came home and placed three packages beneath the tree, all bearing Winnie's name. He was happy as a lark, Winnie thinks, whistling "Silver Bells" and dancing with her by the tree. But now, all weekend, he's been silent, brooding about how they'll pay the January bills. Though he won't admit it, Winnie is certain he regrets buying one small package in particular—the one shaped like it contains the Bulova watch she admired several times in a jewelry-store window downtown.

She watches her husband helplessly, still shushing Sheridan and stroking her hair, knowing she is unable either to change the weather or to steady him toward one direction or another.

Virginia kneels beside Fred, scooping popcorn into the large ashtray Winnie made in a ceramics class.

Chester is still filming when Fred glances up from his squatting position in the midst of spilled popcorn and broken pottery. Wiring his mouth into a tight grimace, he crouches up to his brother and the camera, waving his arms horizontally, as deliberately as if he were a referee signaling a call, an out, in a baseball game. Then he extends his arm and stretches out his palm against the camera lens.

"Oh, Fred. You're just a party pooper." Chester turns off his camera. "A real spoilsport."

SIX

FLYING THE COOP
1956

Elvis Presley's voice blares out, *You ain't nothing but a hound dog,* from Amanda's bedroom. Before the locked door, Virginia stands with her hands on her hips and a frown on her face, talking to her older daughter through the thin wood.

"Amanda, it's time to go. Everybody's ready but you." Virginia says her words between the raps she is making on the door.

Elvis' voice is the only answer . . . *cryin' all the time.*

The attic fan pulls an artificial July breeze through the windows in the house and blows Virginia's skirt into a blue cotton tent that licks her tan legs. "Do you hear me? Uncle Fred and Aunt Winnie are already here. We've loaded up the car. We're all waiting for you." Her mouth contracts into a tight line, and she knocks on the door again, harder this time.

Behind her in the family room, Chester paces in front of the bulky Zenith television set, trying to catch the last few minutes of the baseball game before he and his brother drive their families to the coast. There is a spot near Pensacola on the Florida Panhandle where he takes his family for a long weekend every summer. This year he persuaded Virginia that they should invite Fred and Winnie along, mostly to console them: Ed Jolly has just turned down Fred's suggestion that he expand the store's stockroom to do equipment repairs in the back. "Doesn't sound like much to be disappointed about, does it?" Fred said. "But, hell, I researched that report for three weeks! He's a fool, that's what he is. He'd make enough on lawn-mower repair alone to cover the expansion." He laughed abruptly. "If he's not gonna let me be manager, he could at least let me tinker around in the back."

Now the two of them watch television together, but there is an unspoken tension between them. The television set itself is a sign of the two promotions that Ace Farm Supply has given Chester in as many years. But the television looks odd: Ruby Ann has left her "Winky Dink" green plastic sheet adhered to the tiny black and white screen. Chester likes to watch baseball with the shield attached. He tells Fred it makes the field look green instead of gray.

Today Chester imagines drawing his own game on it, the way his daughter draws her erasable cartoon characters there. The Washington Senators or the St. Louis Cardinals are the nearest thing to a southern baseball team around. But ever since Dizzy Dean left the Cardinals in 1937—almost twenty years ago—it seems neither team ever has a good season against the Brooklyn Dodgers or Casey Stengel's Yankees. But it is a great season, as always, for Dizzy Dean's running commentary on the games. His southern accent makes Chester proud of the whole region. "Who cares if his grammar is correct?" Chester says to Fred, who nods. "The man cares about the game, about the men who play it."

After Dizzy Dean leaves his post, Chester will never like baseball quite as well as he does in 1956. But it will set him free from drinking Falstaff; he feels guilty drinking any beer but the brand that sponsors Diz, even though he likes Jax better. But Chester's loyalty to Dizzy Dean runs deep. Every summer when he takes his family down to the Florida coast, he is careful to pass through the small town of Rinkin, where a young Dizzy Dean once lived long enough for the chamber of commerce to claim him as their own. Their brochures say that during the cotton-picking season in 1920, the Dean family—including both Dizzy and his young brother Daffy—picked up their Arkansas roots and moved to Mississippi. The brochure does not say exactly how long they lived in Rinkin. Now Dizzy Dean Drive runs parallel to the railroad tracks, a dusty avenue leading down to the local ball park.

A weathered billboard outside the town, however, announces only that they are entering "Rinkin, the Pickle Capital of the World." Chester always reverently points out their entrance into Rinkin when he sees the billboard. "This is Diz's town," he says. And Amanda and Ruby Ann look up politely from their Tiny Tears dolls, Nancy Drew books, or later, their teen fan magazines.

"Why don't they put up a billboard for him?" Virginia always asks. "They named a street for him, didn't they? So why don't they change that tacky billboard? Pickles, of all things! Who wants to hear about pickles!"

She asks it every year, until, in 1958, the chamber of commerce will replace the pickle-capital sign with one welcoming travelers to Rinkin, "The Home of Dizzy Dean." Then the billboard will become a point of personal satisfaction with Virginia, as if the chamber of commerce had heard her complaints. On their vacation every year, she will point it out, to Chester's annoyance, even before he can say a word about Dizzy Dean.

This year, since Fred and Winnie are going with them, Virginia is looking forward to pointing out the billboard to them, explaining how it should advertise the town's most famous resident instead of pickles.

If she can ever get Amanda out of her bedroom.

Virginia raps on the door again, as hard as her knuckles will let her. The Elvis record suddenly wails to a halt, and the needle on Amanda's record player rakes across it.

Virginia's voice booms into the silence. "Young lady, I'll have you know you're in trouble. You're in trouble right . . ."

"Yeah, Mom?" Amanda swings the door open. Her head is covered with pincurls held in place with crossed bobby pins. A wad of bubble gum balloons from her mouth, snaps, and disappears in a pink flash between her teeth. "Whaddaya want?"

Virginia taps a fingernail against the crystal of her watch, glaring at Amanda. "Ten minutes. You have ten minutes." She turns away, then swings back just as Amanda's door is closing. "And leave the parakeet some extra birdseed."

Chester watches the remaining minutes of the ball game, secretly relieved that Amanda is holding up their departure. It gives him a chance to be alone with Fred, to cheer him up. He ought to need cheering up, Chester thinks, but he can't really tell about his brother. Fred's either telling jokes or stony quiet and depressed. And how's a man supposed to know what his brother's thinking, anyway?

Holding one of Chester's Falstaffs in one hand, Fred is sunk deep into one of Virginia's overstuffed armchairs. He shakes his head and grunts when Mickey Mantle saunters up to home plate, bat in hand.

"Pitiful, just pitiful," Chester says when the ball sails over the back fence into the bleachers. "You and me oughtta start our own team."

Fred grins, stretches one arm out and feels his bicep. "I don't know. I think my ball days are over."

Chester nods his head in the direction of the front window. Outside, Sheridan can be seen, teaching Ruby Ann how to hold her legs straight when she turns a cartwheel. But Ruby Ann flips over like a little frog, her chubby legs barely in the air.

"We got the cheerleaders already, though," Chester says.

"Looks to me like we're raising us some good ones." Then he snaps his fingers, both hands at once. "Dadgummit, I almost forgot, we'll want the movie camera. Lotta happy moments there on the beach. We'll get some good ones of the girls, doncha think?"

He dashes out and rummages in the hall closet, where he keeps the camera stored, and misses the sour look that crosses his brother's face. Fred stares at the television and takes another sip of beer. He raises his eyes from the screen when Amanda comes dashing through the living room, her round zippered suitcase in one hand and Virginia's old easel under the other arm.

Holding up the easel, she says triumphantly, "I'm going to paint the ocean!" And then, hurrying on, she calls over her shoulder, "Race you to the car, Uncle Fred! Last one to the car doesn't get to go to the beach!"

Through the window, Amanda can be seen yelling something at Ruby Ann and Sheridan. They stop in midcartwheel and race her to the car.

But there is a new sound in the living room: the chirping of a parakeet. The green-and-yellow bird has fluttered out the open door of Amanda's room. A birdcage, its wire door partially ajar, hangs from the hook of its stand in her room like a solitary beacon signaling a ship's return.

"Oh for cryin out loud." Chester's fists are on both hips.

"Get him, Chester!" Virginia's blue eyes are round. She clutches one hand over her heart and then throws both arms into the air. "I'll get a shoebox, that's what!" She scurries out so fast that the rubber soles of her canvas sandals squeak on the floor.

Fred approaches the bird where it perches on the round antenna of the television set. "Here, Tweety," he whispers, cupping his hands in front of him. "Don't be scared."

"I have half a mind to let the damn thing go, what with all that racket it makes . . ." Chester runs a hand through his hair.

"Shhh, you'll scare the little thing." Just as Fred reaches out to cup the bird, it blinks rapidly and flutters over his shoulder, winging its way tentatively back to Amanda's bedroom.

"Well, I'll be darned," says Fred, following it to the bedroom. "Would you come look at this." The parakeet has perched on the top of its cage, it head rigid and straight, and its yellow chest puffed out like a tiny soldier clad in a bright uniform.

Virginia rushes up to Fred, waving a shoebox.

"Not yet," he murmurs, blocking her path with his hand. He reaches one long arm behind the parakeet while it stares beadily at his face. Then he gently cups both hands around it.

"Fred's got it, he's got it," Virginia whispers to Chester, standing behind her with a frown puckering his forehead.

Fred carefully tries to slide both hands through the door of the cage, but it is too small. Using one hand as a shield to block the door, he releases the bird into the cage and gently latches it.

"There you go." He dusts his hands. The parakeet sits now on a wooden swing stained with speckled droppings and stares out at Fred with its black, beady eyes. Its head is cocked in an expression that looks like puzzlement to Fred.

"Almost hate to put the fellow back there," he says softly. "See there how he's looking at me?"

"Oh, I don't think so, Fred," breathes Virginia. "Looked to me like the poor little thing wanted to be back there in his cage. That's where he flew. I think he's looking at you to say thank-you."

Chester hoists the movie camera and grunts. "Well, that's where he belongs, whether he wants to be there or not." The door slams behind him.

In the stillness of the empty house, Virginia gazes up at Fred, and she feels suddenly that she is seeing her husband's younger brother for the first time: the angular shape of his face, his strong chin, the unexpected curl of gray in his dark hair, the surprising hurt in his grayer eyes, a soft look of loss. And she does something that surprises them both, something that will be an unspoken secret between them for several years until it will burst forth out of memory and change their lives: she reaches up and kisses him, not on his cheek but directly on the full curve of his mouth. As if the touch releases some mysterious tension already rising in him, he pulls her to him, almost desperately. Her breasts brush the solid hardness of his chest until he releases her just as quickly and they look at each other in surprise.

"Mommy!" Ruby Ann bursts through the front door, one hand cupped into her crotch. "I hafta go to the bathroom. Tell Daddy he can't go yet." She hurries back out and down the front walk, running like a little squat duck.

Virginia, with a quick shake of her head, chases after her. "Well you certainly can't go in the yard, Ruby Ann! Where are you going?" Dismayed, she watches her daughter scurrying toward the sign that says "Fill Up at Billups," at the new gas station that has just gone up on the corner next door. Ruby Ann turns and crosses her legs, pointing to the wavy glass windows of the room marked Ladies.

"To the pretty bathroom!" she cries, and scoots through the door.

"Honest to goodness . . ." Virginia's voice trails off. She shrugs at Fred, still standing with his back against the doorframe watching her. "Kids. She'll grow up to be a grease monkey if we don't move soon." But Virginia cannot look at Fred as she speaks.

"Don't you worry about that, Virginia Moody," says Fred, his voice barely above a whisper. "If she grows up to be half as beautiful as you are, she'll be doing just fine."

Virginia raises her eyes to Fred's, and in the following silent seconds, she feels that she is breathing the very air he exhales, surrendering her own breath back to him. She glances down at the shoebox she still holds, startled for a moment to see it in her hand. Placing it gently on the top of the television set, she gathers her purse and leaves to join Chester outside.

Chester is sliding the movie camera into the station wagon underneath Sheridan's feet, since Amanda has insisted it would be too uncomfortable under hers. After Amanda's complaints, Winnie had leaned over and whispered to Sheridan that, after all, they are guests of Uncle Chester's, wouldn't she be a sweet girl and offer to let Uncle Chester put the camera on the floor there. Right *there*, where she can use it like a footrest. And before Sheridan can say anything, before she can either protest or agree, Winnie has pointed to the floor of the back seat and told Chester to put it there, right there, it won't be in Sheridan's way. It won't bother Sheridan a bit, Winnie assures him again, loudly. There is a slightly triumphant tone to her voice, an edge through which she tells Virginia that *her* daughter is better behaved than Amanda.

Virginia, though, hasn't paid attention to the undercurrents in Winnie's voice. She puts her things in the front seat, dismayed that Winnie has automatically climbed into the back seat beside Amanda, forcing her to sit in front, between her husband and Fred. She slides across the seat, brushing her skirt down over her knees, finding just the right place on the floor for her purse. She is too distracted by the warmth that Fred's lips have left on her mouth to notice Winnie's accusing tone.

In the tiny rear seat, Sheridan has been sitting alone for several minutes now, kicking her Keds against the camera case and munching one of the mayonnaise-and-banana sandwiches—Ruby Ann's favorite—that Virginia packed for them. She is waiting for Chester and Fred, who has just joined them, to finish loading the station wagon, trying to be the sweet girl Winnie told her to be.

Finally, when Ruby Ann dashes into the back seat, the car rumbles down the two-lane highway, its seven occupants staring out the windows. Virginia chatters nervously to Fred about the time Chester took her to hear Bing Crosby sing at a nightclub in Pensacola. Since Fred nods and smiles down at Virginia with a look that is unusually warm and friendly, Winnie strains to hear what Virginia is telling him—something about a club, her coffee club, she decides—while she pretends to look absently out the window of the back seat, watching the pine trees grow scrubbier as they near the coast.

"This is Diz's town," Chester says when they approach the billboard that announces pickles. The big Plymouth eases over the railroad tracks at the edge of town. He sprinkles the ashes of his cigar out the window and glances into the rearview mirror for a response to his announcement. He doesn't notice Ruby Ann looking up politely and nodding in the last seat. Instead, something else grabs his attention—a tattered banner stretches across the main street announcing an exhibition game between two minor-league teams. Across the bottom, where the wind has torn into the sheeting, are the words "Daffy Dean, Guest Commentator. And Surprise Friend!"

"Well," Virginia says, "at least they put up a banner for Dizzy's brother." She turns to Fred, trying to think of something else to say, something to calm the fluttering that Fred's kiss has still left in her heart. "But you'd think they'd change that pickle-capital sign—you know, the one we passed back there—for one for Dizzy Dean. Especially now he's in the Hall of Fame."

Fred laughs and leans forward to look across Virginia at Chester. "You know what ole Diz said when they elected him to the Hall of Fame? He thanked the good Lord for his good right arm, his strong back, and his weak mind."

Chester, too busy looking at street signs to listen to Fred, nods distractedly. Beside him, Virginia rearranges her skirt across her lap and smiles, relieved that the conversation between Fred and Chester seems just as it would have been the day before, or an hour before, before anything so strange as kissing her husband's brother had occurred. Or did it happen at all? she wonders.

"A strong arm and a weak mind," she repeats after Fred. "Isn't that cute?"

"A weak mind." Behind her sunglasses, Amanda rolls her eyes and groans. "Is that how he got into the Hall of Shame?"

The car creeps to an even slower pace. Chester drapes his wrist over the steering wheel and turns around to face Amanda. "What's that? Don't you make fun of Dizzy Dean, you hear? Or the Baseball Hall of Fame. That's America you're making fun of."

"I think he's cute," Virginia says over her shoulder to Amanda. "He says some cute things sometimes."

Amanda slumps deeper into the back seat. "Dizzy Dean might not have a mind at all. I saw a headline one time on Daddy's sports page after some pitcher hit him in the head with a ball. It said, 'Dean's Head X-Rayed; Nothing Found.' " She giggles. "What do you think about that?"

"Honest to goodness, young lady, I don't know where you get your ideas," says Virginia.

"I saw it myself. It's true," Amanda retorts. "It was in the *Sun-Herald*, on the front page of the sports section."

Winnie frowns at her niece. "They meant they didn't find anything wrong in his head, honey, that's all. And what were you doing reading the sports page, anyway? That's for men."

Fred shrugs. "He may not be a mighty smart man, but hell, I don't care what he's got or hasn't got in his head. He's a damn good ballplayer. And that's all that counts in my book."

"Well, Dizzy Dean sure isn't cute." Amanda squints at the back of her mother's head and snorts, "Mama thinks that dumb ole Milton Berle's cute, too. Good Lord." She shakes her bangs out of her eyes with a flip of her head and settles back into the seat. "That's why Daddy smokes a cigar, just to look like Milton Berle. Put it out, Daddy. It stinks. P-*yew.*" She is fanning the air in front of her face with her hand.

Chester shakes a finger into the rearview mirror. "You're getting too big for your britches. You just settle down."

"You look like a horse when you shake your head like that, not like a young lady," says Virginia over her shoulder, chiming in over Chester's voice. "And don't you take the Lord's name in vain." She starts to turn back but then tosses back, "Milton Berle *is* cute." She glances at Fred and continues, trying, with all the words streaming from her mouth, to build a bridge back to normality, back to the world before she kissed him. "But, after all, the chamber of commerce named a whole street for Dizzy Dean. I just don't understand it. Pickles, of all . . ."

Chester tosses the moist stub of his cigar out the window and swings the car off the main street, turning between the Rinkin movie theater and the post office, where Dizzy Dean Drive begins.

"Let's see what's going on at the ball park. This 'surprise' just might be Dizzy himself," says Chester. He lights a cigarette, and then holds out his package of Lucky Strikes to Fred. "Whaddaya say, Fred? Take a look at the goings-on here?"

"Oh God, Daddy," Amanda mutters, leaning out the window to breathe the fresh air. "First a cigar and now cigarettes!"

Winnie jabs a knee through the seatback at Fred, trying to warn him against agreeing with Chester.

"Sure, sure. Let's see if old Diz is here in town." Fred mutters the last few words through his cigarette, as he fumbles through his pockets for a match.

Virginia punches in the lighter on the dashboard, harder than necessary. "Wait a second, here's a light, Fred." She eyes Chester, wishing now that she hadn't been so enthusiastic about Dizzy Dean. "Really, Chester, the girls will be tired soon. We've still got two hours ahead of us. We need to get there." Suddenly, the hours ahead of her in the car, between Chester and Fred, seem like an eternity. She would like nothing more than to shut herself in the bathroom at home for a long hot shower to ease the tension between her shoulders.

"Oh, we won't be long, we won't be long." Gravel crunches beneath the car wheels as Chester turns off the road.

Now the station wagon rolls into the dusty parking lot of the ball park. The voice of an announcer bellows over the crowded bleachers, echoing past the rows of parked cars, until the sound of his words has an authority beyond what he reports happening on the baseball diamond.

"Is it Daffy Duck?" asks Ruby Ann.

Amanda presses her palms against her ears. "It's too loud. Why do they always shout like that? He sounds just like some ole hick."

"No, it's not Daffy Duck," Sheridan says importantly to Ruby Ann. "It's Daffy Dean. They're brothers."

Virginia reaches back and playfully slaps at Amanda's leg. "No louder than Elvis," she says. "Those rock 'n' roll records you're always listening to. And Elvis is just some Tupelo hick."

"He is not!" Amanda folds her arms across her chest and flounces back against the seat.

Not bothering yet to park the car, Chester shuts off the motor in the middle of the lot so he can hear better. He and Fred listen. As they concentrate, a similar squint wrinkles their eyes, making the resemblance between them stronger.

"Is it Daffy Duck?" Ruby Ann asks again, this time aiming her voice for the adults in the front seat. Sheridan shoots her a condescending look of disgust.

There is silence except for the voice announcing a second strike. A warm summer breeze wafts through the door that Winnie has just opened. She stretches out her leg and makes circles in the dust with the toe of one of her oxfords.

The voice rises. "It's a hit! Lester Porter has a hit! He's roundin first . . . he's slidin into second." A thick roar rises from the ball park while the cloud of dust surrounding second base begins to float away. "He slud right into second base just like. . ."

Fred lets out a whoop. "It's not Daffy, it's Dizzy! That's old Diz, I swear to it! C'mon, let's go." He points a finger at a parking space a couple of rows away and slaps his wallet in his back pocket. "I've got enough for all our tickets. Chester, there's a spot over there right beside that Packard." He hits the dashboard with his palm. "Let's go. This is our lucky day."

As Winnie slams her door shut, Fred turns all the way around to face her. A grin cracks his face, but there is a worried frown in his eyes. "This is a once-in-a-lifetime chance. Ole Diz himself! We can spare it, Win."

Amanda kicks the back of the front seat with her saddle shoe. "Well y'all just better take me to hear Buddy Holly when he comes to Mobile next month then, if I have to waste my time on these dumb ole hicks in Rinkin. Rinky-dink Rinkin."

"You should be glad you're taking a vacation at all, Amanda," Winnie informs her. "You know, once there was a man without any shoes, complaining and fussing about his bare feet, and then he saw a man without any feet at all. He didn't fuss so much, then."

Amanda turns to the window and, just as Virginia glances back, makes a gagging gesture by holding her throat and sticking out her tongue. Behind her, Ruby Ann screeches in delight.

"Amanda! You behave yourself." Virginia picks her purse off the floor and fumbles inside for a lipstick. "And don't you kick that seat again, young lady. You'll hurt the car. You're too big for that."

"Well, Aunt Winnie kicked the back of Uncle Fred's seat, and I was nice enough not to say anything about it," Amanda retorts.

"I most certainly did not." Winnie flushes, feeling like a teenager. There is a short pause while she thinks. "I was just crossing my legs and bumped it, that's all."

Virginia is silent as she smooths a stroke of red over her lips. She clicks the cap back on her lipstick and turns to Amanda. "You can paint the ball game while we watch."

"Paint this rinky-dink town?" Amanda's lip curls. "I'll save my watercolors for the beach, thank you very much."

"Rinky-dink Rinkin. Rinky-dink Rinkin." Sheridan and Ruby Ann chant in the back.

Her chubby fists pounding the seat in front of her, Ruby Ann keeps the beat as the rhythm rises. "Rinky-dink Rinkin. Rinky-dink Rinkin."

Winnie wheels around to them, and shakes Sheridan's shoulder. "You two hush. That's enough of that silliness. See that nice man over there?"

She nods her head at a man standing between two cars at the edge of the parking lot, his back turned to them. "He might hear you, and then what would he think? He sure wouldn't think you're very nice little girls. We're his guests here in Rinkin. We better behave ourselves."

The man turns and dips slightly, his attention focused not on the seven occupants in the station wagon but on the yellow stream he is sending into the dust.

A chortle erupts from Chester. "Winnie, hon, I b'lieve you picked us the wrong host."

Winnie flinches and sets her jaw. Her neck stiffens. "Girls, don't look."

The chant from the rear seat rises again like a cheer that accompanies the sound of the announcer's voice. "Rinky-dink, rinky-dink, rinky-dink Rinkin . . ."

SEVEN

LOVE'S REFRAIN
1964

In the late evening of mid-July, just as the sun is streaking the western sky gold and orange, Sheridan dashes through the front door of Ruby Ann's house. Tucked beneath her arm is a square, flat package. Ruby Ann greets her in a conspiratorial silence, as if there is a mysterious ritual they are about to perform. Together, they pull the living-room draperies shut so that the green leaves on the oak outside are hidden. In the semidarkness, Sheridan tears the cellophane from a new record album. "This one's in stereo. See?" she says, pointing to the word above the title *Meet the Beatles*. "It's not mono like the other one."

"Put on 'This Boy' first," whispers Ruby Ann. She clutches a copy of *Sixteen* magazine, opened to a full-page spread on the Beatles.

The needle skids onto the record, making Paul McCartney's voice jump loudly from the stereo speaker. Ruby Ann races over in her sock feet; one plaid kneesock falls to her thin ankle.

"Be careful!" she hisses. "Mama'll kill me if you wreck the needle. It's a brand-new stereo, you know. Daddy just bought it."

"I know," mutters Sheridan, a hint of envy in her voice. She pulls the curtain aside so that light streams across the record. "I can't find the right groove. Here." She stands back, as "I Saw Her Standing There" erupts into the room. " 'This Boy' is next."

Her eyes closed, Ruby Ann settles back into the sofa, holding a picture of Ringo to her cheek. Sheridan sprawls on the carpet before one speaker, gazing intently at the four faces on the record cover. "It's too bad John is married," she says. "He's the most interesting one."

"You better watch out," warns Ruby Ann. "What would ole Ernie Crenshaw say? He'd make you give his ring back, I bet." In her voice is the taunt of jealousy.

"Ernie wouldn't care. I like John's nose." Sheridan traces its slightly crooked outline on the record jacket. Tightened on her middle finger with a crossed rubber band is an outsize silver ring with the black initial *E*. It wobbles gently as her hand descends John's nose.

"How can you say that?" Ruby Ann's voice rises, incredulous. "Ringo has the best nose." She kisses her index finger and presses it gently to the lips on Ringo's grinning picture in *Sixteen* magazine, leaving an ink smudge just below Ringo's right nostril. The effect is of a nosebleed.

"John's smarter than Ringo," Sheridan retorts. "You can tell by the way he smiles."

"He is not!" Ruby Ann scowls at the shadow that is Sheridan, lying on her stomach on the floor before the stereo speakers. "Besides, what's all this junk about John? I thought you liked Paul the best."

"I like Paul's eyes. But John . . ."

The first strains of Paul McCartney's voice singing "This Boy" filter through the speakers. "Shhh!" Ruby Ann commands, sinking back onto one of her mother's needlepoint pillows, her eyes closed.

Sheridan rises and, wrapping her arms around herself, begins to sway to the music.

"Girls?" There is a light tap on the door, and then Chester enters, the light on his movie camera glowing bright red. He crouches behind the sofa and aims the lens down at Ruby Ann.

"Daddy!" she screeches, jumping up. She clutches the magazine to her chest as if she has been caught without a shirt, exposed.

"Don't mind me, girls," says Chester, sweeping the camera toward Sheridan. Sheridan has sat up and is shielding her face with the album cover.

"Get out of here, Daddy! Go away!"

Chester twists a knob on the camera and abruptly waves at them with his other hand, gesturing to them to go on about their business. "Go ahead, have yourselves a good time. Don't let me get in the way of your fun."

"Fun!" shouts Ruby Ann. "How can we have fun . . ."

"Oh, Uncle Chester," Sheridan whines. "Leave us alone."

Still aiming at them, Chester edges over to the curtains and draws them back. "Why is it so dark in here? There's not enough light . . ."

"We're missing the best song!" shrieks Ruby Ann, as "This Boy" begins to soar above their own voices.

Cheerfully, Chester casts his camera at her and adjusts the lens. "But isn't this a happy moment? Don't you want a movie. . ."

"You're making us miss it!" Ruby Ann's hands are knotted into fists she holds at her hips, her elbows jutting out like skinny wings.

"Oh now," begins Chester, plucking at the knees of his pants so that he can squat for a better angle on them.

"Please, Uncle Chester," pleads Sheridan. "This is our very favorite song."

"Get out of here!" yells Ruby Ann. She throws the magazine at the wall and stomps toward the door.

"Now, that's not going to look very nice in our movie," Chester tells her. "In ten years, you'll watch these pictures and wish . . ."

"I'll wish I could've listened to the Beatles in peace, that's what!"

The door cracks open again. This time Virginia peeks in, a dishcloth in one hand. "What's all this commotion?"

Ruby Ann runs to her and grabs her elbow. "Make Daddy leave us alone!"

"He's bugging us with his movies," Sheridan explains.

The music builds into a swell. *This boy would be happy just to love you, but oh my-yi-i . . .*

"Ohhh, I love this part," Ruby Ann moans. "This is my favorite . . ."

Chester moves in closer, trying to capture the rapturous look on her face. "That's right, honey. Just pretend I'm not here."

A frantic look of desperation and horror crosses Ruby Ann's face. "Mama!"

Virginia taps Chester's shoulder. "C'mon. Let's leave them alone. I think they'd have a better time if we weren't in here, Chester."

Hurt, Chester rises up from behind the camera and turns it off. "In ten years, they'll wish they could see themselves now."

"Not with these looks on their faces," Virginia laughs. "It's not worth upsetting them." She pauses, looking down at the record cover Sheridan has left on the stereo. "They are nice-looking boys, aren't they?"

Ruby Ann stamps her foot, making the stereo needle skate lightly over the lyrics of "It Won't Be Long." It skips from *Every night when everybody has fun . . .* and falls finally into a groove: *I'll be good like I know I should . . .*

"We missed my favorite song!" Ruby Ann shrieks. "And it's all Daddy's fault!"

"You can play it again," answers Virginia. "If you don't ruin the needle." She rubs her dishcloth across a smudge on the stereo, visible in the thin light streaming through the curtains Chester has parted.

From the driveway comes the sound of a car door slamming, and then a voice calls from the kitchen door, "Anybody home?" It is Winnie.

"Oh no," groans Sheridan.

Winnie strolls in, followed by Fred. "Here you are!" She glances at the stereo console with a longing look. "So this is the new stereo! Isn't it beautiful?" She runs her fingertips over the smooth walnut, while Virginia watches with dismay at the fingerprints Winnie is making. Winnie lingers over the words that spell the company in raised gold letters. "Like Braille must feel," she muses, her eyes closed as she runs her fingers over the cool metal. "Magna . . . vox," she quotes, punctuating each part of the word equally.

"Great . . . voice!" Sheridan exclaims. A look of recognition flashes across her face, amazed that some bit of information from a page in her Latin textbook could possibly relate to the outside world.

"I don't want to hear you using that slang, young lady," Winnie grimaces, a perfunctory response as natural as the winces she makes when her beautician teases her hair too close to her scalp during her weekly Saturday-morning appointment. "Sounds like something you got from *Mad* magazine."

"It's Latin," explains Sheridan.

"That foreign lingo is as bad as any," Winnie responds in a flat tone that indicates nothing could possibly surprise her. "How did your new stereo record sound on this?" She is still stroking the top of the console. "Was it worth the extra money?"

"We haven't even heard it all the way through," Sheridan complains.

"I mean, do you guys mind?" growls Ruby Ann, gritting her teeth.

Virginia rolls her eyes at Winnie. "Chester was trying to get a movie, and they got upset."

"I don't blame them one bit," says Fred. "Everybody needs their privacy."

"See?" Ruby Ann glares at her father. "Uncle Fred's so cool."

"We're on our way out, girls," says Virginia, glancing then at Chester, Winnie, and Fred, trying to get their agreement as she nods her head toward the door.

Sheridan bends over the stereo, starting the record again. As the song begins, Virginia pauses, tapping her toe. "This is a catchy tune."

Winnie picks up the album cover. "They look like hoodlums, if you ask me. That hair. And sideburns!"

Virginia laughs. "What could be more innocent than 'I Want to Hold Your Hand'? That's what they're singing. Listen to the words."

As though Virginia had slapped her, Winnie's cheeks immediately redden. "You never know where things'll lead," she snaps.

Fred contorts his angular body into a version of the bossa nova, grinning at Winnie. "There's nothing dangerous about this!" One hand on his belly, he glides his long body about a brief circumference between the stereo and the coffee table.

"Where did you learn that?" A frown twists Winnie's face.

"Saw it on TV," Fred grins, turning as he holds an imaginary partner in his arms.

"Fab, Daddy! Everybody do the twist!" Sheridan swivels her hips, lowering herself into a semisquat.

"I know this!" Flinging her dishcloth onto the stereo, Virginia echoes Fred's steps.

With a sly look, Chester bows behind his camera again and aims it at his brother's back.

Ruby Ann hurls the throw pillow at him. "Stop it!"

Just as she yells, the last note of the song vanishes into the scraping silence of the record grooves.

Fred stops his dance abruptly, suddenly embarrassed in the silence while Virginia continues moving to an imaginary beat.

"The song's over again." Sheridan's mouth sags in despair. "And we couldn't even hear it."

Ruby Ann begins to wail. "We'll probably never get to hear them! You'll always come barging in on us. We'll never have any privacy around here!"

A hopeful expression flashes across Sheridan's face. "The Beatles are coming to New Orleans in September. We could stay in the French Quarter." She throws a thrilled look at Ruby Ann. "We could see the Beatles in person!"

Ruby Ann lets out a shriek of a different sort and falls back on the sofa, her arms flailing. "Oh please! Amanda might come down from the Delta to take us over there. She'll probably even pay for our tickets, with all the money she's been making."

"She'll be married by September, honey," Virginia reminds her, sorrow in her eyes. "She'll be way up north."

Ruby Ann thrusts out her lower lip.

In a soft voice, Fred muses, "Amanda must be making a mint selling those sculptures of hers. Now that's a way to make a living . . ."

No one hears him but Virginia. "Paintings," she corrects him, a pleased gleam in her eye. "She's doing more oils now than sculptures. Like this . . ." She points to a canvas hanging above the sofa. "That's Amanda's. She just sent it." She laughs, "I'm not real sure what it means, but it makes me feel lively just to look at it, the way that little house seems to float across that checkered tablecloth, and those trees dancing behind it. Makes me want to dance with them."

Leaving the others to squabble about the Beatles, Fred leans across the couch to look more closely at the painting. "You know," he murmurs, "it looks like that yellow house Winnie and I rented for a while." He squints at Virginia, then points at the lawn in the painting. "See this blue lady, standing beside the chair here? That must be you, Ginny."

She laughs. "I better put some clothes on, if it is. And get that pretty living-room chair back inside before it rains. Back when I was painting, I drew things like I saw them. But now . . ." She stops, surveying the painting. "Well, it doesn't make much sense, steps going straight up to the sky, and all the seasons happening at once. Look here." She steps back, waving at the upper portion of the painting. "Is that a sun or a moon up there in Amanda's sky?"

"A moon," Fred answers.

"Who knows what it is? Makes you feel like anything can happen, doesn't it? Even right in your own backyard."

"Looks like you could spin right off the globe if you lived in that house." Fred leans closer to the canvas, peering into the solitary window Amanda has painted above the door. "Or disappear inside. You know, I never did like that yellow house much, but it looks kinda special here, the way Amanda's made it look. Where does she get her ideas? You reckon that's the way she dreams?"

Virginia shakes her head. "The only dreams Amanda talks about are integration and voter registration. Honest to goodness, I'm worried sick about her up there in the Delta, what with all those outside agitators and these murders going on. Chester drove all the way up there and couldn't even get her to come home . . ."

"Amanda's a mighty smart girl. She'll take care of herself," Fred slips his arm around Virginia and squeezes her shoulders gently.

"She sure takes care of herself with those paintings." Lowering her voice, Virginia whispers, "Now, I'm not one to brag on my girls, but do you know she sold a painting a little bigger than that for three hundred dollars? Some rich New Orleans banker bought it."

A thin whistle escapes Fred's lips as he examines the shapes of color on the canvas, the narrow yellow rectangle, the raised squares of red across the bottom, the dance of blue and gray in the sky.

A silence sets in the living room, broken by a sigh from Ruby Ann, oblivious to any conversation about art. She has turned to Chester, a plea in her eyes. "Oh please!"

"Wouldn't that be fab? New Orleans! And the Beatles!" Sheridan's hands are crossed on her chest, looking almost prayerful. "Oh, I'd go to New Orleans to see Paul! All the way to Liverpool!"

Chester points to the Magnavox stereo console in one corner of the living room. "But you can hear the Beatles on a brand-new stereo right here! Best seats in the house."

"It's not the same!" cries Ruby Ann, her lip beginning to quiver. "You're always doing special things for Amanda. Mama drove her to Mobile so she could hear Buddy Holly once. I remember that! And you hang her pictures in the living room! You can't fool me. You care more about Amanda. . ."

Virginia sweeps an arm around her younger daughter and squeezes her thin shoulders. "Now, now," she croons. "Don't get that Ruby-red temper of yours fired up so quick. We'll see about it; how about that?"

"What?" Chester's jaw slackens a bit. "See about doing what?"

Winnie backs away, her palms held out before her in a gesture of warding off evil. "Now hold on just a minute. Who knows what street gangs will be over there in New Orleans? You know what happened in *West Side Story.*" She wheels to Virginia. "If you haven't seen it, you ought to, before you talk about taking these girls to a big city."

"For heaven's sake, Winnie. You and Fred went to New Orleans on your honeymoon." Virginia frowns. "It's a beautiful city . . ."

"But we were married. And old enough to . . ."

"Honestly, you'd think you were born old," Virginia snaps and then flushes, shamefaced. "I'm sorry . . ."

Winnie's eyebrows have shot halfway up her forehead. "Well, I don't think I want Sheridan in all that rock 'n' roll . . ."

"If Ruby Ann gets to go, why can't I?" Sheridan folds her arms across her chest.

"Hold your horses, both of you. We don't know about any of this." Chester eyes Virginia. "The girls are in school in September. They'd miss their classes. How about that?" His eyes gleam triumphantly.

"They'll learn more on a trip to New Orleans than in a couple of days of school, what with all the museums and concerts and plays we could take them to," answers Virginia. "Now, I know it doesn't necessarily seem right, what with missing school and all, but it seems like . . ."

A puff of disgust escapes Winnie's lips. "Why, Virginia, what's come over you? Taking the girls out of school! It's the principle of the thing." She sniffs, "Besides, New Orleans is a long way to go just to hear some music. The girls have got the record."

Pointing to the stereo, Chester finishes Winnie's argument. "And a brand-new record player to play it on."

"It's not the same as seeing them! And besides"—Ruby Ann looks to her mother for support—"Mama'll take us, right Mom? She'll take real good care of us. She'll educate us."

"Maybe she'll take us shopping at Maison Blanche," Sheridan whispers, looking hopefully at Virginia.

"Ruby Ann's right, Chester. Seeing them isn't the same as hearing a record," Virginia agrees. "Remember how we saw Frank Sinatra in Pensacola right after the war? Somehow his songs just seemed to float in the air. 'I Couldn't Sleep A Wink Last Night'—that song was magic. The Beatles are no different from Frank Sinatra, when you get right down to it."

A groan comes from Sheridan. "Frank Sinatra! Holy cow!"

"Oh, Mama. Don't you understand anything?" Ruby Ann looks at her, hopeless.

Chester eyes her. "You watch it, young lady. Your mother understands you a lot better than I do right now. You better appreciate it." He lowers his voice and gives Winnie a sidelong look. "Cause I sure don't."

Virginia appeals to Chester. "Frank Sinatra never did us any harm, did he? Why, we used to love dancing to . . ."

Winnie waves the record jacket, impatiently fanning away Virginia's words. "But Sheridan's right. He's different from these Beatles. Sinatra was harmless." Bobbing her head to punctuate her proclamation, Winnie slides the album cover onto the stereo with a triumphant flourish, as if history were a vast land she appropriated for her own private use, laying claim to its territory and pronouncing everyone else an intruder on it.

Appalled to find her mother agreeing with anything she said,

Sheridan desperately appeals to Ruby Ann. "We didn't say there weren't some ways Frank Sinatra was a lot like the Beatles, did we, Ruby Ann? Sure, I mean . . ." She searches for some way she might compare them. "I mean, Frank Sinatra's thin, too. He's got long legs." Her eyes plead an earnest sincerity.

Ruby Ann smirks at her.

"Sending two little girls all the way over to New Orleans while school's in session just to see the Beatles is pure silliness." Winnie glances at Fred from the corner of her eye. "Tell them, Fred. Don't be so quiet at a time like this," she nudges him. "Don't you have something to say?"

Slowly, Fred pulls a Lucky Strike package from his chest pocket and thumps it against the heel of his hand. "I think Virginia's right."

Winnie gasps, and her mouth remains open, a silent cave outlined in pink.

"It's something they'll always remember," he continues, drawing out a cigarette. "Like that time we saw Dizzy Dean over in Rinkin. This sounds like a once-in-a-lifetime chance for the girls."

Regaining her breath, Winnie struggles for words to protest. "But, but . . . think of it! Tickets to a rock 'n' roll show! How expensive are these tickets anyway?"

Ruby Ann proudly thrusts her chin in the air. "My sister'll buy our tickets, I betcha!"

Frustrated, Winnie turns to Virginia, who shrugs. "They can't be all that much, can they? And it's a chance for the girls to see all the big museums. Think about it: they'll see the old French Quarter, maybe I'll take them for a ride on that streetcar of desire. That's such a pretty name for a trolley."

"I still stand where I always did. It's plain nonsense." The heels of Winnie's oxfords suddenly seem more firmly planted in the carpet.

Ruby Ann is practically hopping on the sofa. "But Amanda'll pay for both of us! She's making lots of money now, isn't she, Mama?" Before Virginia can answer, Ruby Ann goes on. "She's selling her paintings like crazy. And Mama'll take us everywhere in New Orleans! I love you, Mama!" Ruby Ann wraps her arms around her mother, beseeching her father. "Oh, let us go, Daddy. Let us hear the Beatles!" She scrambles over to where *Sixteen* magazine lies sprawling on the floor. Gathering it up, she smooths its pages and finds Ringo. "Oh, Ringo, just you wait," she croons.

Disgusted, Chester shakes his head and turns to Virginia. "Look at this. Our youngster!"

"It's like Fred says," Virginia informs him, "you're only young once."

A cheer rises simultaneously from Sheridan and Ruby Ann. Holding the record cover before her, Sheridan sails about, pretending she is slow-dancing with all four Beatles in a victory celebration. "We're going to hear the Beatles!" The words escape her throat not in the loud cheers that are coming from Ruby Ann but in a low murmur of slow belief.

Chester shakes his head in amazement. "Now, hold on. Nobody's decided anything. We're all getting carried away to kingdom come."

"Isn't that the truth?" Winnie chimes in. "Honest to goodness, Fred, you and Virginia both. I just can't approve of it, no matter what you two say. Who knows what hoodlums will be at that rock 'n' roll show?"

Impatiently, Fred flicks his cigarette ash in the direction of an ashtray. "They'll have a good time, that's all. Lord knows, there's not enough of that here in Libertyburg."

"Well, I'd be worried about Virginia at that show, too," snorts Winnie. "It's not safe for anybody."

"I'll go along," Fred volunteers, and amazement sags on Winnie's face.

Chester reaches down and carefully puts his movie camera into its case. He looks up at Winnie as he snaps the lid shut. "Looks like we're the only sane ones left in the family."

From the stage set up in the center of City Park's horseshoe-shaped stadium in New Orleans, Paul McCartney watches a policeman escorting a young girl off the football field, back toward the stands.

It is Sheridan, her long bangs flopping into her eyes. She is wearing a Beatles tee shirt and a plaid wraparound skirt.

Ruby Ann is already scrambling back up the concrete steps into the stadium seats. But other girls have begun to swarm over the fences and down into the field, pursued by policemen. They will either be arrested or, like Sheridan, firmly escorted back to their seats.

"Who's winning?" asks Paul, bending down into the microphone. But Sheridan does not hear the question; she is too busy plotting her escape from the grip of the policeman's hand on her arm. Go limp, she tells herself, remembering the civil-rights workers she's seen on television. They refused to walk to the police van after their arrest for "disturbing the peace" in Birmingham.

But somehow her body will not obey, and with the policeman still holding on to her, she walks back to the stands where hundreds of other girls are cheering her. Behind her, the Beatles launch into "All My Loving." *Close your eyes and I'll kiss you, tomorrow I'll miss you . . .*

"Don't you dare tell Mama about that policeman," Sheridan whispers to Ruby Ann.

But Ruby Ann barely hears her words. She just hugs Sheridan. "At least we tried to get closer to the Beatles," she says.

Weeks earlier, after Winnie and Chester finally agreed to let them attend the concert, Sheridan and Ruby Ann sent in their money orders for five and a half dollars apiece to Metairie, Louisiana, and on one joyous day their tickets arrived in the mail. ("Almost six dollars! My lands!" Winnie exclaimed. "As if we have money to burn on such nonsense." But the decision had been made.)

Just after Virginia and Fred dropped them off at the stadium, Ruby Ann and Sheridan desperately tried to stake out the best seats while Jackie DeShannon sang to a restless, screaming audience. On the ground just before the stage were several rows of folding chairs, reserved for disc jockeys, Sheridan told Ruby Ann. "Disc jockeys and debutantes," she added.

"Well, it's no fair," steamed Ruby Ann. Only several minutes after the Beatles began playing, the two girls raced onto the field to claim their rights.

Now, exiled back in the stands with Ruby Ann, Sheridan holds her heart and stares out at the stage, where four tiny figures bend toward microphones. Ruby Ann is gripping her hair into a wadded ball with one hand, and together they sit in silence, watching the pool of light on a stage far away, as if something from another world altogether is happening just beyond their reach.

Even years later, Sheridan will remember that night in New Orleans as one when her life began to change, when a window opened onto something exotic and somehow mysterious.

The magic of that hour was long fought for by Virginia and Fred. For weeks, Virginia had cajoled Chester about letting Ruby Ann and Sheridan go to New Orleans. Virginia, campaigning by inviting Winnie over for coffee, had found that her sister-in-law had become even more stubborn than Chester. Winnie set down her coffee cup and wiped at the corners of her mouth, suddenly pursed with tension.

"You and Fred both," she said. "Well, I just can't approve of it, no matter what you two say. The girls are too young for a trip as big as that. And who knows what riffraff will be at that rock 'n' roll show? Fred's ready to go out and buy her ticket."

"Fred?" Virginia asked. "What else is Fred saying now?"

Winnie waved her napkin. "Oh, the usual. . . how Sheridan should see the world, have a chance to take in New Orleans. Well, she's got her whole life ahead of her to do that . . ."

After Winnie had dismissed all her arguments, Virginia went to visit Fred at the hardware store. For some reason, she decided to be discreet, pulling her blue Pontiac into an unmetered parking space down the block and around the corner from the store. But how could anyone in town know that she wasn't seeing Fred for some ant poison or light bulbs? She laughed at herself as she combed her hair and smoothed on new lipstick in the mirror on the windshield flap. Frowning, she pulled out a gray hair curling at one ear. She was being silly, she told herself. This didn't have to be some secret mission . . . But Chester would feel betrayed, she knew, if he found out she'd visited Fred to plot their strategies against him and Winnie.

At the hardware store, she waited until he finished with a customer, then leaned confidentially on the counter.

She shook her head. "I tell you Fred, I'm worried," she began.

He clicked the cash register drawer shut, and rested one elbow on it. "Why, what's the trouble?"

"It's this business about Ruby Ann and Sheridan going to New Orleans . . ."

"Aw, don't tell me you're backing out on it, too. I thought I could count on you, Virginia. I'm surprised at you."

"No, no," she said quickly, fanning her hands at him. "I'm worried Chester and Winnie'll keep them from going. The girls are all excited about it now, but it looks like Chester's going to ruin the whole thing." Going to New Orleans would be a "grand opportunity" for Ruby Ann and Sheridan, she added, just as she had told Winnie not long ago.

Fred first agreed with Virginia and then invited her to lunch. "I'll save this for tomorrow," he said sheepishly, putting the sack lunch Winnie had packed for him that morning back in the stock room. Pulling the pencil from behind his ear, he drew his tan straw hat from a shelf and cocked it on his head. "We're off," he said, gathering his gray umbrella beneath one arm and offering Virginia the other.

Despite the dark clouds in the sky and the boom of thunder, they walked down to the diner several blocks away, with Virginia explaining that the Beatles, after all, were a wholesome young group.

"And they're such cute young men," Virginia continued, looking up to Fred for approval. The jut of his strong jaw was set, though, and he looked straight ahead. Suddenly afraid that he'd changed his mind, she shifted her tactic. "Ruby Ann and Sheridan just adore them. They're no different from Frank Sinatra, when you get right down to it," she continued, repeating the arguments she'd begun several nights ago, when Ruby Ann and Sheridan had brought home the Beatles' album. "And he never did us any harm, did he?"

But it wasn't Frank Sinatra or even the Beatles that Fred was thinking about when they settled into a plastic booth at the diner—near the windows, Virginia requested, so she could watch the play of lightning in the sky.

"New Orleans!" Fred shook his head. "What a city! Winnie and I went there on our honeymoon, you know. Course it wasn't as special as New York. Now, there's a city for you. I saw it for two days back during the war. Never dreamed I wouldn't get back there. Hell, I thought the whole world was at my fingertips back then." He drummed his fingers against the table, absently. "Seems like you get stuck, doesn't it, and you can't get out to save your life . . ." He paused and let the sudden, dark look on his face pass. "But my kid? Why, it's her chance to see something of the world, and if we can do that for her, why, what kind of dad would I be to stand in the way?"

"You'll get back to New York someday, Fred." Virginia let her eyes slip to his mouth as she spoke, suddenly remembering one summer day years ago when she had impulsively kissed those lips. What could possibly have possessed me that day? she thought, a quick blush rising on her face.

"I'm not a kid anymore. I'm forty, for God's sake. It's too late for me to see much of the world. I'd rather send Sheridan . . ."

"Too late?" Virginia's voice rose. "Oh my. If it's too late for you . . . well! I do have a few years on you, Fred Bloomer. One or two, anyway. And it sure isn't too late for me to go to New York."

One of the last remaining lunch customers, an old man leaning on a cane, walked heavily over to the jukebox and put in a coin. The voice that burst out was Johnny Gimble's, singing "Time Changes Everything."

Swaying her head to the rhythm, Virginia sang along, a confident soprano. *T'was a time when I thought of no other, and we sang our own love's refrain.* She grinned. "Well, if I don't make it to New York, I sure gotta tell you, Bob Wills and His Texas Playboys bring out the cowgirl in me. Makes me want to dance the two-step just like I was eighteen."

Pushing aside his plate, Fred sank his chin into the palm of his hand and studied her for a long minute. Then he folded his arms on the table to speak. "As long as you've got that sparkle in your eyes, you'll always look like you're eighteen. I remember the day Chester brought you to the farm to meet Mom and Dad—how old was I? Thirteen? Fourteen? Hell, I wanted to marry you myself, just for the twinkle in your eyes."

Behind Virginia's delighted laughter, Johnny Gimble's voice chimed, *The dark clouds are gone, there's blue skies again, 'cause time changes everything.* "I never would've known it," Virginia said. "You wouldn't even say a word to me."

"Now, what did a little old farm boy like Freddy Bloomer have to say to a beautiful young lady like Virginia Moody?"

"But I was going to be your own sister-in-law!" laughed Virginia.

"*Especially* if she was going to be his sister-in-law!" Fred sipped his coffee, watching her over the rim of the mug until he set it down. "You've still got that twinkle, you know," he continued. "It'll be there when you're ninety. And if I'm not pushing up daisies by then, you'll still be brightening up my days with those eyes."

From the jukebox sailed out the last of the Bob Wills song. *Good luck to you; may god bless you . . .*

"Now Fred," Virginia tried to scold him, but her eyes glinted with a different message. For the second time that day, she remembered the warmth of his chest pressed against her as she kissed him that summer day years ago. "Nobody ever knows what you're thinking." She looked at him intently, trying to dispel the memory, as the silence of the jukebox filled the restaurant with a new, somber mood. "Anyway, you're too good to be assistant manager at the hardware store. You oughtta get out of that place."

He shrugged. "'That place' pays my bills. It's not as easy as all that, you know. There's not much to choose from in this town, and Win's sure I'll make manager soon. Jolly's retiring, you know, and who else could he put in but me?" He frowned as he asked it. "Not that I want the damn job, of course—but it'll be good to have the extra dough. Hell, if this town had any, I'd rather drive a taxicab than shuffle boxes and invoices, but . . . ah hell." He grinned at her, but his eyes had turned a deeper gray, mirroring the sky outside. "Win likes it here, she likes the security. It's good for Sheridan, she says, a nice, safe place to raise a teenager, you know."

"Teenagers," Virginia mused. "Ruby Ann'll be one next year. They sure are growing up fast, aren't they?"

"Don't you know it. Sheridan's started drinking coffee in the morning."

"She's going steady with a boy, isn't she?"

Fred nodded somberly. "Some kid named Ernie Crenshaw."

"Is that a fact? Little Ernie Crenshaw. He used to deliver our paper, threw it right up on the front porch, like clockwork, every morning." She smiled, optimistically. "He's a nice boy."

Fred circled his coffee cup with both hands and stared into the dark liquid there. "Winnie found a pack of cigarettes in Sheridan's purse the other day, and now she thinks he's a bad influence. She's afraid he's on drugs."

"On drugs!" Virginia's mouth formed a circle. "Don't be ridiculous. Drugs in Libertyburg? Why, the biggest drug problem we have is the pharmacist's wife."

Fred glanced up sharply from his coffee. "You don't say?"

"Miltown," nodded Virginia. "But the kids? My goodness, it's just cigarettes. Now, even I tried those when I was young, and look how I turned out." Teasing, she put one hand behind her head and batted her eyes. She laughed. "Kids have to try things out. Don't you worry about it."

"Oh, it's not me," Fred answered. "It's Winnie. You name it, she'll worry it to death." He held his fingers outstretched, counting on them with the other hand. "A whine in the commode? It'll mean a big plumbing bill we can't pay. I'm fifteen minutes late to work? Ed Jolly's going to fire me. Ernie Crenshaw forgets a haircut or two? He's a drug addict. Hell, he's just trying to look like one of the Beatles." He shook his head and collapsed his hand into a fist. "And now a half-empty pack of cigarettes in Sheridan's purse means she's going to get knocked up . . ." He looked up quickly, to gauge whether he'd offended Virginia. "Sorry, Virginia. I tell you, though, it's enough to drive a man crazy sometimes."

"Honest to goodness," Virginia burst out, "who wants our kids to stay cooped up in Libertyburg all their lives?" Then she caught herself and laughed, trying to refrain from criticizing Winnie. "Well, I guess Chester does, for one. He can barely talk to Amanda on the phone without making a fuss about when she's coming back home. I'll declare, it's enough to keep her away."

"Oh, Chester's a homebody, that's all. So is Win, bless her heart. She just can't understand what I mean when . . ." Fred raised his eyebrows slightly, and a warm glow of appreciation shone from his face as he drew his gaze up the fitted bodice of Virginia's shirtwaist dress and fixed his eyes on hers. "I'm sure glad there's somebody in the family who understands, that's all. I'd think I was going nuts if everybody thought like Winnie and Chester. Sometimes I think I might go crazy anyway."

"You oughtta take a vacation, Fred. You should go on down to the beach again, like we did that summer . . ." The blush rose again on Virginia's cheeks as she remembered the kiss that launched that trip to the Florida coast years ago, and the way she had spent the vacation both avoiding Fred and watching him from a distance. "Take your swimming trunks and get away from it all. You're a great swimmer," she said, remembering the way his biceps would flash up from the blue water that summer, his body leaving a ruffled white trail in the Gulf. "Just go right by yourself," she added. "Winnie'll understand." When she heard her words, she knew instantly how wrong they were, and wondered briefly why she spoke them about her sister-in-law. To show Fred how different she and Winnie were?

Fred chuckled, a dry humorless sound. "The hell she would.

Why, Win'll ask where I've been right now if she calls the store and finds out I'm not there." He smoothed out the paper napkin he had folded and refolded. "No sir. Winnie wouldn't even want to spend the money for all of us to take a vacation. Me go by myself? Well you can forget that! It's all I can do now to get her to let Sheridan take a trip to New Orleans."

"She's just downright silly," Virginia blurted.

"Oh, she's scared, that's all," answered Fred. "Same as Chester. Scared of what they don't know and things they haven't seen."

Virginia picked a loose thread from the sleeve of her dress and pensively rolled it into a ball. "Funny how you can marry somebody so different from yourself, isn't it? When I was twenty, all I thought about was what a good dancer Chester was, what funny stories he could tell . . ."

"Win kept telling me I looked like some movie star back then. Who was it? Gary Cooper or somebody. I don't think she ever saw me, a lonely kid just outta the army. Hell, I fell for the first pretty girl who thought I was something special." He glanced down at the carvings in the wooden table, the initials of sweethearts. "Of course, I thought Winnie was special too, that shy little smile she had. Yessir, I loved her all right . . . I mean . . ." Fred stuttered slightly. "I mean, I still do. She still thinks I'm special, after all these years. Lord knows why."

Virginia reached out and patted his hand. "Don't look so sad, Fred. You are pretty special, you know. You've got a great family. That Sheridan . . ."

"Yeah, she's a talented kid all right. Damn. I'll just make sure she gets to see New Orleans. I'm not gonna let Winnie get in her way."

"You really think the world of Sheridan, don't you?"

Fred smiled. "You know, sometimes when the alarm clock rings in the morning, I lie there and think about going to that hardware store . . . and then I think about Sheridan. She's going places, that girl. I want her to have the things I didn't have. Sometimes I think I get up in the morning for that kid."

"Oh, Fred." Virginia stared at him intently. His gray eyes

looked tarnished and round and, like foreign coins, flecked with the embossing of a strange culture, making her think suddenly of the faraway places Chester would never take her. But who knew what carving or design might be on the reverse side of those gray coins that were Fred's eyes, looking inward, surveying what mysterious landscapes in his mind? There was a thrill in the thought, making a tiny shiver run down her arms. She blinked quickly to chase the thought away, and looked up at Fred. "Are you really that unhappy? Why don't you quit that job? Find something else?"

Fred shrugged. "I've tried. What is there in this town? Hell, I've only got a high-school diploma, you know. I applied at the bank to be a teller a couple of years ago—now, don't you go telling Chester this. He'll be hurt I didn't go to Ace Farm Supply first. I'd make less at the bank, though, than I do now for Ed Jolly. And Ed gives me a solid life-insurance policy. Real solid." He leaned forward and gazed intently at Virginia. "Doesn't matter what happens to me: Winnie and Sheridan'll live like two queens." He pulled back, one eyebrow raised. "That insurance makes a big difference, I tell you."

"Well, why don't you let Chester get you something at Ace? He'd love to have you work with him. We've got good insurance coverage too. And it'd make him feel so proud, to do something for you."

Fred shoved his coffee cup to the center of the table, making it rattle in its saucer. "A man can't live off his brother. All my life, Chester's wanted to protect me, or do for me, even find my wife for me. I swear, he'd breathe for me if he could. But I can make it on my own."

"Of course you can, Fred. You could have done anything you wanted to, when you were back from the army . . . gone back to college and been an engineer or a doctor. I always thought you were so smart." Virginia folded her arms on the table and leaned toward him. "I still think you're awfully smart."

Fred turned the check over and bent forward to reach for the wallet in his back pocket. "Know why they turn the bill facedown, don't you?" He grinned quickly. "Won't ruin your appetite that way. Yeah . . ."—he pulled out three dollars—"I'm real smart, all right. Coulda been anything, huh? And here I am, pinching my pennies in a diner."

"But you got a pretty sister-in-law with you, and she loves you to death!" Virginia said, patting her hair flirtatiously. "Aren't you a lucky man?"

The waitress stopped at the jukebox, her towel in her hand, and fumbled in her pocket for some change. As she dropped in her coin, she turned to them, the only customers left in the restaurant. "Y'all don't mind a little Patsy Cline, do you?"

Before they could answer, she disappeared into the kitchen, and the crooning of "After Midnight" came floating from the jukebox, as if some sultry cloud had suddenly entered the diner and turned the climate balmy. Virginia tapped her spread fingertips against the table, playing the tune on an imaginary piano. *I keep on walking, after midnight, in the moonlight, searchin' for you . . .* She sang the words beneath her breath, and then hit the table, lightly, with both palms. "C'mon, everybody's left. Let's dance!" She stood so quickly that her skirt swung about her legs, and she held out her hand to Fred.

From the corner of his eye, he gave her a long look, while a smile slowly curled at his lips. Then he pushed back his napkin, rose, and slipped his hand around her waist. Together, they glided and swayed among the diner's empty tables, Virginia's small brown-and-white spectator pumps stepping neatly in tandem with Fred's brogans. He pulled her more tightly to him, so that his knee pressed gently into her thighs beneath the front folds of her skirt, and his fingers spread against the small of her back, guiding her movements.

Lightning suddenly flashed at the window, followed by a boom of thunder so loud it rattled the saltshakers. Then the entire diner went dark, and Patsy Cline's voice raked to a halt in midline.

Virginia thrust herself away, her eyebrows raised in a startled arch. "Just the electricity," said Fred, pulling her back, "nothing to worry about." He danced on, in the silence, to an imaginary waltz.

After a minute, he stopped and smiled down at her, his gray eyes shining now in the shadows of the diner. "We better go," he whispered.

Together, they walked back toward the side street where Virginia's Pontiac was parked, the wind sending newspapers scuttling past their ankles. A want-ad section clung briefly to Virginia's leg, and she kicked it away, making her skirt billow up in a green cloud, showing how the tops of her nylons attached to her garter belt. She batted at her skirt, laughing. And then, with a boom of thunder, the heavy gray clouds in the sky suddenly broke with a pelting, cold rain.

Fred fumbled with his umbrella and held it over Virginia's head, the wind jerking the umbrella inside out so that its silver ribs strained against the force. "This way!" He grabbed her around the waist and steered her across the unmown lawn of an empty house, past the For Sale sign and toward the door of the garage in back to wait out the rain. And, on an impulse brought by the weather, to be alone with Virginia.

In the closed garage, with the rain hammering on the tin roof, Fred brushed Virginia's hair back from her forehead, then pulled out his handkerchief to wipe the dampness from her face. With his hand cradling her head, he pulled her face closer to his until his lips, cool and damp from the rain, met hers. Then his fingers were at her throat, sliding down the collar of her wet dress. He eased his hand down the front of her bodice, pausing at each button, opening her dress until his fingers gently cupped the softness of her breast. It was already too late to retreat or to stop.

After Winnie had served dinner that evening, Fred tried again to persuade her to let Sheridan go to New Orleans. There was a new desperation in his voice. "Think of it, Win. Sheridan's growing up. It's time we let her do things."

Winnie nodded as she gathered the dishes from the table, her mouth in an angry, tight line. "Have it your way, then. You and Sheridan are always making me out to be the bad guy. Well, go right ahead! Go ahead and do it your way."

"Ah, Win." Fred's voice was almost a groan. "You know I love you. You know I want the best for all of us. Why do you make it so hard for me?"

"I know you think I'm holding you back, keeping you here in Libertyburg," Winnie snapped, pouring a great dollop of Palmolive dish soap into the sink. She turned and shook the bottle at him. "We already have the best, that's what I know. We have each other. We have our home." She said nothing else for the rest of the night.

When, the following year, Fred locks himself in the station wagon with the motor running and the garage door closed, Sheridan will remember how he had pressured Winnie so she could go to New Orleans. She will wonder whether he had planned his death even then. Some things, she will shrug years later, you just never know, though, so you give up trying to figure them out.

In 1964, Fred and Virginia win out, though, over Chester and Winnie. Winnie frets over the decision right up until the morning they all pack up Virginia's Pontiac for the overnight trip to New Orleans.

When Sheridan returns to Libertyburg, though, Winnie will tell her that seeing her big smile when she jumped out of the car to give them all the news about the trip convinced her that it was worth every bit of her worry. Sheridan just looked so downright happy, she will say.

But Fred will seem oddly preoccupied and disconnected from Sheridan when she tells him about the concert. His eyes will cloud over, and he will smile, a curious bending of his mouth, as if he is seeing a journey of his own into foreign territory.

EIGHT

THE WEDDING
1964

The smell of gardenias fills Forest Park Baptist Church. In the warmth of the southern summer, their sweetness hangs thickly in the chapel, where wedding guests nod nervously across the aisle dividing the groom's party from the bride's. It is still too early for the wedding march to begin.

The organist, Mrs. Lovelace, sits in her position on the smooth mahogany bench, spinning out the music that Amanda Bloomer has requested. When the final strains of "Blowin in the Wind" still linger in the air, heavy as the gardenias, Mrs. Lovelace pulls the church bulletin left on the keyboard from the Sunday before and fans herself vigorously, trying somehow to fan away the sounds of Bob Dylan's music.

With the fading of the music, the buzz of soft conversations blends with the hum of air-conditioners to make a noise smooth as bees. It is the comforting, anticipatory sound that gathered crowds always make, especially in small churches. On this warm Saturday afternoon of August 29, 1964, the sound would have a visitor believe that this is an ordinary Mississippi wedding, this union of Amanda Bloomer and Paul Michaelson.

A group of Amanda and Paul's friends have gathered at the double doors of the chapel, laughing among themselves about their effort to find the way to this small church in Libertyburg. They are from the Delta Ministry, a civil-rights group in the northwestern corner of Mississippi. Amanda joined them two years ago, after writing a term paper about their voting project for her sociology course at Central Mississippi University. Her professor had given her only a C+ for her efforts, with the sole comment that it was not "objective work." ("Yeah, sure. I should write more like the objective newspapers in Jackson, right?" Amanda had sneered at him, her paper crumpled in her fist, before she stormed out of his office.) But, as Amanda tried to explain to an anxious Virginia and an angry Chester, she had gotten something far more important from her paper than a grade. She had "found herself," she told her parents—and a whole group of wonderful friends from all over the country.

"Libertyburg!" a young woman with long black hair whispers, an ironic smile on her face. "We should liberate *its* polls next!" She pulls her hair back and holds it there for a second in a single cascade above her neck before letting it settle back into the straight frame it forms around her thin face. In the moment that her arms are raised, two damp half-circles are visible beneath the sleeves of her blue blouse, belying the ease of her laughter. Her eyes tense as they scan the rows of pews before her, as if she imagines the ticking of a homemade bomb, there in the organ's sudden silence. She drops her hair and twists the long string of pearls that dangle from her neck almost down to her waist; they coil around her long fingers, then spring loose, then coil again, over and over.

Her companions laugh with her. "But Libertyburg gave us Amanda," a tall, bearded young man says, bending down from his height to whisper into the group.

"Amanda," murmurs a black man in a crisp yellow-and-brown dashiki. "Amanda must be a miracle," he says quietly, almost to himself.

As he speaks, he is scanning the small church, not with the tension of his companion in her blue blouse, but with an alert vision of another kind in his pale brown eyes, an awareness that pulls in rather than a fear that pushes out. He scans the backs of the heads in the congregation, the neat pillbox hats, and the carefully sprayed gray coifs, the hairstyles themselves like pale, stiff caps. His eyes flicker over the people, seeming to capture the crowd there in the brown tunnels of his eyes. His nostrils flare slightly and he moves his lips, as if he is smelling and tasting them, holding the sensations there in his mouth, trying to define whether they are bitter or sour or sweet.

In the rows of stained-glass windows are occasional biblical scenes: Jacob wrestling with a silver-winged angel, David firing his slingshot at Goliath, Christ holding two fish in one hand and loaves of bread in the other. A stretch of red carpet runs down the center of the church directly to the pulpit, and, behind that, to the baptistry, where many of the younger people in the gathering this afternoon were baptized.

It is down that red carpet that an usher approaches them rapidly, a tall young man in a green suit that appears stiff as a corn husk. His sandy crew cut sprouts straight up from his head, resembling the clipped tassels of a freshly cut ear of corn. He is Kenneth Moody, a cousin of Amanda's, the son of Virginia's only brother, and a deacon at one of Jackson's biggest Baptist churches as well. Virginia has insisted that he be included in the wedding party, and in a diplomatic moment, Amanda has agreed—on the condition that her parents understand that the Delta Ministry workers must be guests at the wedding.

Kenneth Moody's frown deepens when he sees the two black faces among the group. The smile, however, never leaves his lips, giving his face the impression of a mask distorted at either end. "The groom's side, I presume?" he asks, and the words are formal, their clipped civility well rehearsed, as the small band eases past him and scatters to both sides of the aisle, where their communication narrows to rolled eyes, elbow nudges, and winks.

In a small dressing room behind the baptistry, Virginia's smile is hung on her face as carefully as the garlands of shiny magnolia leaves draped before the altar. She is helping Ruby Ann and Sheridan with their bridesmaid's dresses, adjusting the voile cuffs at Ruby Ann's thin wrists. She almost loses her smile when Ruby Ann asks what she should do if she trips in her new high heels.

"Should I go back to the foyer and start over?" Ruby Ann wonders, absently watching her mother fasten the tiny covered buttons on her sleeves. "But will Mrs. Lovelace know to stop playing the music when I go back? And what if I drop this?" Ruby Ann thrusts out her bouquet and stares at it in horror. From the look on her face, the tiny pink roses and baby's breath clustered there might have become radioactive. "Do you want me to stop and pick it up or just leave it there and keep on going . . ."

Virginia assures her younger daughter that neither will happen; she will neither trip nor drop her flowers, she says firmly, with a hint of a warning in her voice. To close the subject, she wheels Ruby Ann around to fasten a hook in the back of her gown.

Behind her, Amanda's face flushes with excitement under the white veil Virginia has just straightened. The red beading on it gleams beneath the fluorescent lights.

"Why has Mrs. Lovelace stopped playing? She hasn't even done 'Girl from the North Country' yet! Someone has to go tell her to play it. Someone *has* to go tell her to play it." Amanda repeats her request, the words becoming her own magic mantra to remind herself that the whitened world beyond her veil is still real, still a world that she can protest and change. Her dark eyes are shining from behind the tulle, looking wide despite the rims of dark liner around them. Red lace peeks out above the low neckline of her white satin gown, and edges out again at her wrists, from behind her sleeves, looking like flames that are shooting out from beneath the white satin.

Now Winnie hovers over the bride, a solicitous aunt, shushing her niece about the music.

"We can't have everything we want, dear, even on our wedding day, sometimes." And then Winnie's voice turns gently efficient. Does Amanda have her blue garter on? Where is her borrowed handkerchief? And her bouquet, is it . . . shhh. An usher knocks at the door, two crisp taps, and then there is the muffled sound of his heels down the hall. The organist's hands are poised above the keys.

Virginia turns to Amanda, to survey her one last time. "You look like an angel, dear," she says, her eyes gleaming with pleasure and appreciation. She tugs gently at the red lace showing at Amanda's wrist. "An angel whose wings are on fire."

The music rises in volume, and Virginia quickly checks her lipstick before she and Winnie slip back out to the chapel.

In a few minutes, the bouquet will be tossed, the cake will be cut while a camera flashes, tin cans will be tied, and rice will clutter the sidewalk. Chester's closest friend from twenty years with Ace Farm Supply, Rudy Murphy, will film those rituals at the reception, and will keep filming them even after Amanda and Paul drive off to the Blue Ridge Mountains in southern Virginia for two weeks. The result will be blurred, both because he leaves the focus in one place and because he refers too frequently to the hip flask of bourbon in his back pocket.

His wife, Lucille, has given up keeping an eye on his bourbon. She wipes a tear from her eye—Amanda May, that little tyke—she can just see her in her playpen in that boardinghouse where Chester and Virginia lived in the Delta, or on her roller skates after Ace Farm Supply moved them all here to Libertyburg, getting married! (And—poor Virginia—in a wedding dress with *red* trim!) It is hard to believe, how fast the years are going by, how old they're all getting, even the kids. She glances at her husband, glad he can hide behind the movie camera.

The camera lens spins alternately to the bridesmaids, then to Paul's family, or swings over to Grandmother Bloomer, sitting in a folding chair at the edge of the crowd in her best green silk dress, her sturdy black oxfords a concession to her bunions. The camera collects every expression indiscriminately, absorbing everyone but Fred into the film. Fred is leaning in the corner of the reception hall, or finding a spot in the door where he can watch everyone, shadowlike. Even the gray linen suit he wears, and his black-and-white tie, are unbroken by color.

The camera, however, is capturing everyone else, even—briefly—the small group of Delta Ministry workers. Though Rudy tries his best to avoid them, the civil-rights workers are unmistakably there, a steady presence in the background: they are laughing with Paul when Rudy tries to film the bridal couple, or one of them is crossing the camera's path just as he is shooting the bridesmaids, or they are standing at the end of the cake table, in a huddle to themselves so that the back of a head or a gesturing arm is visible to the camera as Rudy films the cake cutting. They are even less avoidable at the rice throwing, heaving handfuls of the white grains so that they fall like northern snow into Amanda's hair and into the folds of Paul's linen jacket before the two rattle off in their Volkswagen, the tin cans rivaling the sound of the engine.

The small band of Delta Ministry workers cluster at the door, still watching the road where Amanda and Paul's Volkswagen has disappeared. The tall young man pours mixed nuts into his mouth from the cup formed by his palm.

"Time to head out?" He raises his eyebrows at the remainder of the group, dusting his hands together lightly, indicating that he is through with more than the nuts.

The young woman in the blue blouse shakes Chester's hand, giving him the entire group's thanks.

"They're a beautiful couple," she says, as Chester nods, a smile frozen, grimacelike, on his face. She turns to look for Virginia as well, scans the reception hall, and shrugs. She waves to Chester and slips out to the parking lot. And then the small band make their exit as well, quietly, leaving behind the sudden void made by Paul and Amanda's departure.

Oblivious both to the young woman who is looking for her and to the camera that Rudy has trained on her, Virginia retreats toward the ladies' room, her head bowed.

"Why, Virginia . . ." Fred's voice is a whisper, unheard by anyone. He starts to move toward her, but Chester arrives at her side, putting his arm around her shoulder. He murmurs something about a "happy moment" and a "stiff upper lip." Virginia nods and slides from his grasp, continuing on her way. Behind her is her mother-in-law, walking more slowly in her flat-heeled shoes. Grandmother Bloomer has clicked open the gold knob that closes her best purse, releasing the faint smells of both mint and lavender from the old silk lining. Winnie follows her, fumbling beneath the flap of her own white patent handbag. She pulls out a Kleenex just as Grandmother Bloomer waves one of her embroidered handkerchiefs in the air, to unfold it.

From a position near the cake table, Fred is watching them, relieved that the civil-rights workers have left. It is mostly for Chester's sake that he is relieved; his brother's shoulders seem to sag slightly with the release of tension now that the group has waved good-bye. What was the big deal, Fred wonders, just a bunch of kids not much older than Sheridan, all looking scared at first, like they thought somebody could pull a gun on them right here in the church. And making Chester look just as scared . . . A wave of bewilderment washes over Fred when he thinks of his brother, the same feeling that has come over him often during the past month, ever since Virginia visited him at the hardware store in July and something wonderful began in his life, seeing her whenever the two of them could arrange the brief hour and private place. It is something wonderful, though, that gives him such intense nightmares he often wakes in the middle of the night. Sometimes he can look at Chester and feel the most intense love for his brother that he's ever known, as if his heart itself were expanding to embrace Chester and everything he has touched in his life. Often, memories come flooding up, like an entire iceberg melting in his mind, and he can almost smell the firecrackers on that July day he first met Winnie, after the soldiers' parade. Or it is fishing with Chester he remembers, when they were both boys, Chester teaching him to bait the line. The memories make him feel like a man dying, life rushing by so fast and so real that he can almost reach out and grab it. But he is not a man dying, Fred reminds himself. He's a man more alive in the past few weeks than he's ever been. The emotions sweep through him, a wash of gold or red or peaceful indigo. There is so much more than his usual sadness about his job or the emptiness of his life. How had he lived that way? he wonders. Like his very soul had become a tarnished mirror. And now he feels so full of life and energy that the reflections he sees in that mirror sometimes blind him.

Virginia passes by him, looking upset and pale, and Fred watches her making her way toward the swinging door marked Ladies. His mother and Winnie are close behind. He watches his mother and his wife at the door of the ladies' room, each with her handkerchief or tissue out for Virginia. He is proud that he married a woman who knows those secrets, who can efficiently take care of these things. Somehow, on the several occasions of the past month when he and Virginia have met to hold each other again, he has felt closer to Winnie too, as if a sweet sadness has been cast over them, uniting them, even though she does not know it.

A wash of love for all three women suddenly swells his heart, and he feels that his arms could stretch wide enough to embrace Virginia, Winnie, and his mother at once. As the door to the rest room closes behind them, his heart sinks just as quickly as it has risen, as the shutting of the door suddenly sounds like something final and irrevocable.

He shrugs off the feeling. Women's business, he thinks, remembering the mysteries of his mother's Sunday purse when he was a boy, the dime or nickel that might fall into his hands from it, the occasional mint to suck during a sermon, or the lace-edged handkerchief that might appear suddenly at his nose. It had always seemed to hold the same dark secrets of locked bureau drawers or closed jewelry boxes, the mysteries of something powerful and private, with its powder-scented lining sometimes crossed with a safety pin, clasped there in case a repair might be needed. It seemed then that it was in women's purses that life itself was distilled down to its essences, to be doled out, passed on through the discretion of their owners' hands.

He looks over at his daughter. Sheridan's hair has been pulled up into a wreath of curls at the crown of her head, gathered there so that the light now catches the gold in her brown hair. She is laughing with Ruby Ann at the way their long skirts have swept up rice behind them, and her mouth becomes a circle of pink lipstick and even white teeth. Sheridan looks more like the Bloomers than Winnie's family, the Franklins. She is already taller than Winnie, and her brown hair has never had Winnie's reddish cast, the deep auburn that had made him untie her ponytail on their first date, in Chester's old Plymouth. He had wanted to stroke her hair, see how it would tumble over her shoulders and frame her round face. Instead of the open circle that Winnie's cheeks and chin form, Sheridan's face is a series of angles. Sometimes, when he looks at his daughter's face, he sees a resemblance to one of the angular prisms that she is always arranging in her bedroom windows to catch either the morning or the afternoon sun, so that the light in her room is cut into different shapes, splashing tiny rainbows across the walls. Sheridan's chin might turn or tilt slightly, and it seems that her entire face rearranges itself—from heart-shaped to an oval and then to the sharper geometrics of a diamond. Her moods, Fred knows, change just as quickly—and he guesses that he can blame himself for that, just as he sees the angle of his own jaw in her face. Well, he tells himself, she'll be a handful for a man, for some damn lucky man. He watches her as she slices Ruby Ann a piece of cake, watches the quick movement of her slender hands as she lays a pink rosette of icing on a napkin. On her right hand sparkles the aquamarine he bought her for her thirteenth birthday, the March birthstone she'd wanted. ("But honey," Winnie had protested to Sheridan, "it's not your birthstone. Don't you want a topaz? For November?" Winnie had been perplexed, insistent. "That's your stone. A pretty brown topaz." But Sheridan had had her heart set on the blue sparkles of an aquamarine, and Fred had surprised her—and Winnie—by bringing the ring home. "Oh, Fred!" Winnie had cried, dismayed. "Giving an aquamarine to a girl born in November! That's not right. She needs a topaz!" But then she had seen the look in both Sheridan's and Fred's faces, and she had softened, slipping her arm around Sheridan's shoulders and her other hand in Fred's. "Well. You're my two free spirits, that's all. Just alike. If the world doesn't suit you, you two will invent your own ways, won't you?" She had shaken her head. "Will I ever understand it? Aquamarines for November! I declare.")

Gazing out across the reception hall, Fred's eyes are filled with both a certainty and a sadness. For a few seconds, that look creates a vast chasm out of the church hall, stretching as it does from the playful gleam in Sheridan's eyes to the well in his own. He presses the short stub of his cigarette to his lips and takes a deep chestful of smoke, then twists the cigarette's glowing end into the paper plate that holds the remains of his wedding cake. No matter what happens, Winnie will take good care of Sheridan, he assures himself, looking up as Virginia strolls from the ladies' room, her eyes still slightly red. And Sheridan is almost old enough to take care of herself, so grown-up-looking today.

He casts his eyes downward into the ashes and cake crumbs on his plate, the chasm in the room now closed.

Sheridan is displaying the bridal bouquet she fought so hard to catch. Ruby Ann already has a sore rib from her elbow.

"Lucky dog," hisses Ruby Ann. "You know what that means, don't you? You and Ernie'll get married next."

"Ringo," Sheridan informs her cousin, even though she is wearing Ernie's initial ring on her middle finger. The rubber band affixed there to make the ring snug digs into her skin, making the imprint of an X.

"No fair," Ruby Ann grumbles. "I liked Ringo first. Why don't you go back to Paul?"

"Don't you think my mama would approve of a musician?" Sheridan continues, ignoring her cousin. "He may be a foreigner, but at least he's no communist."

They eye Paul's parents with suspicion. Their Boston accents sail across the tides of conversation and infiltrate every corner of Forest Park Baptist's reception hall. Chester tries to exchange pleasantries with them. Something about the Mets. He's been glancing nervously at the door of the ladies' room, waiting for Virginia to rescue him. He wishes Rudy Murphy would quit swinging that damn movie camera around at everybody, but he cannot find a spare minute, a break from these conversations with his new son-in-law's parents, to tell him that the film's run out.

Awkward pauses punctuate the conversation he is trying to have with Paul's parents. Each word feels like a thread in a spider's web from which he cannot extricate himself. In desperation Chester invokes the name of his hero, Dizzy Dean. Now there was a great pitcher. Ole Diz. An even greater announcer, maybe. Yessir. Who cares if he talks like he dropped out of grammar school?

Paul's father nods in agreement, and Chester's jaw relaxes slightly. It is like talking to a foreigner who, by some accident, happens to speak the same language.

Chester has tried hard to keep from feeling that Paul himself seems like a foreigner, a Yankee who came to Mississippi to stir things up, to make trouble, when folks down here get along just fine, no matter what color they are.

("It's too soon," Virginia protested when Amanda announced her plans. "You've known him barely two months! Besides, he's a bad influence." Chester nodded in agreement. In one of many arguments, Amanda finally exploded, "Just be glad he's not black!"

Virginia's face whitened.) When Amanda and Paul return at Thanksgiving, Paul will endear himself to Virginia by discovering that he loves her turnip greens, and she will believe that she has won his heart. But it will be years, one Christmas long after Paul has finished law school in Chicago and opened his own practice there, and Amanda has a tenured position at the Art Institute, before they tell Chester and Virginia about the summer that they met: about the sit-in at H. & L. Green's soda counter up in Jackson, about the bottles of ketchup and mustard poured over Paul's head, the bruises left by billy clubs, or the horrors of car headlights following them on dark Delta roads during the summer of 1964.

But that is later, the telling of these stories.

Rudy Murphy finally finishes shooting the home movie long after the film in the camera is, unknown to him, exhausted. There is hardly anyone left to aim the camera at. Most of the wedding guests have parted, hugging Virginia and shaking Chester's hand, sending good wishes for the bride and groom. A lovely wedding. A delightful couple. Mrs. Lovelace pats Virginia's hand as she leaves, whispering that nothing was spoiled, despite that group of rowdies. It was a beautiful ceremony, she assures Virginia. And the church has never looked prettier.

To extend the festivities, Sheridan has asked to spend the night with Ruby Ann. Fred frowns at the idea, but Winnie approves, glad to have a night alone with her husband. He has seemed so strange lately, so quiet and distant one day, so full of himself and playful the next.

Sheridan and Ruby Ann carefully hang their bridesmaid's gowns in Ruby Ann's bedroom, stretching the cleaner's plastic bags down over the pink voile skirts. A life-sized Beatles poster is thumbtacked to the closet door. Sheridan props her transistor radio in the window to pick up KAAY, the rock 'n' roll station in Little Rock. She raises the antennae so that the Supremes' "Baby Love" suddenly blares out into the bedroom: *I need your love, oh how I do-o. But all you do is treat me ba-ad. Break my heart and leave me sa-ad.*

"Hey Sheridan." Ruby Ann has been trying to pull a comb through the curls that her mother molded that morning with hair spray. Now she stops and folds her arms. "How far do you think Amanda let Paul go before tonight? I mean, do you think they've done it, already?"

Sheridan shrugs, remembering instead Amanda and Paul's friends, the strange group of blacks and whites together who appeared at the wedding, seeming awkward and confident at the same time. Rather than Ruby Ann's slyly inquisitive smile, she sees instead one of Amanda's unfinished paintings from college that she has left propped against the wall in her bedroom down the hall, an unfinished collage of black faces like a dark flowing river or a long waving flag.

"Well?" asks Ruby Ann impatiently, plucking out a wad of hair from the comb. "How far do you think they went?"

Now it is Paul's faded green Volkswagen that Sheridan sees, with its Massachusetts license plates, and its bumper stickers, Equality for All Americans, and Vote for Freedom! above the tin cans and wedding streamers. It looks like it has gone many places. It is always covered with dust, as if he has traveled down roads she can hardly imagine. How far *could* he have gone in that car? All the way from Boston? Or, she fears, all the way back, forever, with Amanda? Would Amanda let him go that far? It is all somehow mysterious.

NINE

A GRAY UMBRELLA 1965

The late afternoon sun slants through the dusty venetian blinds in the Green Lizard Lounge, tucked down an ivy-covered embankment off the highway outside Libertyburg. At a table in a dark corner sit Virginia and Fred, the only customers in the place. Foam mottles the inside of an empty beer glass in front of Fred. Beneath it is an envelope with the emblem of an airline in the upper left-hand corner.

"Have you lost your mind?" Virginia watches Fred with caution and fear, the same way she might watch an erratic car on the highway. "That's the craziest idea I've ever heard."

"Look," Fred says. "I want this to be the best damn birthday you ever had. Forty-five, now that's an important one."

Virginia's face colors. "I wish you'd stop reminding me. I already know how old I am today."

He thumps the envelope. "This is our chance. We go to New York and start over, you and me. I can make enough money driving a cab in the city to support us. We can live cheap at first, till I make enough to support Winnie too. And our kids? They're old enough—they can come stay with us just as long as they want. Not that it'll be easy . . ."

"I can't just up and leave my family, leave Chester. What would they do without me? What would I do without *them?*" Her fingertips at both temples, she shakes her head. "Oh, I knew I shouldn't have met you here today! I told you last winter, the last time we met, we couldn't keep the secrecy up. That was three months ago. Nothing's changed."

"Yes it has!" Fred cries, excitement in his voice. "I found a way that we can make it. I've got money—we can tell Chester and Winnie. My marriage has been dead for ten years, Win knows that, she *must*. We'll come clean, you and me."

Virginia runs a hand over her cheek, suddenly grown pale. "Oh, Fred, no. We can't do that."

"You said we couldn't keep hiding. But I've found a way . . . you *do* still love me, don't you Ginny?"

"Why, yes," Virginia stutters. "But I can't give up my life. Oh, Fred. I care so much about you, but . . ."

Fred rakes his chair back abruptly. "*Care* about me. So it's that you just care about me now, huh? I thought you *loved* me . . ."

"Wait now. Hold on. Don't go getting mad at me again. I *do* love you, you know that. But for six whole months, you put me through the wringer. Besides all my worrying about Chester and Winnie, you were either deep in the blues or as happy as a clam. There wasn't much in between. And now this! New York? Oh, come on."

"If you love me, you'll come."

"How can I do that, Fred? It's crazy. All last fall you gave me so much, but . . ."

"It's been almost a year already," Fred informs her. "It'll be a year come July."

"No. As far as I'm concerned, it ended last winter. But you gave me six solid months of the most exciting . . . Do you know how I looked forward to meeting you those times when we had a chance to get away, out to the park last summer and fall—oh, it was glorious under those maple trees!—or to the fishing cabin down at the farm last winter? That was heaven. And New Orleans. I never knew how good it could be. My heart beats fast, just remembering it."

"Remembering it? Is that all you want it to be? A memory? We can still be together, we can make it . . ."

"But don't you see? Just the *way* we had to get together those times . . . what we did was wrong. It made me feel dirty, even when it was wonderful. To go back home to Chester afterward? Lord, I felt lower than a bucket at the bottom of a well. I love Chester. He'd be so hurt."

"I love him too. But you and Chester are no good for each other. You know that. He doesn't even know who Virginia Moody is. When I see him sitting there watching that TV, not even looking at you, not even listening to what you're saying . . . Oh, Ginny. You married the wrong brother, that's all. Chester isn't the right husband for you. He never was."

"He's never made me feel the way you make me feel, it's true. There've never been fireworks with Chester, but that's not his style . . ."

The waiter, a young man in blue jeans and a tee shirt, walks up with a full pot of coffee.

Virginia places her palm over her cup, still nearly full from the last refill. "No, thank you," she smiles. "I've had plenty."

She lowers her voice as the young man moves away. "Don't you see . . . Chester and I have too much behind us, I understand him too well."

Fred lifts the beer mug halfway to his mouth, sees that it's empty, and slams it back on the table. "I thought you meant it when you said you wanted another kind of life," he hisses. "You gave me the hope to change everything, to risk it all for you, and now you're going back on me."

"Think what would happen if people found out . . . I told you last winter we can't go on."

"Who *gives* a damn what folks think?" Fred explodes. "I thought you told me we couldn't keep on like we *were*, keeping secrets. Well, I'm giving you the chance to try it again, different. We'll tell them, we'll stop hiding . . ."

He stops. Virginia is shaking her head, pressing her hands to her ears. A tear escapes her lashes, and she catches it quickly with her napkin.

"Well, hell," he whispers, "I guess I never deserved you anyway. Not you or Winnie. I'm a worthless . . ."

Virginia raises her head and looks him full in the eyes. "Stop it! Much as I care about you, Fred, I swear I'll never understand you, never know what makes you tick. I can't take it anymore. I'm in over my head. One minute you're on top of the world, the next you're talking about how worthless your life is . . ."

"So you're telling me I really *don't* deserve you, right? You don't want me anymore? Is that what you're telling me? It's over?"

"Oh, Fred. It was such a mistake. We couldn't go on, and we sure can't desert everybody here and go moving up to New York City. What would it do to our families? Chester would never get over it. It would break Winnie's heart. Oh heavens, Fred." Tears rise again in her eyes. "What on earth have we done? Just think about it . . . I'm so ashamed of myself. We'll live with this forever, and I guess the loneliness of that is our punishment." She pulls a tissue from her purse, wipes her nose, and continues, more firmly, "We have other people to think about, that's all there is to it. There's more to life than the excitement of a moment . . . We've already *made* our choices in life. Don't you see?"

"Ah, now you're sounding like Winnie. Okay." Fred stuffs the airline envelope into his pocket and pulls out a small gray velvet box. "I guess you don't want this either." He snaps open the lid. Inside gleams an emerald, raised on a gold band. A circle of tiny diamonds sparkles around the stone.

Virginia gasps and shrinks away. For the horror in her eyes, the ring might have been a tiny coiled snake.

"Happy birthday," says Fred, a defiant challenge in his voice. "It's your proper birthstone, you know. Not the emerald, of course. But the others. Diamonds for April."

"Why, how in the world did you get that?" A new look of fright folds across Virginia's face. "What's going on, Fred? Airplane tickets? An emerald ring? Have you sold something? Did you remortgage the house? Oh no, Fred. Tell me you didn't . . . not for me . . ."

"Is that the only way you think I can buy something beautiful for you? You think I'm just some jerk, some good-for-nothing lout . . ."

"Oh, don't talk that way. Please. You've gone on like that too many times. Why do I have to keep telling you what a wonderful man you are? Well, I'll say it again. You are. I was just scared you'd mortgaged your house."

"It came from Ed Jolly. He owed me some money," Fred answers.

"Ed? He borrowed money from you?"

"He's been borrowing from me for years. See? I'm not the failure you think I am." Defiantly, he slings one arm over the back of his chair and crosses his ankle over the other knee. A hole has eaten at the sole of his shoe, and Virginia glances away quickly, as if she might protect them both that way.

"No, Fred," she sighs. "You're not a failure. No man as sensitive and generous as you are could be a failure. If we'd met before I was married . . ."

"We did."

"Oh, don't give me that!" Exasperated, Virginia clenches her fist. "You know what I mean. If it hadn't been for Chester, if things had been different . . ."

"So it's over, that's what you're saying."

A look of relief passes over Virginia's face. "It's what I've been saying, Fred. And I can't accept that." She nods down at the ring. "It's not right."

"Well. I guess I got to get on home." The words come with an edge of sarcasm, as he pushes the velvet box toward her. "You were worth it, anyway, Ginny. You just remember that." He stands and reaches for his jacket, slung over the back of the chair. "Happy birthday, hear?"

He strides quickly across the wooden floor, making it creak beneath the rhythm of his brogans. Just as Virginia starts to cry out after Fred, the waiter returns with his pot of coffee and the double doors that lead to the parking lot bang shut.

The next day, as Virginia is leaving the house to go to her coffee-club meeting, the telephone rings. She dashes back in to answer. Fred's voice greets her, but he does not say hello.

"I'm gone," he says.

"Fred? What do you mean, you're gone?" Virginia's words catch in her throat. "You're not going to New York, are you? You didn't tell Winnie . . ."

"No. Nobody knows." Fred's voice cracks. "Oh, Jesus Christ, Virginia, I'm in big trouble. I've gotta come see you."

"To the house?" Virginia asks. "I've got my coffee club in a few minutes . . ." Then she pauses. It is the sound of Fred's voice, the urgency. "They can do without me this time. Come on over."

At the sight of Fred getting out of the station wagon in her driveway, Virginia thinks that something has happened to Winnie or Sheridan. It is the way he moves, the way his shoulders are hunched when he slams the door shut. It is something larger than the two of them.

Fred sinks into Chester's recliner and lowers his head into his hands. He breaks into sobs.

"Fred?" Virginia sits on the edge of the arm, rubbing his back. "What's happened? Is it Sheridan? Winnie?"

"I've been caught," he groans. "Jolly knows."

"Knows what?" she breathes. And then the emerald-and-diamond ring, the plane tickets, flash into her mind. "Oh, Fred. Oh no, Fred."

His hands are covering his face so that his voice is muffled. "I've been doing it for three months, ever since you said we couldn't keep hiding things. I wanted to find a way to make it work, dammit."

"How much did you take, Fred?" Her own words seem to come in slow motion to Virginia, spelling a reality that sinks into her chest and makes her breath difficult.

"A couple thousand. Slow, every night a little." He punches one fist into his palm. "I do the damn books. I never thought he'd miss . . ." His voice cracks again. "Oh, what am I gonna do?"

Virginia's eyes dart about the room as if searching for an answer in the record jackets on the stereo, the family Bible on the coffee table, or the framed photographs of Amanda's wedding on the mantel. Finally she asks, "Has Ed Jolly called the police?" A wave of nausea lurches in her stomach as she says the words.

"No," Fred moans. "He just called me in, first thing this morning, before I could even put my lunch sack under the counter. What could I *do?*" The word stretches out like an anguished groan. "I told him everything."

"Everything?" Virginia thrusts her face down to his.

He waves her away. "No, no. Not about us. About the money. I told him I needed it for Sheridan's college education." Anger surges up in Fred and colors his face. "Dammit, the old bastard's been underpaying me for years. He *owed* it to me, the son of a bitch."

"What's going to happen?"

"He's firing me," Fred tells her, looking up at her for the first time. Now his face is white, his eyes red rimmed. "You know what he said? That he'd thought I was his most loyal employee, all these years. Twenty years! Said he wouldn't go to the police, long as I pay him back. But who'd have thought I'd stoop low enough to steal from him, he asks me. The old coot! He's been stealing from me, as far as I'm concerned. No raises, putting in that barely grown kid of his as manager instead of promoting me! I've had it!" He laughs bitterly at his own words. "Oh God, *have* I had it!"

"Have you told Winnie yet?"

"No."

In the long silence that follows, Virginia strokes his back in the same rhythm she makes when she irons Chester's shirts, gently smoothing out the creases. Fred holds his forehead, his eyes closed, in a posture like someone praying. He suddenly drops his hand and twists around to look at Virginia.

"I'll tell Winnie the same thing: I took the money for Sheridan. But now what, Ginny? What do I do now? I've got to repay the money. How the hell do I do that?"

"You can take the ring back. Couldn't you get the money back for it?"

Fred shakes his head abruptly. "No. That's yours. When I pay the money back to Jolly, it'll be yours fair and square."

"I don't want it, Fred. How could I ever wear it? I've been hiding it under the electric blankets in the cedar chest. It's worth more to you . . ."

"I already feel like a dog. Don't make me sink even lower."

Virginia pauses. "Where did you buy it?"

"You think I'll tell you so you can take it back yourself? It doesn't mean any more to you than that?"

"Fred! Be practical. This is an emergency. I don't need the ring. You need the money."

"All I need is work, then I'll pay it all back."

"Maybe you'll find yourself a job you like better. Maybe there's a silver lining . . ."

"Oh hell. Who are you fooling? Jolly's not gonna give me a recommendation for any job in Libertyburg. I don't have a thing to my name now." He breaks into a sob. "Oh, Ginny. What kind of man *am* I, anyway? How does a man make such a mess out of his life? I'm a fool. A fool and a thief, that's all I am. I even tried to steal my brother's wife." His last words are choked by a sob, and he dissolves into tears, weeping first into his hands, then, as she pulls him to her, into Virginia's lap.

"No, Fred," she strokes his hair. "I wasn't there for the stealing. I was there taking you, too." She bends down to his ear and whispers, "Because I love you, Fred."

She holds him tightly, trying somehow to contain his sorrow that way, and cradles him against her body the way she rocked Ruby Ann, years ago. His breath is warm against her neck. Even years after Fred has killed himself, when she thinks of him she will remember first the wet warmth that his tears and breath formed against her neck that afternoon in late April.

A late-spring thunderstorm taps against the windows of the Orion funeral home. Ed Jolly, sitting alone in the back row, stares off into the gray space beyond the rain-streaked windowpanes. When a crack of thunder suddenly rocks the chapel, he flinches and fixes his eyes again on the preacher, Brother Stebbins. The other gatherers there, a small group of mourners with an occasional black hat dotting the surface, appear numb to the weather. Umbrellas drip at the end of the pews, looking like markers placed there to reserve the seats.

From behind the screen separating the family comes the muffled sound of Winnie weeping. Chester is holding her hand. At Winnie's other side sit Ruby Ann and Sheridan, who is wearing the blue linen dress that was her Easter outfit two months before. It matches the blue of the aquamarine ring on her left hand. She has thrust both her hands, though, between her knees, squeezed tightly together, wrinkling the front of her dress. Her whole body is hunched and drawn, as if she can somehow protect herself that way from the pain around her, from the sting of the air itself.

In the pew beside Chester, Virginia holds herself erect, a monogrammed handkerchief clutched in one hand. Her other arm rests on Mother Bloomer's thin shoulders. Sitting there between Chester and her mother-in-law, she feels acutely how *small* the family seems, this row of six drawn faces. She wanted to wear sunglasses today, to conceal the dark rings and red rims around her eyes. And then she realized it was her entire self she wanted to hide, and that was impossible.

Beyond them, through the wooden slats of the screen, Fred lies in a brown metal casket, brass handles at either end. His face is pale and puffy, unlike the angular lines that had always defined his cheeks and jawline. In a comforting moment, Virginia realizes that the casket looks oddly like the old Chevrolets Chester used to drive when he was a salesman for Ace Farm Supply. The funeral director had pressed Winnie and Chester to buy a fancy walnut casket, but Winnie was adamant: Fred would want something plain and simple, she insisted. So now his body lies inside the brown metal box, and Virginia is thinking that he looks for all the world like he is about to travel somewhere in one of Chester's old brown company cars. Then she thinks that that is an odd thing to be thinking, and her mind searches for a thought that does not seem strange.

In the viewing room the day before, Winnie burst into tears at the sight of Fred, and her knees suddenly sank so that her entire body swayed and then dipped. Tears streaming down her own face, Virginia grabbed her and held her. "That's not Fred there, you know that," she whispered. "He isn't in this room, honey." And somehow, whether it was the sound of her voice or the words themselves, Winnie had stilled. Watching Virginia and her mother, Sheridan huddled at the end of the casket alone, her arms wrapped tightly about her waist, her eyes wide and dry. At the far side of the room, Ruby Ann watched her uncertainly, biting her lip, her blue eyes glistening. But she stayed where she was, frozen, unable to move to Sheridan, staring at her cousin even as a young funeral attendant moved between them, bringing in flowers, great shoots of gladiolias or bouquets of gardenias. Then, with his straw hat in his hand, Ed Jolly had quietly entered, nodding to Winnie. "I'm mighty sorry," he said awkwardly. "Fred was awful good to you and Sheridan, I know that." Avoiding looking at the casket, he glanced about. "Guess my flowers aren't here yet. I ordered some sent." He shook his head. "I just wish things had been different. This is awful hard for me."

With an edge in her voice, Virginia responded, "I'm sure it is. It's hard on all of us."

Tears filled Winnie's eyes again. "I guess we all feel guilty, don't we?"

Then, in an impulsive rush, she and Ed Jolly told each other at the same time, "It wasn't your fault."

Drawing back in surprise, Ed stared at Winnie. "*My* fault?"

"None of us are to blame," Winnie replied weakly.

Ed continued to stare at her. Then Virginia touched his arm. "Thanks for coming, Ed."

Now, at the funeral, Brother Stebbins leans on the pulpit before the congregation. "He was an honorable man," he is telling them, "a family man, devoted to his wife and to his daughter. Fred Bloomer was one of the finest citizens of our fair town."

What if they knew? wonders Virginia. What if they knew what Ed Jolly—thank God!—has promised he will never make public? What would Brother Stebbins find to say about Fred then?

The day Fred confessed the embezzlement to Virginia, he left Virginia's house a few minutes before Ruby Ann was due in from school. He drove home, surprising Winnie in midafternoon as she washed the dishes that had collected from breakfast. He told her then about losing his job and stealing the money—for Sheridan, he explained, so she could go to any college she wanted. While he talked, Winnie silently went around the house, from room to room. With Fred following after her, explaining and pleading, she pulled the blinds and locked all the windows and doors, a ritual that kept her rising hysteria in check until the entire house was sealed in shadows. Then she collapsed on her knees on the kitchen floor, sobbing into the wet dishrag she still held.

That was a month ago. In the weeks between, Fred stopped by Virginia's house several times, and each time, it seemed, he was more hopeless. Even the filling station didn't need him, he whispered desperately, the words themselves struggling to rise above his grief. Not the drugstore, the five-and-dime, or the Jitney Jungle either. Winnie had gone to the Penney's store at the new shopping center and gotten herself a job at the credit counter. Since then, he told her, Winnie had sealed herself up in her own sorrow until she, too, had shut him out. And Sheridan? Afraid that Sheridan might hear the news from someone else if the word got out, Fred and Winnie told her how Fred lost his job. Angry and hurt, Sheridan insisted that she'd never wanted to go to college anyway. She got an after-school job, working every afternoon at the ice-cream parlor downtown. ("She pities me," Fred told Virginia. "You can see it in her eyes. My own daughter! That's the worst of all.")

The last time he came to Virginia, three days before his own funeral, he said little, wanting only to be held. He held her in his arms so tightly she thought her breath would be pressed from her lungs. He whispered, "I'll always love you, Virginia. You remember that." Moving slowly, his face pale and drawn, his eyes dry, he left. That was the last time Virginia saw him.

It is Fred's voice that Virginia is hearing, not the drone of Brother Stebbins' words. "You were worth it, Ginny," Fred is telling her. "You just remember . . ." Her mind is cluttered with fragments of the past, with ways that the present might have been different. If only she hadn't gone to visit Fred at the hardware store last summer, if only she had pushed him away in the abandoned garage (if only it hadn't been raining!), if only she'd made it clearer last winter that it wasn't just the secrecy that was unbearable to her, it was the whole idea of hurting the family. If only . . . The tears break through her thoughts, and Chester turns, startled at the sound. He sits there in his gray suit, then, one large hand still holding Winnie's, the other stretched now on Virginia's knee. The laughter grooves on his face, running in half-moons from his eyes, around his cheeks, and down to his mouth, seem to be etched deeper today. They make his face appear like an inappropriate mask, concealing all but the solemn, weary dullness in his eyes.

In the white limousine that follows the hearse en route to the cemetery, Chester blurts in a whisper to Virginia, "I'd have given him the money. Why the hell didn't he just *ask* me for it?"

For a moment, Virginia shuts her eyes and squeezes his hand. "I'm sure Fred knew he could count on you." She stares beyond Chester's profile out the window at the kudzu-covered trees lining the highway. They have left Libertyburg behind now, moving in a slow route toward Pine Grove Cemetery. "You gave him everything you possibly could, honey." They near the Green Lizard Lounge, almost hidden down a gravel drive beneath the highway embankment. When the sign looms up, she turns her head away.

"Nice of Ed Jolly to come," Chester comments absently. "Wasn't it, Win?"

A hard glint shines through the sorrow in Winnie's eyes. "And why shouldn't he? Fred worked for him for over twenty years."

"That's right," says Virginia. "There are some things anybody would do. It's human decency."

At the cemetery, Ed Jolly hangs on the outskirts of the crowd gathered beneath the canopy. As the casket is slowly lowered into the fresh earth, he shoves his hands into his pockets and pulls out his car keys. With the rain beginning to increase in volume, he edges up near Winnie's chair, touches her elbow gently, and nods to her. Then he is off, trudging a wet, grassy path between the graves, rain dripping off the felt hat he has pulled down low over his eyes.

After the casket disappears into the grave, Virginia reaches down beside the folding metal chair where Winnie still sits, her head bowed. She picks up the gray umbrella there that Winnie has brought, recognizing it as Fred's when she opens it up. As Winnie rises, she puts her arm around her shoulders. Together, they walk slowly toward the funeral company's white limousine, the rain rolling from a gray umbrella not quite large enough to shield them both.

TEN

THE HERMITITE
1965

It is one of those deep summer nights in mid-July when people in Libertyburg wonder how they survived before they had air conditioning. Sometimes that is all people talk about, what it was like when all they had were fans and how these young people today can't possibly imagine it, here with all the modern conveniences in 1965. It is the sort of conversation that Winnie and Virginia often have, especially now that Virginia comes by several times a week to talk aimlessly to Winnie, to take her mind off things, off Fred's "accident," they call it. Those conversations annoy Sheridan. All that talk about fans "bugs" her, she tells them. Bugs the everlovin *hell* out of her, she tells herself, hating the way, when the sky finally grows dark after the long July days, the night looms ahead, emptily.

This is one of those deep summer nights. Except that tonight Winnie isn't talking about anything.

The fireflies are just beginning to flash outside the house when Winnie begins to close up the living room in preparation for bed. She has the blues again, Sheridan can tell by the way she walks. Sleepwalking, it looks like, with Winnie drifting around in a dream that Fred haunts. Sometimes she looks like a ghost too, aimless and pale, sleeping off the weeks since she found Fred in the closed garage, slumped over the steering wheel of the station wagon, the motor still running. She refuses to drive the car now, even to the grocery store or to church.

"Sheridan," she often says, fumbling in her purse for a couple of dollars and her key ring. "Run over to the Jitney Jungle and get yourself something for supper." But most of the time Winnie doesn't even think about errands like grocery shopping.

She hands Fred's car keys over to Sheridan just before dinnertime. It is a gesture that gives Sheridan freedom from the world into which her mother disappears when she goes back to her bedroom around eight o'clock, as soon as it starts to get dark. It is a world filled with Fred's half-empty bottles of Old Spice in the medicine cabinet, with his hunting vest, shirts, and blue Sunday suit hanging in the closet. Often, when Winnie opens the closet to get dressed, she lingers there, holding one of Fred's loose sleeves to her cheek, smelling its familiar musky scent. In the mornings, the first thing she sees is his key chain without the car key, still lying on the oval pewter tray atop the chest of drawers where he would empty his pockets at night, and sometimes her first thought is, Where is Fred? Has he already taken the car to work? And then the events of the past several weeks tumble in on her, so quickly that she sags back onto the bed.

In the evenings after Winnie retreats to her bedroom, Sheridan doesn't see her mother again until Winnie starts shuffling around the kitchen making her coffee twelve hours later, the pockets of her robe bulging with Kleenex, her eyes swollen.

Sheridan is glad to see her pulling the blinds already tonight. They slap against the windowsills with a shush, signaling that she can slip out early in the station wagon. Six weeks ago, her steady boyfriend, Ernie Crenshaw, came to the last day of school with passion marks on his neck that a cheerleader gave him after a baseball game, and now there is little to do on these long summer nights. But most of the time Sheridan tells herself that she is glad to be alone. She doesn't even want another boy calling her, giving her his oversize ring to wear just so he can unbutton her blouse at the drive-in. And ever since the Libertyburg *Sun-Herald* headlined her father's death in a lower corner of the front page, Sheridan avoids even her friends, leaving the phone off the hook and taking detours so she won't have to drive past the crowded pizza parlor on Main Street or the Teen Center near Libertyburg High. She quit her job at the ice-cream parlor because too many of her friends came in, with curious or pitying stares, and now, every morning, she reports to work for a few hours at Lucille Murphy's beauty shop, mixing henna packs and learning to do manicures.

The station wagon is her escape from it all. Winnie always runs the air-conditioner so high back in her bedroom that the noise drowns out even the sound of the car cranking up. Then, when Winnie's bedroom door is closed and her lights are out, Sheridan heads out the highway, down the back country roads where there is nothing but the speed of the car, the sound of rock 'n' roll on the radio turned way up, and the feel of the warm wind flooding against her face while she barrels through the hot summer of 1965 on thirty-two-cent gallons of gasoline.

That is how Sheridan finds out about the hermaphrodite down at the swinging bridge near Ambrosia, Mississippi. She stops off to get gas at the Gulf station down on Highway 53—Winnie gives Sheridan her credit cards too. The attendant sizes her up when she gets out of the station wagon. He is hunched monkeylike over the pump handle, looking as if he is performing some unnatural act with the car.

"Your eyes botherin you?" He squints his eyes into slits and tilts up his head so he can see out from under the blue brim of his cap.

Sheridan just looks at him.

"Well they're abotherin *me,*" he cackles, slapping his leg. And then he takes a second look, edging close into her face.

"Say, ain't you kinda young to be out and about by yourself? Where you headed to? You ain't going down to the swinging bridge, are you?" He spits into the gravel. "Too many kids going down there. That ole critter down there never hurt nobody."

He shifts the handle of the gas pump, jiggling it to get out the last drop. "Well, you just be careful if you going to see that there hermitite. You ain't meeting some boy down there, are you?"

He is giving Sheridan what she calls the creeps, but she is, nevertheless, curious. A hermitite? Was this some kind of religious group or something? One of those anti-Christian cults she hears Winnie tell Virginia about? A shaved-head Tibetan, maybe, who's somehow wound up in Mississippi?

She asks at the truck stop down the road when she stops for a cup of coffee.

The waitress shakes her head, and her coil of yellow hair wobbles. "Some say it's half man, half woman, but I don't believe 'em. There ain't no truth to it. Hon, as long as I've lived here, there's been a story that he run off from a circus and holed up down there at the creek so they wouldn't find him. Buncha folks used to run a bet about who could get a picture of it, one that would say . . . you know . . . if it's man or woman. Nobody never did get it." She looks up from under the yellow hood that her bouffant hair makes over her face. "He comes in here sometimes, don't say hardly no word to nobody. He's just a ole tired man, been living off crawdads and catfish too long. Been alone too damn long. Shouldn't nobody just live all by theirself. But I reckon he likes it."

The jukebox explodes with sudden rock 'n' roll, and she jiggles away to the Big Bopper's "Chantilly Lace." "Leave him alone, hon," she tosses back over one bony shoulder. She wrenches her body into a version of the twist like some rubber band all wound up and suddenly let loose. She twists over to the next table and then she quits just as quickly as she began. She pulls out her order pad and pencil for the two men sitting there. They look as if they are used to her.

They are staring at Sheridan, not at the waitress. Sheridan thinks they are staring at her hair, since she dyed it red a couple of days ago, just for a change. Winnie noticed it, and she was mad for a while, saying it looked like pink food coloring. But then even the spark of anger was gone in Winnie.

Sheridan shakes her hair at the truck drivers and stirs another spoon of sugar into her coffee.

"You don't need that sugar. You look sweet enough as it is to me." One of them winks at her and takes a deep swig of the beer that has been set in front of him.

She sips her coffee, wondering whether it would be bad manners to leave as soon as she was served.

"Cat got your tongue?" He wipes his mouth with the back of his hand and winks again.

"Mabel been tellin you about that queer thing down there on the river? You wanna go see it, honey?" The other one turns his chair around to face Sheridan.

Years later, Sheridan will remember that shirt he is wearing. Big red checks cover it, and the front is unbuttoned just far enough to show his curly chest hair. His friend is skinny, and a cheap Kodak hangs from a string around his long neck. His eyes are green and so large that they seem to pop out of his head when he winks. She will have to describe the men to the police, so she will remember those details long after the night has passed.

"Yeah, it sounds weird." Sheridan flounces her new red hair again and looks at them straight in their eyes—head-on, she thinks to herself, so she won't look scared. "Where does it stay?"

They look at each other, both trying to read the mind of the other. The skinny one speaks up first, his Adam's apple jerking up and down in his neck. "Well, we'll just take you down there, sugar." He lifts the camera around his neck. "We'll get a picture of you with it, win you a bet, maybe. It's not too far from here, you just take a turn to the left down the road, takes you far as the river bottom, and he's down there. Lives in a little cabin with fishlines out in front."

Sheridan's hands are trembling as she sets the cup back in its saucer. She isn't about to get in their pickup truck and drive down some dark, muddy road to the river with them. She may be doing some crazy things this summer, but getting in a truck with two strange men to take a picture of some half-woman/half-man is beyond her boundaries.

"Thanks for the offer." She smiles at them politely. Winnie has taught her always to be polite. But when they grin and start to push their chairs back, she adds, "But I'll just go myself. I've got a car. I don't need a ride."

Their faces fall into mean expressions, and the big one raises his bushy eyebrows at her. "Well, you just be careful down there," he growls. "Some say it's a dangerous critter. Teenage couple got shot a few years back. They never pinned it on nobody." He is giving Sheridan a stony look that tells her he doesn't care about what happened down there, he is just mad he can't be in on it. He mashes out a cigarette on the floor. The neon light that announces World's Strongest Coffee outside the window is flashing on his face now, turning his features red, then yellow, then blue, a kaleidoscope arranging itself on the topography of his bulbous nose, his creased forehead.

Sheridan is getting what she calls spooked. She puts down a quarter for the cup of coffee and walks out. The waitress is twisting again. She has dropped a dime in the jukebox for the Everly Brothers' song "Bird Dog" this time. *Hey bird dog, get away from my quail, hey bird dog, you're on the wrong trail . . .* The skirt of her uniform has worked its way up to her pear-shaped bottom, and the tops of her pink stockings show. She does not look to Sheridan as though she cares much about what shows. Later, the waitress will tell the police she didn't notice when Sheridan left.

Outside the crickets are making noises as if an invisible factory might be hidden in the trees. There is a cool, musty smell coming up from the river, that almost tastes like swamp water when Sheridan licks her lips. She has heard that the black churches have baptisms down there in the river. She can just imagine it: whole lines of children and adults dressed in white marching down to the river and then streaming back muddied from washing their sins away, singing about heaven and angels. But that, she thinks, is another world entirely.

Sheridan cranks up the motor of the station wagon, and the radio blares out. It is Peter and Gordon: *I don't care what they say, I won't stay in a world without lo-ove . . .* In the rearview mirror, she catches a glimpse of the red checked shirt moving quickly toward the car. A hand taps on the passenger window and Sheridan turns the music down and leans over to roll down the window, just a little, so she won't make him angry. But it appears to her, soon enough, that she has made him mad anyway.

"Why, sugar, what you skeered at? You mean you ain't gonna open this door?"

She knows one thing: she sure doesn't want to make him any angrier. "I'm on my way home, sir," she lies. And then another sentence seems to come, unbidden, from her mouth: "My daddy'll be awful mad if I don't get his car back soon." She smiles and waves the same kind of white-gloved wave that homecoming queens at her high school give from the back of convertibles in parades—the kind majorettes never get to give, with their hands full of spinning batons. The car eases away from him.

His friend has joined him, and she can see them in the rearview mirror for just a second, standing there frowning at her, looking hateful, until the road replaces them. Then all she can see behind her is a tunnel of kudzu vines unfolding as she speeds along, the radio blaring loud, for company.

Sheridan thinks about that hermitite all the way home, past the Green Lizard Lounge, at the edge of town, where her parents used to dance when she was still young enough to need her cousin Amanda to baby-sit her. Now, though, the lounge is considered notorious by the townspeople, who stay away even in the daytime—it's gone to the dogs, they say, too many country boys looking for a fight on the weekends. She speeds past the parking lot, full of pickup trucks and rusted Fords. She passes the new sausage plant, the shopping mall with both a Penney's and a Sears, the Forest Park Baptist Church with its three fellowship halls and new spotlight for the pulpit.

All the way, she thinks about how much she needs to talk to the hermitite. Is he really half-and-half? What was the circus like? How did he escape? Why do people drive from all over to see him? And—most important of all—how does he stand living so alone, with only himself for company?

She decides to get Ruby Ann—since she is almost two years younger, Sheridan is sure she can persuade her—to go with her to find him. Ruby Ann is good at asking nosy questions, and Sheridan figures if she herself gets tongue-tied with too much to say, Ruby Ann can find out what they want to know—or think they want to know. And maybe Ruby Ann can bring her father's movie camera along, the small portable one he bought to replace the old World War II–vintage camera.

So Sheridan has it planned out by the time she gets home, back to the dark house. Driving the station wagon into the garage is like the description she used to hear her father give of the obstacle courses he ran in the army. That's what he used to say: that he could hardly get the car in, for all the junk that had accumulated there. His old hunting rifle is still propped in one cobwebbed corner, and the headlights graze it before they bear evenly on the wall ahead. As quickly as the light hits the gun, a thought flashes into Sheridan's mind: Why couldn't he have done it that way? Why did we have to find him all limp and pale, his mouth slouched to the same side that his whole body had listed to behind the steering wheel that morning, his lips pink and soft like a woman's, open and emptied of breath as if his mouth were some pool drained of water and she could suddenly see the mysterious bottom of it? His face had appeared caught in a cry that she'd never even been able to hear until he was silent. Why *that way,* the thought comes again, uninvited, why didn't he just take the gun off to the woods like a soldier and . . .

Sheridan is maneuvering the station wagon well, avoiding her old bicycle on the right, the power mower on the left. She has scraped the fender against the mower so many times that little shreds of the Goldwater in '64 sticker on the front bumper are littering the concrete. But not tonight. Smooth as a hot knife through butter, she thinks. Deft, she often calls herself when she needs the praise. So she congratulates herself on a deft parking job as she turns off the ignition and clicks off the headlights tonight. She passes the dark window where Winnie's air-conditioner protrudes, dripping cold water in a steady rhythm.

She has to wait a week until Virginia will give Ruby Ann permission to go out. To the drive-in, Virginia thinks, to see the Beatles in *A Hard Day's Night*. And even then she insists that Ruby Ann must be back by ten-thirty. So Sheridan tries to make good time when she picks up her cousin. They take the paper sack of popcorn Virginia has made for them and, while she is still in the kitchen, they slip to the hall closet to smuggle out the home movie camera. As they shove it into the station wagon, Sheridan can see her Uncle Chester lying in the backyard hammock. Since his brother died, that is where Chester often spends the evening, watching the last of the light fade. Tonight his binoculars are to his eyes, focused up into the tree. A bird, Sheridan thinks.

And then she cranks the engine, and they are off, the camera rattling gently in its case on the back seat.

"I'm not nervous," says Ruby Ann suddenly, after several silent minutes. "Nothing bad's gonna happen." She has been chewing sticks of gum until she's gotten all the sugar out, and throwing them out the station-wagon window until two whole packs are gone. When she isn't fishing for another piece of Doublemint, she fiddles with the radio dial, trying to find Little Rock or Memphis stations through the static.

"We don't have to do this if you're not up for it," Sheridan tells her, suddenly feeling she should make a generous gesture. "We can go to the drive-in, and I'll just come back myself some night."

She can tell Ruby Ann is hesitating, embarrassed at acting like some dumb little cousin, but scared of the hermitite, too.

"What's *really* on at the drive-in?" Ruby Ann pretends that the idea has just struck her. "*My Fair Lady* was at the Tri-Screen a couple of weeks ago, and I missed it the first time around. It might still be on." A hopeful look crosses her face. "We could see Audrey Hepburn, instead of some ole weird thing that doesn't even know if it's a girl or a boy."

The generosity that Sheridan has been feeling disappears when she hears her cousin actually take her up on it.

"Look," she says, "if you don't wanna go, just say so." They are already ten miles down the highway toward the truck stop, and Sheridan really doesn't want to have to come back by herself. "Besides"—she glances over at Ruby Ann—"*My Fair Lady*'s off."

Ruby Ann tosses her last piece of gum out the window and sighs. "Okay, let's go." She turns and sits up straight in her seat, like some kamikaze pilot bracing himself for the crash.

They are quiet, then, the car lights slicing ahead into the night, the sound of the crickets grating from the kudzu-covered trees lurking beside the road—giant misshapen monsters, they look like, creaking with the frustrated noise crickets make. Ruby Ann has turned off the radio, surrendering to the static that crackles between them and those faraway stations with their strange-sounding disc jockeys and all-night programs.

It is as if they aren't connected to the world, just speeding along through the tunnel of kudzu and asphalt that the highway becomes just north of town. Sheridan lets her hands fall to the bottommost curve of the steering wheel, and it seems that she isn't even driving anymore, just letting the station wagon be pulled along by invisible horses who know the way, with her and Ruby Ann sitting reinless in the buggy. They rumble over gravelly stretches in the road that make sounds like the noise in a seashell at the beach, that secret sound that almost insists on silence.

Sheridan can see Ruby Ann's face out of the corner of her eye. It is dappled with moon shadows that shift back and forth, with the patterns of leaves that shape and reshape like liquid lace. There is a funny feeling deep in Sheridan's chest. She feels as if she is watching Ruby Ann and herself float along in some underwater memory of sound without meaning.

They pass the Gulf station, with its one pump and rusted Coca-Cola machine and its three public toilets: men, ladies, colored. They are getting close to the truck stop, near the road that is supposed to turn down to the river on the left.

Sheridan glances over at Ruby Ann when they pass the neon light at the truck stop, the three words flashing first in a succession of red, yellow, and blue—World's—Strongest—Coffee—and then together, three blinks in unison.

"We gotta start watching for the road to the river now. First one on the left, just like I said." Sheridan grips the steering wheel a little harder.

Ruby Ann just nods. She is so resigned to her destiny tonight that she doesn't even bother to look over at her cousin. The sprinkles of shadows across her face have converged into a single darkness that hides her features from Sheridan, so that Sheridan can see only the shape of Ruby Ann's head move, assenting.

And then Sheridan spots a break in the trees on the left. The car lights swing across the road, flashing into the bank of kudzu vines and then down a muddy passage sloping off into the woods and down to the river. She releases the steering wheel and lets it spin through her fingers while they bounce and jostle first into one rut, then into another. She has to back up once when a tree branch catches in the fender.

Ruby Ann's voice cuts through the sound of the car making its way into the woods. "Sheridan, I don't see a blasted thing. And there's no way we can turn around on this road." Her words come out slowly, as though she is carefully stringing them on a thread. "I think we ought to turn around just as soon as we're at the river. We ought to go back home."

The road is getting muddier and flatter, and the river smell hangs stronger in the air, a dampness that clings to Sheridan's skin, and makes her think of the greasy musk-scented bath oil that sometimes lines the tub after Winnie has had her bath. The trees are opening up again.

"We're there," she says, pointing ahead. "And there's the old bridge."

Ahead of them hangs a single lane suspended across the river under wooden poles. Planks lie across it, curling at both ends, refusing to lie flat. In some spots the boards have given way entirely. Sheridan flips the headlights on bright. Through a couple of holes in the bridge, the river is visible, glistening silver under the moon. A cypress knee sticks through the bridge where one of the planks has rotted out—but Sheridan decides that the station wagon will make it around that spot. It's just a little hole, she thinks.

"Think it's okay to cross?" She thinks she can make out a little cabin on the other side of the river, a square shadow against the trees. She tries to breathe slowly, to still the pounding in her chest.

Ruby Ann screeches when Sheridan slips the gear into drive. "Stop! Stop it! Sheridan, so help me, if you drive across that thing I will never, never go out with you again. Not even speak to you again. If we live. And if I die, I swear I'll haunt you!"

The shadows have completely lifted off Ruby Ann's face now, and she stares, horrified, at the bridge ahead, her face itself looking like a full moon, round and shining in the light. Sheridan shifts into park, and heaves a sigh at her cousin.

"Okay. Have it your way. We'll walk across then. How's that?" Sheridan slings the strap of the movie camera over her shoulder, tucks her clutch purse under the car seat so no one will steal it, and reaches around to lock the back door.

Ruby Ann still sits there, biting her thumbnail, clutching her purse in her lap.

"You coming? Or you wanna wait for me?" Sheridan has swung her legs out of the door, and she turns around to her cousin.

Ruby Ann glares at her. "I'll come. But I'm not leaving *my* purse here." She swings the strap of her shoulder bag up over one shoulder and steps out into mud. They make their way toward the bridge, the mud making sucking noises at their feet. Ruby Ann almost loses one of her shoes—new black leather flats she has just worn to the Fourth of July sock hop at the Teen Center—but she slips it back on and plows ahead.

Some of the boards on the bridge have come loose entirely, the nails pried up like rusty splinters. Someone has left old fishing lines tied to the poles—at least Sheridan guesses that is what they are. Pieces of rotted string hang down, still and dry.

"Watch out for loose boards." Sheridan glances over at Ruby Ann. She stretches her thin legs from board to board, pausing to pick out the safest looking ones. She is wearing madras Bermuda shorts that are baggy on her, making her legs look like sticks. Sheridan suddenly feels sorry for her. Her new flats are caked with mud, and her mouth is set in the same determined grim line that she used to put on her face when she was learning to ride Amanda's bicycle, wobbling slowly down the driveway, deliberately crashing before she could careen into the street.

"Hey, Ruby Ann." Sheridan thinks she will lighten things up. "Remember how you used to fall off Amanda's bike? You look just like that now."

"Shut up, Sheridan."

They keep picking their way across in silence. Even the crickets have grown silent. A few fireflies flicker in the bank ahead of them, disappearing and then flashing again in unexpected places.

And then an explosion comes ringing out—like some giant firefly blowing itself up. Everything becomes bright in that second, the way lightning engraves things on the mind or a photograph snatches a second out of time. Sheridan sees the curled plank she is about to step on, even the grayed knot in the board. Ruby Ann's arms fly up in that instant as if she is pleading to the sky. The cypress stumps in the river seem to rise up out of the darkness like parts of a monster's body half-submerged in the water. And then it is dark again, totally black this time, and Sheridan can't see anything for a few seconds.

A voice comes out of the blackness, a high-pitched whine.

"Don't y'all come no further. Don't you take one more step this-away."

"Don't shoot us." It is Ruby Ann, but she is whispering. She keeps trying, but it is only a croak. "Don't shoot. Don't shoot."

Then, from the far side of the bridge, a flashlight beams into their faces, and Sheridan can't see anything again through its blinding ray. Not even Ruby Ann. The bridge sways and groans beneath their feet as if someone has stepped onto it—and the light gets nearer.

The voice comes from behind the light. "What you two gals doing out here? You come to see me? What do you want from me? This ain't no place for young kids." The light is only a few feet away, and Sheridan can slowly make out a shape behind it.

The next voice she hears is her own, coming from her mouth in words she does not know how she is forming. "Are you the hermitite? I heard about you, I wanted to talk to you. I'm Sheridan Bloomer, and this here is my cousin Ruby Ann Bloomer. We're pleased to meet you. We didn't mean to bother you, we just wanted to visit you. I'm all alone too, see my dad just died. But we'll leave if you want us to. We didn't mean to bother you. I just wanted to ask you a few things . . ." She is clutching the camera, forgetting why she brought it, and what she wanted to ask.

Ruby Ann's voice is stronger now. "Don't shoot. Please, God. Don't shoot us."

The light swings out of their faces and before them stands a squat little man with a hat slouched down over his eyes. A few wisps of gray hair lie matted against his neck. He looks them over, his head cocked to one side like a pigeon. An oily shirt hangs out of his pants—khaki, the color of river water.

"What did you want to know?" His voice sounds like one of Sheridan's grandmother's old scratched-up Victrola records played on high speed.

She looks at his face—greasy, beardless, and rutted with wrinkles. The eyes shine out at her like two raisins that have baked to the surface of an oatmeal cookie. A smell of fish grease hovers around the three of them standing there in a triangle in the middle of the bridge. Ruby Ann tries to reach for Sheridan's hand, but her arm freezes midway, forgetting its destination.

The hermitite's eyes flicker to a spot behind them and turn colder. Sheridan knows even before she hears the voices who is standing back there, and whose deep voice begins to speak.

"So you come back. Now what for? What do you nice girls want out here?" It is the one with the bushy eyebrows and the red checked shirt. Sheridan doesn't hear his words so much as she hears the sound of his voice coming nearer, and footsteps. Before them, the hermitite slowly raises the shotgun to his face and takes aim through the squint of his left eye.

"Now you wouldn't do that, would you?" It is the green-eyed man with the Adam's apple.

His companion's bushy eyebrows raise into a single hairy line and a chortle rises from his throat. "He don't have the *balls* to do that . . . Why, we brought him some company again, didn't we? Ain't you gonna be nice to your new friends here?"

The hermitite's gun moves steadily from one man to the other and back again, its aim focused just beyond Sheridan and Ruby Ann.

The fireflies crackle with a new electricity, as if they are sending out a desperate sign language to invisible angels.

Blam! The blast whizzes past Sheridan so close that she can feel the heat and then the bridge tremble. In the seconds that follow, there is silence and then a moan. The checks on the red shirt are filling into one solid color, leaking down the front from a point at the shoulder. He is still standing, watching the color grow there on his belly, the fingers extended on his hands as if even they are surprised.

Then the whole bridge shakes and quivers. Ruby Ann screams and flings herself at Sheridan. Everything is splitting, and the river surges up around them, a beast awakened.

Sheridan will never remember quite how they got back to the

bank. She and Ruby Ann cling to each other, pulling and clawing their way up the muddy side of the river. Something slimy disappears from under Sheridan's hand once, slithering away into the warm water.

Ruby Ann finds a cypress root sticking from the bank, and they haul each other out of the river on it. Sheridan's shoes are lost in the water. So is Chester's movie camera. It is settling into the mud at the bottom of the river. The river bottom will eventually claim the camera until only the lens protrudes, periscopelike, above the mud and it is a curiosity for the catfish.

"Oh God, Sheridan." Ruby Ann's voice is cracked with tears. "Are we okay? Are we okay?" Mud plasters her hair down against her face, and her eyes peer out, wet and terrified.

The only thing Sheridan can think of is getting back to the safety of the car, getting out of there. She pulls Ruby Ann to her, and they are hugging each other, half crying, half laughing. The hermitite comes flopping out of the river, the hat swept away, the shirt clinging to his chest. And even through the shock of those minutes, another shock registers in their minds. Breasts! Two orbs swing beneath the hermitite's shirt as it scrambles up the riverbank on its stubby legs.

She is crying too. "The bridge is gone." Her hands clasp and unclasp. "The bridge is gone. Oh." She clutches at her head, her chest, bends to grab at her knees, even, in a strange protest danced to the river. "Oh, oh, oh no. The bridge is gone."

The Victrola needle has caught in a groove; she keeps dancing the same steps to the same rasped words. There is a deep scratch just beneath her right eye, and the blood is beginning to dribble down over her cheek in streaks like Indian war paint.

Sheridan and Ruby Ann stare, their arms still around each other. And then Ruby Ann moves to touch the hermitite's shoulder. "C'mon," she says. "The car's over there. Let's go."

The distance to Libertyburg seems shorter than their drive out—now that they know their destination. Sheridan heads straight for the new Baptist hospital on the edge of town. She is silent, feeling the rough ridges of the accelerator beneath her bare foot. In the back seat, where the movie camera was, the hermitite giggles softly and then gently sobs, alternating the sounds until Ruby Ann passes her the paper sack of popcorn that Virginia made for them to eat at the drive-in.

The only sound for a moment is the crunching of popcorn. Somehow, it is a soothing sound to Sheridan, as if she has captured all the crickets in the world right in her own back seat and tamed them.

Ruby Ann turns around to face the back seat. "What do you do? How do you live down there?"

"I fish," comes the answer, between the noise of chewing. "Them two crazy men on the bridge, they took my vegetables to farmers' market for me, till they done started stealin my money, cheatin me. *Men.*"

"So you're a lady?"

A half-chewed piece of popcorn flies from the hermitite's throat when she coughs, spraying the back of the seat. "Nobody called me *that* in a damn long time," she says, and it sounds as if the Victrola has sped up yet another notch. "You let somebody call you *that* and it's gawn start all kind of trouble. Nawsir," she shakes her head. "I can do without it."

"So what are you, then?" persists Ruby Ann, oblivious to the glares Sheridan shoots her.

"I already done tole you. I'm a fisher. I'm a farmer. The rest is just a buncha games folks play. Don't let nobody tell you no different, you hear?" A snorting noise erupts from her nose.

"Yes ma'am." Ruby Ann turns back to face the road.

Under the bright fluorescent lights of the emergency room, Sheridan and Ruby Ann tell their story to an intern and nurse on duty. The nurse gives the hermitite a sedative and helps her onto a stretcher. Then a hospital official calls the police to take their report. Sirens blasting, the police race to the river to survey the damage, to see if they can find any bodies to match the descriptions Sheridan and Ruby Ann have given them.

As they wait for their parents to arrive, Ruby Ann eyes Sheridan awkwardly, sadness in her eyes. "Hey, Sheridan?" she begins, "I wouldn't ever haunt you, Sheridan. I'm sorry I said that." She pauses as Sheridan gives her an affectionate smile. "I mean, I don't think dead people would do that, anyway, do you? Especially if they're your family. There's probably nothing to worry about. I'm sure Uncle Fred wouldn't."

Winnie comes in through the glass double doors of the emergency room, her high heels clicking on the linoleum. Chester and Virginia are on either side of her, their faces white and drawn. Sheridan has not seen her mother walk that fast in months. How thin she is! It is a mild shock to Sheridan, the folds that her mother's skirt make beneath the belt around her waist, and the thin whiteness of her upper arms.

Winnie strides right up to Sheridan and hugs her, pulls her head against her shoulder and rocks her, smooths her muddy hair.

She drives Sheridan home through a night soothed now with a gentle rain. And Sheridan is just happy that Winnie is behind the wheel, driving her home just like her father used to do. It was a deft move, she tells herself, not to drive across that swinging bridge. Losing the movie camera is bad enough, but how could she explain the station wagon in the river?

ELEVEN

HOLIDAY SCREENING
1969

Outside the closed blinds in Virginia's dining room, the branches of the sweet gum tree bend silver with ice. A thin layer of snow covers the brown Bermuda grass like a pale quilt and then makes a white mound of the Christmas tree, lying on its side at the edge of the yard. It is an unseasonably cold winter in January, 1969. It reminds Winnie of one winter in Libertyburg during the war, when the cold edge of the wind would rattle the windows like enemy soldiers.

Through the slats of the blinds now come thin rails of afternoon light—enough light for Virginia and Winnie to thread the movie projector they have lifted to the center of the dining-room table.

Judging from the small squares of film they have held to the bare light bulb in a lamp they unshaded, the movie they will see was taken on the Fourth of July at the Bloomer family farm near Millsdale. It will be 1961. Or so they imagine.

"You know," Winnie says, taking a sip of the sherry Virginia has offered her, a celebration of the new year. They would have a toast, Virginia said, to the old home movies they have just found in the attic beside the Christmas decorations when they stored them away for the year. "I declare. That looked just like Fred there, holding that ole rifle he used to hunt ducks with. It's the way he was standing, you know, so tall, with his foot propped up on that stump. My, he used to love duck hunting out on his folks' farm. Made him feel like a boy."

"Him and Chester both. Like two little boys when it came to hunting." Virginia nudges the tip of the celluloid through the last gate, snaps it shut, and looks at the blank wall that will serve as their screen. "Now, then!"

In the silence, patterns of light dance on the wall above Virginia's china collection. Winnie sips her sherry again, as carefully as if the amber liquid were a sacrament for the showing of the silent pictures.

And then the wall dissolves into 1961, the present sinking into the past so rapidly that Winnie's heart flutters. A barn looms up in the square of light on the wall, at an angle as if Virginia and Winnie were sitting on the ground directly beneath it.

Winnie squints. "My lands, what is that up on top? It looks like a dog dancing on the roof of the barn. A little bitty dog."

"How much sherry have you had?" Virginia laughs. "It's the weather vane."

"Oh." Winnie crosses her leg over one knee and swings her foot. "Well, it's so grainy-looking it's hard to tell what's . . ."

"It's that old rooster weather vane Chester helped his daddy put up there back in the thirties," Virginia continues. "Looks like it's going crazy, doesn't it? Turning every which way. The wind must've . . ."

Then two figures form on the wall. One of them postures with a rifle slung over his shoulder; the other one, a taller figure, aims his gun toward the sky, his foot resting on a tree stump. It is not Fred.

"It's Harold," Winnie says, her voice sinking and her foot still now. "That was your brother, Harold, standing so tall."

Then the camera opens to embrace a third figure, his back to the lens. He is squatting to load bullets into his rifle from a tin on the ground. Only his arm can be seen in motion, reaching to the can for bullets, then clicking them into the rifle. In the distance behind the three men, grainy cotton fields stretch into a horizon closed in gray.

"Mother Bloomer took these, I think. She sure loved to tinker with that camera," Virginia says. And then she glances sideways at Winnie. "That's Fred she's aiming at there, with his back to us, loading his rifle."

"He's loading his rifle," Winnie repeats. Her voice caresses the words, as if loading his rifle were the sweetest thing in the world. "Wish he'd turn around and look at us."

Two small figures streak up from behind the camera and the picture spins into the sky, briefly, then focuses again on two little girls, laughing and jumping in front of the lens.

Sheridan's mouth frames the words: "Hi, Grandma!" Then she crosses her eyes and stretches the corners of her mouth with her index fingers to make a face. She runs off again, leaving Ruby Ann to smile shyly into the camera. She raises her baby doll to the lens and moves its hand, making it wave to the camera. She giggles and skips away after Sheridan, and then it is the three men with their rifles again, their backs to the camera, heading toward the horizon.

"I can't believe Sheridan's all grown up." A tear trembles in Winnie's voice. "And gone so far off. I'm just worried sick about her."

"Oh now, Win. San Francisco's not the end of the world. She'll get herself a good education out there and then come back home. You'll see. How could she turn down that scholarship?"

"It's a pretty funny scholarship, if you ask me," sniffs Winnie. "Acting! Oh, don't get me wrong"—she turns quickly to Virginia—"we sure appreciate everything Chester's done, helping out with the expenses. And you giving her that gorgeous emerald ring! That was some going-away present, I'll tell you. Diamonds on it! You know, Sheridan told me that ring made her feel just like she could conquer the whole city."

A smile pulls at Virginia's mouth. "That's why I gave it to her."

"Well, it was mighty sweet of you, but you shouldn't have bought something like that. It was too expensive."

"Sheridan's like one of our own, you know that."

"It's a mighty good thing Fred's insurance paid off, what with . . ." Winnie's voice fades as she gazes into the gray horizon in the movie. "And with you and Chester, well, Sheridan's a lucky girl. I hope she makes her education worth all this expense and travel."

"Sheridan's going to do awfully well out there in school."

"But, for goodness' sake! She could have gotten herself educated right here in Mississippi, in something sensible like teaching. Or social work. Now what kind of job is she going to get acting? And what kind of people is she going to get mixed up with? I just know she's going to find some boy out there she wants to marry. She doesn't even sound like she used to, the way she says her words. And she's lost too much weight living in that dorm. She even turned her nose up at my Christmas cookies last week. Pecan crispies—they used to be her favorite kind. After I told her how hard I'd worked on them, shelling all those pecans by hand, she still only ate a couple. Kinda hurt my feelings, to tell you the truth."

"All the girls are on a diet. Even Ruby Ann says she is, and she's always been thin as a rail. It's just a fad. Don't worry yourself so much, Win. Sheridan's only eighteen. She's too young for you to fret about her marrying a Yankee like Amanda did. Besides, even if she does, look how happy Amanda is."

"But she's so far away. I don't know how you stand it." Winnie sniffs again. "All I can say is, I hope to heaven it's just a fad. Those ragged bell-bottom blue jeans and then those short skirts. Honest to goodness, I don't know which is worse. I declare, I wish she'd come back home . . ."

"She will, Winnie." Virginia pats her hand and rises, her eyes following the movie on the wall until she enters the kitchen.

In the solitude, Winnie rises to move closer to the movie so she can see the retreating figures better. She leans against the wall there beside the pictures, imagining that she can get inside them, transport herself through the last eight years into 1961. With one finger, she traces the outline of the trees against the horizon, where Fred and Chester and Harold grow smaller and smaller until they disappear. Even after the three men have gone, the camera lingers on the acres of soybeans stretching up to the woods, as if the men might return. Or as if something visible only to the holder of the camera, to the mother of Chester and Fred, were happening in the empty field.

Winnie drops her hand to her side, still watching the window into 1961, watching the land that Fred had plowed until he left for the army and never returned to work the field. A flaw in the film begins to flicker through the picture, a series of singes that ripple across the rows of soybeans, making the scene run liquid, the land swelling into a sea swimming with amber ghosts. The flawed movie seems more real now to Winnie than the flat, still picture of the motionless field. She knows it without needing to form the thought: as if the picture had become the sign language of ghosts, flickering there on the wall in light and shadow, telling her in their secret code that her memory of Fred is not the snap of a shutter, not sealed in her mind in a photograph, but rather running fluid in a thousand fragmented images, constantly reshaping their mosaic. As Winnie watches the movie on the wall, she begins to see not 1961, not the Millsdale farm, but another scene from her memory. It is a honeymoon trip she and Fred took to New Orleans in 1946, a weekend trip to the city to hear its music, see its lights, to lie curled together, exploring each other's bodies, in a French Quarter rooming house. She remembers even the blue linen suit she wore, the gardenia in her lapel, and the way the city lights glowed from the wrought-iron balcony of their room, glittering like electric jewels or jazz fragments, neon notes they improvised on that holiday, before clocks began disapproving of them, ticking their dismay to Fred, putting wrinkles around her eyes and repeated rhythms to their lives. And a baby in her lap. In her mind now it is not the cold 1969 of Virginia's dining room or the 1961 in the movie frames of the Bloomer family farm but it is New Orleans in May, 1946. She can even hear the music, the black saxophonist on the corner beneath their window playing a version of "Sentimental Journey" that fragments the tune into a musical mosaic. She remembers the new dance that Fred taught her up in their room, bending his long legs so he could hold her close while he spun her about the floor. They had collapsed, laughing, on the bed, and then the laughter dissolved into kisses, into the warm closeness, the familiar strangeness, that was her new husband. And then another memory nudges at her mind: the drive back to Libertyburg, a missed turn. In the darkness of an unfamiliar road, Fred suddenly wheeled the car to a stop, cursed, and shone a flashlight on the ragged Louisiana road map Chester had lent him. The turn to Libertyburg was sunk deep into a crevice in the paper, nearly invisible. In the crease of Chester's old road map, it seemed, they had lost their destination.

Now Winnie touches the horizon on the wall again, remembering the bravado and despair that tumbled into one single wheel in Fred.

The swinging door leading to the kitchen suddenly bangs. At the sound, Winnie quickly withdraws her hand from the pictures and studies her fingernails.

Virginia returns, the bottle of sherry in one hand. The door whishes behind her, once, then twice, before it settles into stillness.

"What did I miss?" she asks, refilling both glasses. She settles back into her chair.

"I declare," says Winnie. "This nail polish sure doesn't last long. It's already chipped."

Fireworks are exploding on the wall in silent black and white.

"There you are, Winnie!" Virginia points to the picture. Across a younger Winnie's face dance shadows as she lights a sparkler and then bends down to hand it to Sheridan.

But Winnie isn't interested in the image of herself, eight years ago. She is still thinking of Fred, disappearing into the gray horizon. "Where were the men going off to? I can't believe we let them get away with going hunting on the Fourth of July." A disappointed frown creases Winnie's forehead.

"They were heading toward the river when I went to the kitchen. I don't remember what they came back with, do you, Win? I guess we cooked the nasty things, whatever it was." Virginia shudders and wrinkles her nose.

But Winnie is listening to her own memories again, not to Virginia. "Fred was baptized in that river when he was twelve. And now it's all polluted. Honest to goodness, sometimes I don't know what the world's coming to. All these assassinations last spring, young people on drugs rioting in the streets, those Black Prowlers up North acting like they . . ."

"Panthers," Virginia says. "Black Panthers."

Winnie flaps her hand dismissively. "Well, whatever they call themselves. Might as well be prowlers, the way they want to kill us all off. And look at our own kids! The Democrats can't even have their convention without the college students tearing the streets up." She sighs. "And now even the Blue Moon River is polluted. What in the world is next?"

Virginia shakes her head. "Maybe it was Fred's baptism that polluted it, washing all his sins away. We all need a good laundering now and then."

Winnie's shoulders square. "All that oily foam and grease that's floating down there on the river now? I don't think that's what sin looks like. And I don't think a twelve-year-old boy . . ."

"Oh, Win. Don't be cross with me. I was just trying to lighten you up. Who knows what sin looks like?"

"God does." There is still a snip in Winnie's voice. She lifts her sherry glass to her mouth, takes a dainty sip, and then rolls the stem between her fingers, staring down into the liquid. Her chest feels as if it has become a deep well, the water rising from below until it bursts out in words. "I still miss Fred. God knows, sometimes I still think if I'd just been a better wife . . ."

"No!" Virginia shakes her shoulder lightly. "You can't say that, Winnie. It's not true. You were the best wife Fred could ever have had. He loved you. He loved you more than anyone else in the world. You have to believe that, Winnie. You weren't responsible for how Fred died. No one could've helped him, not even you, the best wife . . ."

Staring into her sherry, Winnie is barely listening. "And now Sheridan . . . I don't know if she'll ever be back home to stay." Her fingers are wrapped about the stem of her glass now, clutching it. Her voice tightens. "But how you can say that about Fred's sins, I'll never know. It's making fun of his memory, that's what it is."

Virginia's face sags downward and her chest falls as if the breath has been knocked from her. "Oh, Winnie. I was just trying to lift our spirits up. I never meant . . ." Virginia's words collapse into silence as tears rise in her eyes.

But Winnie's shoulders have begun to shake gently, and she covers her eyes with one hand.

"Well, look at this! It's my two favorite ladies!" Chester's voice booms from the living-room door. His footsteps rattle the teacups against their saucers in Virginia's china cabinet.

"Man, it's colder than an arctic icebox out there. What do we have here? Movie time?" He pauses behind Winnie and slips a spearmint Chiclet into his mouth. The gum is a replacement for the cigars he has made a New Year's resolution to give up.

He puts his hand on Winnie's shoulder, watching the Fourth of July celebration that Winnie and Sheridan, and now Ruby Ann, are having in 1961. "Well, will you look at that."

Ruby Ann plays with her doll on the grass while Sheridan dances around her with sparklers and bends down to kiss the top of Ruby Ann's head.

"Now, isn't that a sweet one," says Chester.

Winnie's shoulder trembles beneath Chester's hand and he bends down quickly to look into her face. "Why, Win? What's the matter?"

Winnie's and Virginia's tears form a gentle sound track for the celebration taking place on the wall.

"Oh now, girls. Girls." He stretches over to rub Virginia's shoulder and eyes the two half-filled sherry glasses on the table. "You girls had a toast to keep warm this afternoon, huh?"

"We're okay, Chester." Virginia reaches out and takes Winnie's hand. "It's just not easy to see your children grow up, that's all."

The square on the wall blooms into full white light, and the last of the film strip flaps around the reel, slapping the projector in a noise that sounds like forced applause to Winnie.

She runs a finger beneath both her eyes and looks up at Chester. "We're okay, Chester," she repeats, and squeezes Virginia's hand.

Chester turns off the projector and wraps the film around the reel, pulling it snug. He opens the canister lying on the dining table, fits the reel inside, and snaps it shut.

"If you gals say so." Chester unplugs the projector, wraps the cord into a knot, and lifts both the projector and the canisters. "I'll put these back in the attic."

He starts toward the hall, then turns back at the door. "Tell you what. I'll take you gals out to a movie tonight. A brand-*new* movie. And we'll go to dinner too. How does that sound?" Without waiting for an answer, he winks at them and heads down the hall.

Winnie lets a smile ease across her face. "Let's go see that Cary Grant movie at the Regal Palace." She turns to Virginia. "I swear, he still looks as young as he did when he made *Holiday* with Katherine Hepburn. Remember that old movie?"

TWELVE

A PRIVATE HISTORY 1975

By Virginia's cloth kitchen calendar, the one that hangs on her refrigerator door, it is June 21, 1975—summer solstice and a new moon at the same time, it says. She notices it when she slams the refrigerator door shut, making the calendar fall from the magnets that hold it to the door.

Since the new moon promises a clear night sky free of lunar light and she has been teaching herself the constellations from a book that Ruby Ann gave her last Christmas, she decides to walk the dog at midnight, when the twins of Gemini should be rising on the horizon. What a treat a late walk would be for Smitty, the terrier, she tells herself.

It will also be a good chance to walk off some anger, she thinks. She is mad at Chester for misplacing the old home movies she wanted to show at the Fourth of July family reunion. At least forty years, gone! she was thinking when she banged the refrigerator door shut, sending the calendar to the floor. That morning at breakfast, Chester had confessed that he had searched everywhere for the movies but he couldn't remember where he might have stored them. It was just too damn long ago, he said, stirring his fried egg into his grits. No telling where those things are.

A sick feeling has stayed with Virginia all day, and tonight her stomach still feels tight, "just like it's tied into knots," she would tell Chester if she felt like talking to him.

So now she plans a solitary excursion under the North Star, the Big Dipper, and—if she can spot them—the twins of Gemini. To relax, she tells herself, forget the lost memories.

When Chester drops off to sleep watching television reruns, Virginia hooks Smitty to his leash, surprising the dog into a scrambling frenzy. She shushes him, stroking his back, so they won't wake Chester, already in his pajamas and slippers. Chester is dozing in his reclining chair, his pink hands folded over the snore in his chest. With Smitty straining on his leash, she sets out to identify some new stars.

Pine Street glistens under the arcs of the new streetlights that Mayor Bucknell ordered installed within Libertyburg's city limits two years ago. Though it had been a controversial move that had cost him the next election, Virginia has grown to appreciate the lights, especially the way they make the street look like a mysterious river at night. And in the midsummer, when the maple trees are full in the front yard, the light on the corner shines through the leaves and dapples the yard with strange shadows that seem to move with the motion of the porch swing when she and Chester stay out late talking, perhaps debating the merits of the streetlights, the political mistakes of Mayor Bucknell. Chester believes that Libertyburg should be kept a small town, and he laughs at Virginia's memory of how he thought it had been a city when they'd moved there from the Delta countryside over thirty years ago. He has worked hard to defeat Mayor Bucknell, making telephone calls and delivering pamphlets about the dangers of too much progress. Virginia has not told him that she voted to keep him in office.

Now Virginia holds out the palm of one hand so she can block out the streetlight and see the stars beyond it. But the movement of a figure on the sidewalk catches her eye first: it is Ralph Cole, walking his terrier—a cousin of her own dog.

Libertyburg is, after all, the sort of small town where all the pets are related. She and Chester have lived here since the forties, enough time to measure events by what dog they had during certain years, and enough time to measure the town's growth by the swelling ranks of the people who have owned their dogs' relatives. Libertyburg, though, is still the sort of small town in which one could expect no fellow expeditioners on a moonless midnight like tonight.

She recognizes Ralph more by his walk than by his face, hidden as it is in the shadows of sweet gum trees. He lumbers along with his knees bent slightly out, but he has, she notices, a lift to his heels when he steps. It is unmistakably Ralph Cole.

"Well, what do you know," Ralph's voice calls out softly, as if the words, too, were in shadows. "Virginia Bloomer."

Their dogs sniff at each other, reestablishing kinship and familiarity.

Feeling nervous (what would people say if they thought she walked her dog late at night, all by herself?—that Virginia Bloomer was getting just the slightest bit, you know, odd? that her two daughters had finally driven her batty?), she tugs on Smitty's leash and smooths her short brown curls with the other hand. For a brief instant, she wonders if her gray roots are already showing.

"Smitty needed to get out," she smiles. "And it's such a lovely night. It's the shortest night in the year, summer solstice."

"Is that a fact?" says Ralph, hitching at his belt. "Well, what do you know." He stands beneath the full beam of the streetlamp now, his thick hair combed back from his face so that it is black and glossy in the light. A fine stubble peppers his face, gathering into a darker spot at the dimple in his chin.

"Smitty sure did want to get out," Virginia says again. "Honest to goodness, sometimes he just can't be still when he's all cooped up."

"You know, their grandmother died last week," Ralph nods down at the two terriers. "The Johnsons were fixing to put her to sleep, but she beat them to it. Had a mind of her own, right to the end, they said."

Virginia reaches down and pats Smitty in sympathy, and then laughs at herself. "Funny how we think they know things, isn't it?"

He laughs, and then they are walking together, pulled by their dogs in the same direction before Virginia realizes it.

"To tell you the truth," says Ralph, "it's the stars that get me out on a night like tonight. Just look at them." He sweeps an arm up at the sky as they walk in the brief darkness between streetlights. "Clear as a bell."

"Why, Ralph? You don't mean it." Virginia gazes at his profile, turned up toward the sky. "I've been learning the constellations, myself. I'm looking for the twins of Gemini tonight, but it's a little early for them."

"Who knows what's up there? A couple of those lights that look like fuzzy stars are really whole other galaxies, you know. Who's to say what might be out there?" He is gazing down at the far end of the street, as if the horizon there promises more than another sidewalk and another row of houses. "Could be whole other kinds of creatures out there, things we can't even imagine." He chuckles at himself and winks at her. "Course Shirley thinks I'm a little touched."

In the darkness around a forsythia hedge comes the erratic glow of fireflies, making red designs in the shadows. The stillness of the night seems to surround Virginia, and the sweet smell of magnolias on the air comes stronger and fresher than in the daytime, like an invitation into the mysteries of the night hours.

"I never was one to laugh at what I don't know," Virginia says softly.

They turn down Maple Way, a narrow, bricked street where the soft light of the streetlamps is barely able to reach through the thick foliage of the overhanging trees. In a flower garden that lines someone's front walk stands a gnarled magnolia tree that sends its smell out like a secret told on the cool night air. A window is lit in the house behind the garden, a square of yellow that frames a woman sitting at her kitchen table with a cookbook in front of her. It is the only window lit on Maple Way, and as Virginia passes it, the solitary woman and the smell of her flowers seem like conspirators in her adventure tonight.

Guided by their terriers, Virginia and Ralph turn down another narrow street, then cut through an alley, then cross to another, wider street. Their arms swing side by side; once their hands brush in a way at once accidental and intimate, and Virginia's first impulse is to ease over to widen the space between them. But she surprises herself by refraining from that impulse, enjoying this unexpected nearness, the smell of Ralph's lime after-shave, the familiarity of chatting together while the rest of the town sleeps behind drawn window shades. And it is somehow delicious to wonder if their hands are going to brush again.

The wet smell of the night reminds her of those high-school dances in her hometown, Millsdale, back in the thirties. Chester would take her home so late that sometimes the dew sparkled on the ground. They would sit in the porch swing, then, Chester rocking it with one foot, talking about his plans for the future while her family slept in the darkened house. Once they fell asleep together in the swing, her head on his broad shoulder. They awoke when the sun was beginning to streak the eastern sky and a neighbor was already calling his cow. There was a freshness, then, a forbidden mystery in the night's smell, even in the smell of Chester's starched white shirts, a mystery even more in the tentative touch of Chester's hand against her skin. Anything, it seemed, could have happened.

But not, she thinks, the kind of thing that *did* happen, some ten years ago.

She glances over at Ralph, and his nearness stirs a memory that seems to strike at her chest: the shadows in a closed garage, rain pattering on the tin roof, thunder shaking the fragile walls, Fred brushing the rain from her hair and face. And then his mouth finds hers, and she remembers how, at that moment, a memory flashed into her mind: that summer day with a parakeet chirping behind them in the empty house, thinking, Oh yes! She can smell his Old Spice after-shave, feel the roughness of his beard against her chin. This time, in the privacy of the abandoned garage, there is more: his fingers ease down the bodice of her wet dress, unbuttoning it until she can feel his hand against her breast. He stoops so that he can kiss her throat, and then his lips are there at her breast, warm against the cool dampness of her skin. He unbuttons his shirt quickly and removes it, his muscles rippling across his strong chest, and he holds her tightly against him, his hands slipping down to caress her hips before he spreads the shirt on the grassy floor and they descend together. He needed me! she wants to cry out now, to the deserted Libertyburg streets. He was lonely and scared and he needed me! It should have ended there, she thinks, just as she has told herself many times since. But they could not forget it, the discovery of each other, try as they might to let both the exhilaration and the pain go. He needed her, he would tell her, in a telephone call, or in the back of the hardware store, or in a truck stop at the edge of town where they would meet for the "world's strongest coffee"—"Charles Atlas coffee," Fred would say, making a typical joke. Things were too god-awful, he told her, without having her to at least talk to. He'd be hanged first if he'd go back to that damn store, he would tell her in the kitchen on Sunday afternoons when he would join Chester to watch a football game. Virginia was everything to him, he told her one afternoon in the back of the hardware store. He had laughed cynically. She was everything all right—his salvation and his damnation. And then, months later, while she sat under the hair dryer at Lucille Murphy's beauty shop, Lucille came running over, pulling at her arm to summon her to the phone. Chester was sobbing so that she could barely understand his words, something about Fred and the car and the motor left running.

She remembers those lost home movies again, but the sick feeling has gone. Instead, she feels an odd sensation of freedom, as if she could live her life over again, invent her memories out of nights like tonight.

Ralph is telling her about the house he and his wife, Shirley, are building in a new suburb. "There'll be room for the grandkids in it—we've got four now, you know—and a place for them to swim. It's right down there near the pond—lake, we used to call it when I was a kid." He smiles down at Virginia and shakes his head. "Sometimes I think the whole world is getting smaller."

As if in answer, the sound of a siren begins to make its way toward them, swelling in the silence like a light getting brighter.

"Now, who in the world could Sheriff Demand be after?" Ralph clucks his tongue. "High-school kids, I reckon. No telling what kids are up to these days."

Guilt stabs at Virginia. She feels suddenly as if she's been caught at enjoying his smell of pipe tobacco and after-shave, at appreciating the affection she sees in his smiles. The siren wails to the entire town that she has been admiring the outline of Ralph Cole's profile in the dark, even the lean movement of his legs as he walks, the way his pants shape around his thighs. Vaguely she has been conscious of the bicep gently bulging beneath his shirt sleeve.

Now, horrified at herself, she turns away so abruptly the leash slips from her hand.

Ralph stoops to pick it up and laughs again. "Sirens make you nervous?"

The headlights of the sheriff's cruiser swing around the block in two long slices and cut past them, followed by the black-and-yellow car. It stops, midblock, and slowly backs up to them. Virginia can see Sheriff Demand's thin neck straining out from the window and his elbow jutting out.

"Mrs. Bloomer?" he asks, his eyes shifting over to Ralph. "Your husband . . ."

And then Chester is out of the car, waving the sheriff on, the elastic of his green pajama bottoms visible above his belt. "It's all right. It's her."

He walks over to Virginia, his slippers softly slapping against his heels. "I've been worried to death. What's going on?"

"You called the sheriff? My lands, Chester, I just went out to take Smitty for a walk."

"After midnight?" He runs his hand over the smooth top of his head, exasperated. "Who on earth walks their dog in the middle of the night?"

Ralph Cole wraps his dog's leash around his wrist, draws him nearer by tugging on it lightly, and wishes them a good-night.

Chester is still jealous when they crawl into bed. "Ralph Cole, of all people. Now, how did you meet up with him?" And, for the third time, Virginia tells him, this time stretching her arm across his broad chest, twining her fingers into the gray hair curling at the throat of his pajamas.

To forestall any rumors that Sheriff Demand's wife, Molly, or—worse yet—Shirley Cole, might start (the town, after all, has teeth), Virginia tells her coffee club the story, carefully justifying her excursion by saying that Smitty broke his leash on the front porch and ran off into the night. "And, do you know," she laughs and taps her knee lightly for emphasis, "there was Smitty's cousin, strolling down the sidewalk with Ralph Cole, just like he was looking for Smitty."

But even long after Chester and her coffee club have forgotten the episode, she will remember June 21, 1975, in her own most private history of her life, as the night her husband caught her with another man.

THIRTEEN

NAMING CONSTELLATIONS
1986

The iron clumps in rhythm on the plaid shirt Virginia is pressing for Chester. Beneath the hissing of the steam, she aimlessly hums a hymn, "How Great Thou Art," happy that part of her family has already arrived tonight in Libertyburg for the reunion picnic in a few days. No one, she thinks, sang that old hymn better than Elvis, not even Kate Smith. But the only person she might possibly admit that opinion to is Amanda, who has been reminiscing about Elvis ever since she arrived from Chicago.

Amanda and Paul stopped in Memphis to tour Graceland on their drive to Libertyburg, and their thirteen-year-old son, Nathan, has hardly stopped talking about it: the jeweled cape so heavy Elvis couldn't even wear it, the twin black Italian cars with keys made of solid gold, the hallway lined with platinum records, the engine from Elvis' favorite airplane, the *Lisa Marie,* on display in the parking lot. Amanda had thought it would be fun, a "hoot," to take Nathan to see Elvis' home, she said, but then it had all been poignant and somehow touching, the garish stained-glass peacocks in the living room, the marbled mirrors, the televisions in every room. She'd been moved by the exposure of the man behind Elvis the star, living in what must have seemed like splendor to Elvis the country boy from Tupelo, Mississippi, who had found himself the hero of millions, a young man who told the Memphis Chamber of Commerce that his "every dream came true—a hundred times."

"Did I tell you about the three television sets Elvis had built into the wall in a row?" Amanda sits on the bed, trying to entertain her younger son, Matthew, her two-year-old, by letting him play with the silver Mexican bangles on her arm. She became pregnant with Matthew when she and Paul reconciled after a five-month separation. "Three of them. He got the idea from the way LBJ would watch the war, you know, all three news channels at once. But Elvis watched football that way, all the games at the same time."

Standing at the ironing board, Virginia lets her free hand follow the movement of the iron, smoothing out the creases in Chester's shirt. "How did he keep up with so many games at once?" She shakes the iron, checking the water level.

"Honestly, Mama, why don't you let Daddy iron his own shirts?"

Virginia slides a sly look at Amanda. "To tell you the truth, honey, he wouldn't know how. I'd just have to redo them."

"Why do you always try to take responsibility for Daddy? He could *learn,* you know. He's not an idiot. He doesn't do enough for you."

Steam from the iron has collected on Virginia's forehead, and she runs her palm upward across her face, toward her hairline. "That's a mighty big statement," she says quietly. She sits down in a rocker and drops her hands into her lap. "He does things for me you never see, honey. Your father is a stable, loving husband—and I've always known I can count on him. He's good-hearted right down to his bones. I wouldn't hurt him for the world."

"Well, Mama? I know that." Amanda searches her mother's face, looking for clues to her sudden meditative mood.

"After all the places you've lived, that may seem like a boring life to you, but . . ."

Amanda starts to protest, but Virginia cuts her off with a wave of her hand. "There was a time I wanted more exciting things out of life, oh, you can bet on that. But when you have somebody who loves you, well, that's the most important thing you can have."

"What did you want out of life, Mama?" Amanda sets down Matthew, her face quietly shining at Virginia. "You're always doing for other people, for all of us, but you never think about yourself. You're such a saint."

"Oh, I'm not a saint, honey. All of us walking the earth are just human, making our mistakes. But I'll tell you one thing: you say I take responsibility for Chester. Ironing his shirts isn't taking responsibility for him. No, ma'am," says Virginia firmly. "You can't do that for anybody, no matter how much you love them. Sometimes you have to set people free to make their own mistakes, even to hurt themselves if that's the direction they're bound." She rises and picks up the iron again. "Much as it hurts," she adds.

"Well, Daddy doesn't make too many mistakes, does he? I mean, he was never like Uncle Fred, was he? Out to hurt himself?"

"No," Virginia replies, abruptly. She glances up and smiles. "So you and Paul seem awfully happy. You are, aren't you, honey?"

"Things are better," answers Amanda. "We just got busy, didn't have a lot of time for each other. I never dreamed he'd start seeing his secretary, after hours. What a boring cliché. He could at least have been a little more inventive." She sighs, watching Matthew push a rubber ball against his mouth. "But it's over, all of it. I know he never stopped loving me."

"Oh, honey," Virginia's eyes glistened at the hurt in Amanda's voice. "You'll get over it. You just have to set things like that aside, put them behind you. Paul may have let his eyes wander to somebody else, but it sure doesn't mean he ever stopped appreciating you. Or wanting you." The iron hisses again as she glides it down the blue striped back of another shirt. "You know, sometimes somebody else can help you appreciate the person you really love, the person you want to spend your life with. Sometimes that's just what it takes. And Paul's young."

"Forty-five's old enough to know better."

"Now I know that probably doesn't seem so young to you, but believe me, when he's older and wiser he'll look back and realize the foolish things you can do when you're young. Lord knows, we all do things we regret. We just have to learn to forgive each other, and forgive ourselves."

Amanda has been observing her mother closely. "You've had an affair, haven't you?" The words come with a tone of wonder, and she watches Virginia's face color. "Oh, Mama. And you chose Daddy, didn't you? Did he know?"

As if a word is stuck in her throat, Virginia's lips open and close once, then twice, noiselessly. "No. And I would've chosen Chester no matter what," she says finally. "He's my husband."

A quiet smile curls at Amanda's mouth. "I love you, Mama," she says, almost a whisper. A loud thump comes from the corner of the bedroom where Matthew has been playing, followed by a wail, and Amanda hurries to pick him up. "Shhh, shhh," she breathes into his wispy hair. "You're all right. You're not hurt. It's okay." She says the words again, reassuring herself this time.

When Matthew has quieted, Virginia continues, "A good marriage isn't anything to throw away, even when it seems like it's more pain than pleasure. Sometimes you and Paul worry me still." She sighs. "I know Paul does for himself around the house—I bet he probably does more than you do. I don't know how you find time to do it all, keep up your painting, teach your classes, tend to both Nathan and Matthew." Virginia runs the tip of the iron around Chester's collar. "I declare, I'm afraid you try to do too much—do you really leave enough time for each other now?"

"Oh, Mama," sighs Amanda. "We've worked it out. You don't

need to worry. I just don't want to talk about it." She grimaces and tosses her hair over one shoulder. She still wears it in the long, straight style that she has worn for years, but two silver streaks curve now on either side of her face, framing it like wings. "Is that what happened to you and Daddy? He didn't leave enough time for you?"

The iron hisses rhythmically around each button down the shirt front. "Oh, Chester's always had time for me. He's always made the time to barbecue outside or take me to a ball game."

"But those aren't things *you* like to do." Her green eyes narrow. "What *would* you have liked to have done? What kinds of things did you do with this other man?"

Virginia lifts the shirt and rearranges it on the ironing board so that one wrinkled sleeve is stretched across the top. "Tell me more about Elvis' house. Three TV sets?"

Amanda gives her mother an ironic smile that Virginia, her head bent to the ironing, misses. "Okay," she shrugs. "I guess I'm the one who's intruding now, right?" She pauses, twisting one of her bracelets slowly around her thin wrist, looking at her mother. The silver-haired woman standing there ironing her father's shirts suddenly seems like a stranger to her, someone full of her own secret ambitions and private frustrations that may never be known to her, to her own daughter. "But, Mama," she adds hopefully, "I'm always here if you ever want to talk."

The iron releases a sigh of steam as Virginia sets it down. "We're talking right now, aren't we, honey? That Elvis sounds like a downright TV addict. Three of them?"

In a gesture Virginia has seen many times when her daughter suffered either real or imagined slights, Amanda thrusts her chin up and squares her shoulders. "Oh, he had more than that, all together. Fourteen or something, scattered throughout the place. But the funniest thing was the plane engine in the parking lot. They had this bronze engraved plaque underneath that said, '11,200 pounds of thrust.'" Amanda puts Matthew on the floor and watches him grab a bureau-drawer handle, trying to pull it open. "Nathan got a big kick out of it. He wanted to ride it, but the guard wouldn't let him. I can't believe the plaque really said that, can you? "'11,200 pounds of . . .'"

"Pure thrust!" Nathan pops into the bedroom door, gyrates in his tight jeans so that he looks more like Michael Jackson than Elvis, and disappears. Amanda laughs.

"Amanda?" Virginia turns and frowns. "I don't believe I'd laugh at that." She reaches down to unplug the iron. "That's just too suggestive."

"Oh, Mama. That's the same thing you said about Elvis thirty years ago." Amanda yawns and rotates her head to massage her neck. "Oh boy. I'm worn out."

Chester appears in the door and scoops up Matthew in his arms. "Too bad you're too little to come fishing tomorrow morning with your daddy and big brother and me!" He ruffles Matthew's thin brown curls and taps the round tip of his nose with his index finger while Matthew squirms to get down. Chester lowers him to the floor and lifts the bait box he holds in the other hand. "Bet I've got some pretty playthings for a little boy in here." He starts to unlatch the box.

"There're hooks on those things, aren't there, Daddy?" Amanda frowns. "Don't let him have them."

"Oh, I'm not going to give them to him. I've raised a couple of little ones in my time, you know. He can just look . . ." But then Chester stops, his mouth open in midsentence. "Why, what in the world . . ." He lifts out a small tin canister. "Virginia, would you take a look at this! It's our movies!"

Stacked in rows in the bait box lie the canisters of home movies that Chester stored years ago and then forgot. Now he remembers: the icy gray afternoon in January almost twenty years ago when he stored the movies that Virginia and Winnie had found beside the Christmas decorations in the attic. In his bait box, he thought, the movies would store well, insulated against dust and dampness. And, he remembers thinking, they would be protected against being found and watched again anytime soon. He didn't want to risk seeing Virginia and Winnie upset, the way they'd been that January afternoon. And he didn't want to take the chance of seeing his brother in the movies, either. The four years since Fred had died hadn't been long enough then, back in 1969, to watch him without risking his own tears. Better to bury the movies for a while, he thought, leave them alone to lose their bittersweet edge.

"And we thought they were gone!" Virginia reaches out to touch the bait box, but her hand stops in midair. The movies might disappear, she suddenly feels, if she touched them.

"My wedding's in there?" Amanda's eyes dart to the bait box. "I never saw that movie, never saw myself being a bride."

Virginia laughs. "That's exactly what you used to say when you were a teenager: 'Mom' "—Virginia raises her voice, imitating Amanda's—" 'I just can't see myself getting married.' "

Nathan wheels to his mother. "Really, Mom? That's what you thought? You didn't want Matt and me?"

"I changed my mind." Amanda winks at her son and reaches out to tug on the lock of hair that Nathan has carefully spiked up at his forehead.

"Well, the wedding movie didn't turn out right, you know, honey. It came out all fuzzy. Rudy Murphy didn't know how to work the camera right." Chester is searching his memory even as he speaks, though, for Fred: Fred marching in a soldiers' parade, Fred hunting on the farm, Fred in a Hawaiian shirt, operating the camera, Fred swimming in the Gulf waters, refusing to come out and get in the picture. Chester's memory comes up without a face every time. Did he ever film his own brother? Or did Fred escape, slip away from his grasp every time?

"Oh, you're in here many times, Amanda. Not just as a bride," Virginia breathes. They are all hovered around the bait box now, whispering. It gives Virginia the sudden feeling that they've entered a tomb and found lost treasures. "You and Ruby Ann . . .

Sheridan. Oh. Are all the movies here, Chester? All of them?" Virginia's face glows.

Chester takes the box to the bed and begins prying open the top canister with the blunt edge of his pocketknife. "Well, we'll just take a look and see."

But the strip of celluloid he lifts from the first tin is withered and brittle.

"Oh, shit." It is Nathan, who has returned with Paul to see what the stir is about. Amanda is too absorbed in the film dangling from her father's hand to send him the perfunctory frown he would ordinarily have gotten. "That's your and Dad's wedding, Mom? It's all shriveled up."

"No, it's something else." Chester is holding the strip up to the ceiling light.

"Well, that's good," says Paul, laughing. "A shriveled wedding seems like bad news about a marriage, doesn't it? Think it's an omen?"

There is a glint in Amanda's eyes. "It depends on when it withered, I guess," she says.

Unsure if they are teasing each other, Virginia offers up a gentle laugh, to smooth over what she thinks might be tension. "I'd say when a twenty-year-old marriage can start all over with a brand-new baby that you're doing more than okay." She is relieved to see Paul reach out and massage Amanda's shoulder.

Chester tilts his head back, his mouth slightly ajar, his reading glasses perched on the tip of his nose. "Looks like . . ." He lowers the film and grins at Virginia, standing beside him, still holding the shirt she just ironed. "It's one of Ruby Ann's little birthday parties, hon."

"But can we see it? It's so battered up." Virginia touches the end of the movie, and a dusting of decayed celluloid powders to the floor. "Are they all this far gone?"

More carefully now, Chester opens the next container and lifts out another brittle film strip. "It's not as bad." he says, turning it gently in his hand. "But it's not good, either."

"What's that one?" Nathan glances up at Chester. "Is that Mom and Dad's wedding?" He stands on the toes of his high-topped tennis shoes, peering into the celluloid squares. "That's when you were getting beat up by the Klan all the time, wasn't it, Dad?"

"Beaten up," Paul corrects him, slipping an arm around his son's shoulders. "And not all the time. A couple of times."

Wadding one hand into a fist, Nathan scowls. "I wouldn't let em do it to me. I'd kill those suckers first."

Chester raises his eyebrows at his grandson, and pushes his reading glasses up on his nose. "That was just a few bad people down here, now Nathan, that business about the KKK. Most of us here in Mississippi didn't know how bad it was for folks like your dad."

Paul stoops to pick up Matthew, who has been clutching at the leg of his jeans, hoping to be held, wanting to see what has been happening above his head. "Don't worry, son." He reads Nathan's frown. "It won't happen again."

"I declare," says Chester, shaking a film strip so that it dances. "It *is* the wedding. Look here! It's the bridesmaids, Amanda!"

Peering over her father's shoulder, Amanda studies the pictures. A fog seems to envelop the figures there, as if they are evading the memory of the camera, erasing the boundaries of their faces and blending their bodies into the silver light the camera recorded around them. In the air above their heads hangs a spherical shape of flowers, a bouquet tossed by the bride's unseen hand from somewhere behind the camera. The three figures with their arms outstretched wait to receive an omen of their romantic fortune, their flashlight into the future, into the dark unknown beyond 1964. In the frames of cracked celluloid, they still wait.

Amanda laughs, remembering. "Ah yes. The bridesmaids. They really fought for that bouquet."

Chester is prying open another canister, then another, to find that the years have touched all the movies in the same way.

"Ask Jacob what to do when he and Sheridan get here," Amanda says. She takes the end of the film Chester has just pulled out and examines it, feeling its stiffness, its reluctance to divulge whatever secrets it holds. "If anybody would know whether these could be repaired, Jacob would."

"That's it, Chester!" Virginia rubs his arm. "Ask Jacob to fix them. Then we could show them at the reunion next year. Wouldn't that be fun?" She claps her hands. "Can you imagine how surprised everybody would be?"

"Now, let's not all get our hopes up. Jacob's a busy man . . ." Chester replaces the lid on one of the canisters, snapping it down with a click of authority, signaling a certain finality. "But we'll see."

Paul pats Matthew's back and eyes Amanda. "He's asleep, isn't he?" He turns so Amanda can see Matthew's face, wrinkled in sleep on his shoulder.

"Isn't he a little doll?" Virginia smooths back a curl that has fallen across Matthew's forehead. She beams over at Amanda. "He's been so good tonight."

Amanda nods. "He slept most of the way today. But he's so tired." She strokes the pink curve of his upper arm, curled against Paul's neck. She glances at Paul. "Mama made up the baby bed in Ruby Ann's old room."

"Where's Ruby Ann going to stay?" asks Paul.

"She'll just have to be quiet, I guess," Virginia answers, "but she can sleep in her own room, of course."

"We've always said our daughters will have their own beds to come back home to any time they want," Chester bellows with a pointed look at Paul, before Virginia can give him a shushing glance.

In the stillness that follows their footsteps down the hall, Virginia and Chester replace the films in the bait box while Nathan watches. "There aren't any movies of me, are there, Grandpa?" he asks.

"No, I'm afraid not. And none of Matthew either. I didn't have my movie camera anymore when you two were born," says Chester.

Nathan flounces on the bed. "So what happened to it? Did it break? Why didn't you get another one?"

A sigh escapes Chester's lips. "Well, I'll tell you, son," he says. "Somebody got to playing with it and it got lost. Accidents happen. But I ought to get another one." He turns to Virginia. "Nathan's right. We ought to get us another movie camera."

Virginia is hanging the shirt she ironed for Chester to wear tomorrow. "You've said that for years. I ought to just *buy* you one. Maybe I'll put it under the tree next Christmas."

Amanda and Paul return, still on tiptoe and in hushed voices. Amanda taps a finger to her lips. "He's asleep." She massages her shoulders. "Boy, I'm about as tired as Matthew. What a drive."

"I don't know why y'all don't fly." Virginia rubs Amanda's back. "Course I'm glad to have all of you no matter how you get here, but it seems like . . ."

"It's the scenery, Mom. We really enjoy it."

"You wind up seeing parts of America you'd never see otherwise," Paul says. "It's educational for Nathan."

Virginia shrugs. "Well, you two have always done things that don't make much sense to me."

Chester snaps his fingers, both hands at once. "I made some punch for y'all, and here I am about to forget to offer it." He winks. "A little bourbon in it."

"Shhh, Daddy. Not so loud." Amanda taps her finger against her lips.

Chester gestures to the kitchen and whispers, "I'll get everybody a drink out on the patio."

Outside, they settle into the lawn chairs Virginia bought for the family reunion two years ago. Nathan sinks into the hammock stretched between two trees just beyond the edge of the patio. The smell of fresh pine straw rises up from the dampness of the grass that Chester mowed early that morning, before the sun had rippled down in heat waves over the yard. From the pine straw comes the rhythmic hum of crickets. In the darkness now, the pine trees form a canopy of shadows above them, a lacy tent through which the stars are visible.

Virginia points up through a couple of pine branches and draws a triangle in the air with her finger. "See there?" she says. "Those three bright stars that make a great big triangle? That's Vega, Altair, and Deneb. Deneb is the best one of the three. It's in the Swan constellation. See how bright it is?"

"God, Mama, the next thing you'll be into is astrology," laughs Amanda.

In the darkness, Virginia blushes and makes a mental note to remove *Your Year in Planet Transits, 1985* from the bookcase in the den until Amanda and Paul leave. "The constellations don't have a thing in the world to do with astrology," she answers, an edge in her voice. "That's planets, mostly."

"You don't really believe that stuff, do you?" The laughter still plays in Amanda's voice. "You're just kidding around with those tarot cards, aren't you?"

There is silence, and Amanda begins again, more gently. "It would mean that we're not really responsible for what we do, wouldn't it? That we could do anything and blame it on the stars, or on fate?"

"Of course we're responsible for how we act," Virginia replies. "But there are some things we just can't help." Her chair scrapes the patio as she shifts. "There are some things in this world we can't avoid happening. Things we don't know how to prevent until they've already happened."

"Well, you sure do know the constellations, don't you?" From a far corner of the patio comes Paul's voice, his presence marked by the red glow of his cigarette, moving occasionally in a leisurely arc to his mouth. "I'm impressed."

"I learned them years ago. Remember that book on the constellations Ruby Ann gave me one Christmas?" Virginia's voice is soft in the night now, as she confides to the three faces she cannot see. "It took me a whole year to learn them all, waiting for them to come around in the sky by the seasons. I had to take it by spells, learning some in the summer, some in the fall . . ."

"Take it by spells? What does that mean?" asks Nathan.

From the darkness comes a chuckle from Amanda. "Spells," she repeats. "That's just the way people used to talk here in the South. It means she did it a little at a time."

"*Used* to talk?" says Virginia. "Don't make me sound so old." She pauses, and then asks quietly, "I guess it does make me sound countrified, doesn't it?"

"Makes you sound like a witch, Grandma," says Nathan, "casting spells . . ."

Suddenly yellow light floods the patio. Chester appears at the kitchen door, holding a tray of glasses. Amanda shields her eyes.

"Turn it off, Daddy. It's too bright."

"Y'all aren't getting eaten alive by the bugs?" He pauses, his hand on the light switch inside the door. "I put this special light in to keep them away. Mosquitoes don't like yellow."

"No, it's fine, sweetheart," Virginia says. "We're looking at the stars."

Chester distributes the glasses he's brought, filled with a golden punch, and then flips off the light switch. The shadows return to the patio. His laugh comes nervously in the new darkness as he settles into his chair. "You telling the future, hon?"

Amanda's voice answers. "The future's not in the stars, Dad. Mama says that's in the planets." She sips her drink and the clinking of her bangle bracelets disguises Chester's patient sigh. She tilts her head back. "So what else is up there?"

A voice comes from the hammock. "Who cares about constellations? I wanna see something radical. A shooting star." There is a brief pause. The hammock can be heard creaking in rhythm. "No, a satellite. I wanna see a satellite."

"Where's the North Star?" asks Paul. The red tip of his cigarette moves up to his mouth, glows brighter for a brief moment, and then makes a crimson arc back to the arm of his lawn chair.

"Paul wants to know how to get back home!" Chester exclaims.

Virginia searches the sky and then points above her, just north of the bright star she's pointed out as Deneb. "Somewhere north of Deneb, that brightest one up there," she says. "You can always find it if you know where the Big Dipper is, though. It points right to it—the cup part, not the handle." Though no one can see her, she draws a map of it in the air with her finger.

"She'd never get lost on the ocean, would she?" It is Chester's voice, booming out. "Just like having a compass. Sure glad I married her."

They fall into silence, there in the darkness, as they watch the sky through the web of pine branches. The crickets and the creaking of the hammock are a lulling rhythm.

"There are some wonderful stories up there, some real adventures." Virginia's words slide into the silence. "Andromeda's up there, and so is Perseus, trying to set her free from the chains her daddy put on her for being too pretty. After all these thousands of years, he's never quite able to reach her. I always like to think I'll look up there one of these nights and they'll be riding away on Pegasus, the stars of Andromeda and Perseus clustered right there together between the horse's wings."

"That's a beautiful thought, Virginia." A quiet note of surprise sounds in Paul's voice. "Quite a powerful image."

"Oh, if you think that's powerful, you should hear the story about the serpent holder. He's the biggest one up there, stretched out all across the sky in the summer, scattered out so far you can hardly put together the stars that make his body. He's so big you'd almost never notice him. Isn't that a funny thought?"

"The big guys are like that. They'll sneak up on you that way." It is Nathan, still swinging the hammock.

There is a clapping sound as Amanda slaps at a mosquito. "So what did this serpent holder do that made him so important he fills half the sky? Did he rescue somebody from the serpent or was he terrorizing people with it?"

"Oh no. He wasn't scaring anybody. They say the serpent holder is the only constellation that was a real person once—some doctor way back," continues Virginia. "But the story is that none of his patients ever died—just think about it. He even thought he could raise Orion from the dead, but Hades got so mad about it that he had the poor doctor taken off the earth and put in the sky as a constellation. Wouldn't it be something if you looked up there and Orion started dancing, moving all around in the sky, coming alive?"

"Like my home movies," Chester's voice booms proudly into the darkness. Then his words soften. "If we can just see the darn things."

Virginia pats the spot where she thinks Chester's hand lies on the arm of his chair, but she touches aluminum. "Jacob will fix them, sweetheart. Don't worry."

A laugh comes from the corner of darkness where Amanda sits. "Just think about what Mom's saying though. Wouldn't that be wonderful? All those myths scrambled up into new ones."

"I'd put Elvis up there," says Nathan. "He's a myth, isn't he?"

"It's hard for me to think of him as a myth now. He seemed so real at Graceland, like such a vulnerable man living in such an isolated little world," says Amanda. "He doesn't seem like some larger-than-life star anymore."

"The Elvis constellation." It is Paul's deep Boston accent. "That's a good idea. Let's pick out the stars for him."

"The shape of a guitar would work. Or a hound dog," Virginia suggests, searching the sky for the appropriate dots of light.

"Oh now. The sky's too pretty the way it is to think about that." From Chester's chair comes the clink of glass against glass. He is setting his drink down on the table beside him. "And besides, if you don't like those up there, why, we've got our own stories right here. And we've got our own stars." He sighs, a deep sigh of pleasure. "We've got our movies back."

The warm night folds around the small group, gathered in silence now on the patio. The red bud that is Paul's cigarette falls to the ground and goes out, leaving the darkness to swell about them.

FOURTEEN

DETECTIVE MOVIES 1986

On an unseasonably rainy October evening in Los Angeles, Jacob carefully gathers damaged home movies in loose coils around his wrist. He is sitting at the desk in his editing room, thinking absently about the lives contained in the withered frames he holds. Sheridan's mother and Aunt Virginia and Uncle Chester are collected in them, among others. There are a few faces he barely knows there, in the old movies. He vaguely recognizes some from trips to Mississippi, but even those faces are so altered by the years and by the condition of the movies that the people seem like strangers.

He remembers his wedding, that loose configuration of staid ceremony and unbounded celebration that marked his initiation into the Bloomer family. How foreign and familiar they all seemed at the same time! It was not the most relaxed of gatherings: there he was in his Mexican wedding shirt, assured by Sheridan that it was fine not to wear a jacket in the heat of the late Mississippi spring. "The ceremony's in a *garden*, for heaven's sake," she had said. "Of course the shirt's okay. It's not formal." But all the family men were sweating in their suits. Even the daisies tucked in Sheridan's hair wilted. He smiles at the memory of the men's attempt to be buddies with him, at their jokes about the wedding night, or the constraints of married life. No one but Winnie knew that he and Sheridan had lived together in a San Francisco apartment for two years while Sheridan studied acting and he completed his film degree. They were going to move to Los Angeles and be rich and famous, he remembers. It was a fantasy they laughed about, a dream they toasted on the rare occasions when they ordered champagne, but there was a serious current beneath the laughter and the toasts—a commitment to themselves, to their work. In the last few years, Jacob thinks, that commitment has grown even stronger, though the wealth and critical acclaim have not come. "Sheridan and Jacob, they've got their feet planted firmly in the air," Chester grinned before their wedding. "They'll be a good pair, won't they?" How little they knew him, Jacob thinks now. Or, for that matter, how little they knew Sheridan either.

"Hi, babe. How's it going?" Sheridan's voice echoes down the hallway, and then the door to his editing room swings open. She stands in the doorway, lifting her rain-streaked sunglasses to the top of her head and slipping her car keys into the pocket of her jeans with the other hand. She has just arrived home from a rehearsal of the Chekhov play she's gotten a part in. Rehearsing the play "jazzes" her, she says, especially the comic role she has. It is a stretch for her, but it still leaves her with energy to spare.

Ruffling Jacob's hair, she reaches over to kiss his cheek, then peeks into a frame of the film dripping from his hand. "You got my past in your hands." She laughs and sings a line from a gospel song, holding one fist to her mouth, microphone-style. *He's got the whole wo-orld, in his hands . . .* She does a bop step and gives him a mock punch on the upper arm.

Jacob eyes her, still wrapping the film. "You're in a good mood."

"So that means you're not. Right? Don't tell me you're still grouchy about doing this stuff for Uncle Chester."

"Take a look at this, would you?" Jacob rubs his thumb over a tear in the film. "Chester must've tried to project this through his damn lawn mower. And I'm supposed to save it?"

Sheridan reaches for a strand of the film. "Stop whining. Lord knows there are enough martyrs in here already." She shakes the film at Jacob, and squeezes its sides together. "It still feels crunchy."

"Hey, don't do that. It's fragile."

"Ah yeah. Subject to decay." She slips a hand down the neckline of her tee shirt and shrugs a bra strap back into place. "Well, hey, I'll try not to ruin your bad mood."

She steps toward the door but pauses as a damp wind outside swells through the editing room's sole window, rattling the thin slats of the venetian blinds. Outside, the top of the corner street-light has almost disappeared into a silvery fog that carries the smell of rain. Sheridan reaches over to close the window but stands there for a moment instead, her hand on the sill, feeling the cool night breeze on her face, remembering the first southern winds of autumn, the cool reassurances that the season of hot days and balmy nights was ending. There was magic, it seemed, on those whimsical winds that blew away the summer.

The home movies themselves seem to contain some of that magic. Since the footage arrived the week before, Sheridan has hardly been able to pass the editing room without stopping in to sort through the canisters or to check on the strips that Jacob has treated.

She has begun to feel that she is giving a great private party, checking to see if everyone has arrived, what costumes they are wearing, what year or event they have brought with them, there into her own home in Los Angeles, where she can scrutinize them to her heart's content, without the risk of being observed or judged, herself. She has decided that she will go to the next Libertyburg reunion, the following summer, to be present at the showing. "Two years in a row!" she exclaimed to Jacob. "Can we stand that many reunions?" But it all has the flavor of a great play opening, and how can she possibly miss *that,* she asked him, a note of glee in her voice. Privately, she feels like both the director of that play and an anonymous critic.

Jacob, though, is not as pleased with the new cache of films. They arrived many weeks after the reunion in July. After a couple of months of hoping that Chester had forgotten his promise to send the remaining movies, Jacob pushed them from his mind.

Then he found the package propped beneath the mailbox, covered with round purple stamps announcing it was "insured" and "fragile." Inside, a letter from Chester explained why he was late sending the films, apologizing for the delay. He'd taken them up to Jackson, he wrote, to some photography specialists, to see what they could do. He'd hoped he wouldn't have to bother Jacob. But no dice, Chester wrote, his handwriting looping across Virginia's monogrammed stationery. They had just scratched their heads and suggested he "write the company." And what company might that be, after all these years? Chester had wondered. It was no dice again. So here they are, wrote Chester. Could Jacob fix them up? How about some of that Yankee ingenuity?

Already, after only a few treatments, the film is beginning to get more supple, a little less likely to splinter or break. But he still doesn't know if he can get it back into shape for Chester's projector at the reunion next spring. He has already begun to ask himself how he's gotten suckered into it, why he ever agreed to try.

There has been no sign of Sheridan in her majorette uniform. He has found some film of what looks like a parade of soldiers, and another so blurred he can't tell what celebration is taking place. A wedding, maybe. Another holds a baseball game with a tiny batter angling for a pitch, shifting his body as the ball comes past. The next few frames dissolve into the bleacher crowds, as if the filmmaker briefly forgot the movie he was making and cheered the batter on. But there is not a hint of Fred yet, though there is still footage he hasn't looked at, canisters even Sheridan hasn't pried open.

He doesn't know if he wants to look at the rest, though. What a lousy burden the whole thing seems, especially since Chester has told Virginia that the film can be fixed by the next reunion. The old guy wasn't able to keep the secret he'd planned as a surprise for his wife. When the phone rang the day after the films arrived, it was Virginia, making sure they hadn't been lost in the mail. And now Sheridan, too, has such hopes for the "family play," as she calls the assortment of movies. Everyone, he thinks, has jumped on the home-movie bandwagon, all with their different reasons—nostalgia or narcissism or some vague desire to justify or complete themselves, he imagines.

A jagged edge of lightning cracks across the sky, lighting their faces in stark white. Sheridan steps back from the window and rubs her upper arms with both hands. "This is spooky weather. It sounds like the sky's going to explode any minute."

Jacob curls the last of the film around his forearm. "Check this out," he tells her, holding out a film strip. "What's going on here?" He hands Sheridan the round jeweler's magnifying glass he uses for his film editing.

"Get a load of this," she says, squinting into the glass. "It's Mama and Aunt Virginia wearing Hawaiian costumes. You can tell they're trying to get along, can't you? Look how Mama has her hand planted on Aunt Virginia's shoulder, and how positively grim she looks. Just because they married brothers, they're supposed to be sisters. What a bummer for those two."

"They get along now well enough, don't they?" asks Jacob. "Or are they just being polite? I can never tell with you southerners."

"Oh, they've found a way to appreciate each other. But only after years of practice." She laughs and then frowns, her mood suddenly shifting. "Look how young they are. My God, they're probably a lot younger there than we are now. What a thought." She looks up at Jacob. "That's depressing. Why's that depressing, do you think?"

Jacob leans over to look at the film. "So that's Winnie? It doesn't look much like her."

"Well, she's probably all of about twenty-five there. It's depressing," she says into the movie, as if she is scolding the black-and-white characters. "Why does that make me sad?"

"I don't know. Because you think you wouldn't have been friends with her if you'd known her at that age and she hadn't been your mother?" Jacob shrugs. "What's this outfit Virginia's wearing? It's really strange."

But Sheridan ignores him, looking off with a pensive expression at the rain against the window. She snaps her fingers suddenly, breaking off her reverie. "There's a photograph of this!"

Thrusting the film strip into Jacob's hands, she dashes out and returns with a small cardboard box balanced on top of a blue leather album. "Here!" She flips the stiff pages of the book, the pages making a clapping sound like a slow rhythmic beat of applause by a single pair of hands. She flips past color photographs of herself and Jacob, of their New York friends waving to them from an East Coast dock, past California scenes of herself at a San Francisco beach, eyeing the camera coyly, her hair blowing across one cheek, her arms folded against the thick green sweater she is wearing. There is Jacob grinning with his brother as they playfully wrestle on New Year's Eve in New York, blurring the picture with their jostling. The scenes slap by, a quick succession of colors and faces, until the photographs become black-and-white, entering another place, another time. The sound grows slower as Sheridan scans the pages more carefully, skimming the rows of old photographs. Her finger stops on a small black-and-white photograph, tapping it.

"This one," she says, bending down over the desk. Jacob's head meets her own over the page, his dark curls brushing the curtain of brown hair that hangs past Sheridan's shoulder. "It's not very clear. Daddy had an old box camera that took crummy pictures."

He frowns at the photograph. "You're right; it's the same thing. That's a grass skirt Virginia's wearing. Was that a forties style or something?"

"I don't think that was ever a popular style in Mississippi," Sheridan answers dryly. "Though if it was, Aunt Virginia would've been the first to wear it." She laughs. "And if the muumuu Mama's wearing was ever in fashion, then this must've been taken five years later."

"Think it's Halloween?" asks Jacob.

"No. Adults never dressed up for Halloween in Mississippi like they do here. Not back then, anyway."

"Not unless they wore white hoods and carried crosses to go trick-or-treating, right?" Jacob snickers.

"That's a cheap shot. Can't resist a jab, can you?" Sheridan flips her hair over one shoulder and turns back to the album. "Look at the print in this muumuu." She shudders, a hand over her heart. "Not exactly flattering, is it? Wonder what Uncle Chester and Daddy were wearing. I can just see Uncle Chester in some loud Hawaiian shirt, puffing one of those awful cigars he used to smoke. I bet Daddy was behind the camera, directing it. Just think, Daddy could have been a film director if he'd had half a chance."

"Virginia was pretty sexy, wasn't she? Check out these legs of hers." He slips a sideways look at Sheridan, a teasing sparkle in his eye. "Think she ever cheated on Chester?"

Sheridan smiles at the two faces in the photograph. "You know—this sounds terrible—sometimes I kind of hope so. But I doubt it. I can't imagine who it would have been with. It's more likely Uncle Chester left some broken hearts behind when he was a traveling salesman for that feed company. A waitress, maybe, or a clerk behind a rooming-house desk. But Aunt Virginia has her passion, too. I've even seen it break through her repression. Mostly when she gets mad, though."

"Virginia angry? She's always so soft-spoken."

"She doesn't have tantrums or anything. I used to know Aunt Virginia was angry with us kids when her jaw would start working. Her voice would hardly change, but boy, these little muscles . . ." Sheridan taps the sides of her jaw with both index fingers. "They'd twitch like crazy."

Jacob laughs. "Unlike you. You just explode."

"And then," Sheridan continues, "pots and pans in the kitchen would start clattering a little louder than usual. If she was really outdone with us, she'd just up and leave the house. Mama said Virginia was really angry when Uncle Chester lost the home movies a long time ago—the whole town gossiped about the fight they had. Their little terrier, you know, Smitty, ran away one night when he was a puppy because they were arguing about the movies, Mama said. Aunt Virginia had to go running out in the middle of the night to rescue the dog."

She gives Jacob a playful punch on his arm. "So look out, kiddo. Passion and repression. It's a dynamic duo. Which is one reason you better whip this film into shape. In her own subtle way, Aunt Virginia'll whip you into a thousand shapes if you don't." Sheridan mechanically shrugs her fallen bra strap back onto her shoulder again and grins as she does a dance step around Jacob.

A tight smile stretches Jacob's mouth as he surveys the film canisters on his desk. "I didn't have any idea Chester was such a home-movie freak. There must be tons of these here."

"Oh, he loved them all right." Sheridan sweeps her sunglasses from their perch on her head and waves them by one stem, punctuating the air with circles and swirls. "But he always wanted us to be like some family from a Hollywood movie or a TV sitcom." She giggles. "Uncle Chester Knows Worst."

"So the movies were Chester's fantasies, is that what you're saying?"

"Oh, don't get me wrong. It was terrific fun to watch them. Mama always said that's why I wanted to be an actress, because Uncle Chester's screen wasn't big enough for me."

"Aha." Jacob's eyes twinkle. "So they were *your* fantasies."

Sheridan laughs. "In a way. Uncle Chester used to let us kids play with his old camera, after he bought the portable. We'd pretend we were Marilyn Monroe or Elizabeth Taylor. Ruby Ann always wanted to be Ingrid Bergman after she saw a rerun of *The Bells of St. Mary's* on TV."

A wet breeze gusts through the crack Sheridan has left in the window, banging the blinds against the sill. A ragged fragment of a home movie, a piece that Jacob has clipped off to smooth the edge, sails to the floor near the chair leg.

She bends to rescue it and fingers the rough edge, thinking. "We all loved the movies Uncle Chester made. Even my father liked to watch them, as long as he wasn't in them. He sure hated for anybody to turn the camera on him."

"I hope he's here," says Jacob, frowning into the canister he has just filled. The movies lie, now neatly coiled and smoothedged, in concentric circles, shades of gray, black, and almost-silver. From hooks above the desk, other scraps hang in uneven lengths like strings of fish caught on a single line.

Fantasies, thinks Sheridan. That is what they are: a multitude of her family's fantasies. Her own memory is like a vast fishing net thrown behind her life, collecting the shadowy vagaries of the currents and streams—and the very shadows that have escaped that net, it seems, are precisely what have found their way into her family's net, so that they all have their separate trails of memories.

"Look at this," she says softly, opening the brown box she has brought in along with the photograph album. Inside are old letters, carefully tied in ribboned bundles or wrapped around with crumbling rubber bands.

"What's that?"

Sheridan pulls out a yellowed envelope, addressed in a slanting scrawl to Miss Winnie Franklin, 604 Sycamore Street, Libertyburg, Mississippi. In the upper corner is a three-cent stamp, canceled with a purple circle: Pensacola, Florida, October, 1945.

"What're you doing with your mother's mail?" Jacob teases her.

"I told you about this, a long time ago. It's a box of letters and other stuff Mama threw away after Daddy died." Sheridan picks up a dried corsage from which the flowers have long fallen, leaving a stream of faded red ribbons and a couple of tiny satin hearts.

"Winnie didn't want this?"

"She sure didn't. I was putting out the trash one morning—it must've been only a few months after Daddy died, and there was this box, mashed down under the trash-can lid with his after-shave, and"—Sheridan pauses—"and with Mama's diaphragm. I hardly knew what it was, then. I thought it was a compact or something, so I opened it. Who knows what she was going through, thinking there'd never be anyone else."

Sheridan strokes the ribbons on the corsage. And there never *has* been anyone else, she thinks, though a couple of men have tried to court her mother, tried taking her to dinner or sending her candy on Valentine's Day. Winnie has shrugged them off: Homer Wadsworth from the church, she said, why what woman in her right mind would be interested in a man who yelled out, "Amen!" to the preacher like some country hick? And George Pringle sending her Valentine's chocolates: he was nice enough, she said, but my word, when in the world had he seen the inside of a church? What would people say?

"I guess nobody was as good as Daddy," Sheridan says, carefully replacing the corsage. She lifts another envelope from the box. "There aren't too many of these letters. Most of them are from the fall of 1945, before Mama and Daddy married, when Daddy moved off to Pensacola to look for work in the oil industry."

A tiny heart has been drawn in blue ink on the back of the envelope, so that the open flap splits it. Sheridan remembers the contents of the letter without rereading it, the angled handwriting that tells of wanting to buy a house on the beach and move Winnie to Florida after they marry—he has picked out the house, he wrote, one with green shutters, a backyard that slopes off down to the beach, a big kitchen, and a garage that is attached to the house with a screened-in porch—a breezeway, they call it. Now if he can just get a definite word from the oil company on a job. "'Maybe next week,' they say," Fred wrote. His letters stopped in December, when he moved back to Libertyburg ("Even Florida gets cold," he said in the last letter, "especially when you're alone") and went to work at the hardware store until he could find something better.

Jacob frowns at the letter in her hand. "What did Winnie think about you having these?"

"I meant to tell her right after I found them, but then I couldn't, I just couldn't, not with the diaphragm that had been with them. So I stuck them in the top of my closet, behind my shoeboxes. And then when I was older . . . well, how could I throw them away?"

"You mean she doesn't even know you have them?"

"Oh sure. She does now. I told her when she came out here a long time ago. She didn't even remember throwing it out. I told you about it, don't you remember?" Sheridan shrugs. "God, nobody remembers anything. To tell you the truth, she didn't seem very interested. She glanced at one letter, and then wanted to go to a movie."

Jacob laughs. "Winnie and her movies."

"I think that's why she and Aunt Virginia finally became friends—all those movies they're always seeing." Sheridan replaces the top on the box and ties a piece of string around it in a bow. They were the only clues she had, she thinks, when she was sixteen. The letters and photographs boxed up here, together with the isolated memories of her father, the memories that might make sense of the lifeless body in the garage that morning. And always, it was her father's frustration she found, even there in the impatient handwriting: the job that wasn't offered, the loan that couldn't be paid off in time, the vacation they couldn't take. Later there were her father's retreats into silence, into his hunting trips, and the escapes, always, from the probe of the camera. She tucks the box under her arm and starts to leave the room.

"In a way, this feels like a real archaeological expedition, doesn't it?" asks Jacob, gazing at the pensive look on Sheridan's face. "Peeling back the layers that must be here, sifting through them, sorting. And trying not to damage the ruins. It's going to be a real responsibility."

The headlights from a car outside flicker briefly through the slats of the blinds. The shadows make a pattern of bars that travel through the room, and though Sheridan can't see them, across her own face. Instead she sees only the image sliding across the wall, and it makes her think of some old detective movie from the forties. Her Uncle Chester's home movies suddenly seem as mysterious, the endings as unknown, the characters shrouded in shadows.

Sheridan's eyes melt on Jacob. "Exactly. That's what it is: an archaeological expedition."

FIFTEEN

ILLUSIONS OF MOTION
1986

Christmas in Los Angeles always seems ridiculous to Sheridan, a confusion of symbols, of palm trees and Christmas wreaths, of Santa Claus and surfers becomes absurd to her. Some of it has to do with the special holiday tours of the stars' homes. Entire busloads of tourists rumble down their modest street on the way to the posh neighborhoods of the stars. And then the fans start to see celebrities everywhere. If Jacob ventures outside to wash the car or bring the newspaper in, someone will inevitably call out to him to ask if he isn't Al Pacino. Or Dustin Hoffman, maybe?

Once, an elderly woman wearing a baseball cap emblazoned

with #1 Mom leaned out the bus window when Sheridan was watering the lawn. Was she famous, Number-One Mom wanted to know. Was she a star?

No, Sheridan said, waving her hand at the house. If she were, she'd be living in a mansion, wouldn't she? Only her namesake was famous, Sheridan thought—her mother had named her after a movie star from the forties, Ann Sheridan. Most people in the 1980s barely recognize the name of Ann Sheridan, of course. Why hadn't her mother named her Ingrid or Rita or Vivien? Then Sheridan immediately regretted her thought. She might not be famous, but she was important in the way that it mattered, among the people who counted in her life. So were all those people on all those buses, traveling through her neighborhood in search of a star, a brush with the immortality of fame, stories about the Hollywood gods they could tell their own neighbors.

Now the season of the holiday tours has begun. Buses painted with the stars' faces inside Christmas wreaths make daily pilgrimages down the street. Joan Collins or Tom Selleck may go smiling by at any moment, framed in holly. It makes Sheridan want to go back to the South for the holidays, but the closest she can come to a visit this year is the home movies that Jacob has been restoring for the reunion next spring. He has already transferred some of the movies to videotape, but Chester keeps foiling the completion of the project by sending more films that he's found in the attic. Jacob has finally given up putting them in chronological order. Two bright red canisters arrived last week, and at first she put them in the refrigerator, thinking they were Christmas cookies or fruitcake. When she opened one, hoping for her mother's pecan crispies, her heart sank at the coils of yet more movies.

One of those canisters contained a Shriner parade she had twirled a fire baton in, back in 1959. Jacob has enlarged a couple of those frames so he could give one to Winnie for Christmas and hang the other on the wall of his editing room. The other canister held an Easter-egg hunt from the early sixties, Amanda's high-school graduation, some children playing at a beach, and a Tupperware party Virginia had given (*"A Tupperware party!"* she and Jacob hooted when they identified the rituals there). There are still other movies she hasn't looked at. Some of the footage at the bottom of the canister, Jacob has said, is in such good condition that he doesn't need to treat it.

A week before Christmas, she pulls into the driveway after mailing gifts to Mississippi and to Jacob's family in New York. Just as she slams the car door shut, herds of tour buses trek past, their passengers craning their necks at her. All that public anonymity makes her homesick for Libertyburg, and she wishes Jacob would return from the film studio soon, to commiserate with her. She nurses her pangs by brewing herself a cup of sassafras tea in her best china. The tea reminds her of the summers on Grandmother Bloomer's farm in Millsdale, before Grandpa Bloomer had his heart attack, when he could still take his granddaughters fishing in the river. Along the path they used to take, their fishing poles and cans of wriggling worms in hand, stood weatherbeaten sheds: the old smokehouse, the chicken coop, the corn barn, an enduring geometry against the horizon as natural as the oak and sweet gum trees lining the path. How serene those old gray shacks seemed, she thinks, remembering the way her father, after Grandpa Bloomer died, often slipped into them on some mysterious mission or other, looking for feed for the remaining cattle or some tool for the tractor. Her father seemed to become someone else then, she muses, remembering how at ease he seemed on the farm, how fluid even his walk became as he strolled from one task to the next. All his talk about wanting to get a job in a city—that was just empty bravado, after all. He would never have moved the family, even if he'd had the chance, would he? He should never have left the farm, she thinks. *Then I would have been a country girl, with horses and a garden with magnolia trees and gardenias and narcissus blooming in the spring. And I might still have a father.* Her eyes soften at the way her life might have been, and she opens the door to Jacob's editing room, pensively sipping her tea.

At the sudden rush of air, the strips of warped negatives hanging above Jacob's desk twist on their clamps, catching the light. Like skeletons dancing, she thinks, sinking into the swivel chair. Or ghosts. She sets her tea down and unclips one of the film strips. It is two pieces of slightly different grays that Jacob has spliced together so he can transfer them to video.

She holds the first segment up to the light and recognizes the footage of Dizzy Dean's baseball game. From the aging frames, the noise and smells of a summer noon some thirty years ago grow in her mind. Her father stands on his toes, trying to catch a glimpse of Dizzy Dean. Chester sees it all through the lens of his camera, trying to zoom in and focus. The memories well up, engulfing her, until the present moment, the very room where she stands, becomes the memory, and the Los Angeles traffic sounds outside, the shadow of the hanging ivy across the wall—these are the ghosts.

What a random conglomeration, she thinks, this invention of memory, this stretching of the years into a tangible celluloid fabric. Chester wanted these memories for Virginia's sake. They are her past, he said. But these strips of partly disintegrated celluloid hold as many pasts, as many interpretations, as there were degrees of focus on Chester's camera. In the last frame, the pictures of the ball sailing over the outfield dissolve into the first scene of the Easter-egg hunt. The children, it appears, are searching for the baseball to put in their baskets. Sheridan smiles to herself, wondering if Jacob was injecting his own sense of the ridiculous into the home movies. She raises another coil that has been spliced together.

Part of it is the beach footage from one of their summer weekends in Florida. Three children bounce in the waves, surrounded by their inflatable floats. Sheridan loops the film up, past her cousins and herself swimming and diving, gathering shells, and, in the last scene, overturning buckets of sand to build castles. She holds it closer to the light. Streaks of rain dot the frame, and in the bottom corner Ruby Ann's sand castle has washed into the water.

Then Virginia appears, wiping her daughter's tears with the corner of a beach towel. Three frames of rain and tears slide by, and then it is three years later, 1959, and Sheridan recognizes Amanda's high-school graduation. Virginia is adjusting the tassel on Amanda's graduation cap and then turning to wipe her own eyes, to brush away what must have been tears. At the end of the footage, the lines of the Libertyburg High School Class of 1959 march confidently and solemnly into a row of clowns in a 1947 Shriner parade.

She laughs, glad that Jacob has found the continuity he has been searching for—a continuity not in the chronology of years but in absurdity, in this random tumble of memory. Scattered across the desk, and now on the videocassette on the shelf above her, is an entire universe where the years dance past on the discord of desire and illusion, where home-run hits sail into Easter-egg hunts with treasures as ephemeral as Ruby Ann's sand castle.

Sheridan draws out more film, searching now not for ends that match but for that moment where the rituals of these years blend into a disharmonious whole. Above her head, the strips of dangling film seem more like flags from a foreign country, proclaiming a certain sovereignty of place and time all their own.

Later that night, a full moon begins to slant through the blinds of Jacob and Sheridan's dark bedroom. The unexpected light wakes Sheridan up, and at first she thinks a car is parked outside, with the headlights shining through the window. The light, though, is too gentle for that, and her body relaxes into the realization that it is only the moon outside.

But her mind refuses to relax. Thoughts of the holidays coming up begin to tumble, the presents she still needs to buy, the conversations she's been having with Winnie about Christmas. A light bulb seems to brighten uncontrollably in her brain, burning away the dream she can already barely remember. Something about an old house, she thinks, trying to grasp the remnants of it. Was it on fire? Had she set the fire herself? But the dream is gone, lost like some elusive shadow crossing her psyche.

She folds back the down coverlet on her side of the bed, softly so she won't wake Jacob. She eases her feet to the cold floor, and slides into her slippers, thinking about pouring herself a glass of apple juice.

On the way down the hall to the kitchen, she passes the editing room. Moonlight strikes the narrow strips of home movies that Jacob has replaced on the hooks that evening. The natural light transforms them into ornaments, shimmering there in silence with a silvery light that seems to come from within their own square frames, as if they have a life of their own, a certain serenity.

Skeletons or flags? she thinks. No. This time they seem more like Christmas ornaments. They draw her in, toys for her restless mind, there at three o'clock on a cold December morning.

Alone in the dark editing room, Sheridan stands and leans against the back of the swivel chair, making it creak gently in the silence. The hanging ivy that she has moved to the window to catch the morning light trails its leaves down to the sill, making a web of shadows across the desk. In the moonlight, the room seems to have a secret life of its own, a deep stillness that washes over her like water. Even the items there—Jacob's sunglasses lying on the desk, a half-empty coffee cup, the embroidered pillow lying in an adjacent chair—seem like the props of a play that have been discarded backstage and have somehow taken on their own life in the absence of a script.

Sheridan switches on the Tensor lamp at Jacob's editing table, making a small pool of yellow light there. Beneath it, she settles herself into the swivel chair and pushes aside Jacob's sunglasses. She studies the frames in the last strip of celluloid that Jacob has hung that evening. This is from among the film that Jacob said had remained curled in the bottom of the canister in nearly perfect condition. If the half-decorated cedar tree in the first frame is any indication, it is Christmas, or almost Christmas.

Recognizing the house, she draws the film closer, turning it first this way and then that, to measure its contents in the light. The small yellow house is where her family lived until she was seven, when they moved to a place closer to Chester and Virginia. She vaguely remembers the double windows in the living room that are visible there in the frame. The windowsill jutted out into a shelf that seemed wide to her at age seven. It was three hand-widths deep then, broad enough for her to use as a stage where her dolls acted in plays against the backdrop of the front yard. Her mother's brocade window draperies were perfect stage curtains. Every Christmas, the tree stood in front of that window, just as it does here in the film.

Holding the edges of the celluloid between the thumbs and middle fingers of both her hands, Sheridan lifts it high so she can rapidly run her eyes down each frame:

the tree
the tree
the tree
the tree

And then the tree dissolves into another scene: her mother and Virginia sitting side by side on a couch, lifting up something that looks like a long chain, reversed to black in the negative.

Sheridan slides her fingers down the strip of film in a fluid motion and draws another length of celluloid to the light. Identical frames fade into one another like a series of ellipsis marks, a holding pattern that Sheridan quickly scans until the pattern begins slowly to shift, sliding into new pictures.

In a sequence of several frames, her mother is standing up from the sofa. Then the camera seems to run the movie backward, and Winnie sits again in virtually the same sequence of movements. The pictures come alive in slow motion, Sheridan thinks, every movement breaking down into multiple gestures, each requesting a separate interpretation, each asking if this is precisely the right way the movement should be performed and remembered. Every nod or shrug fragments into the intersection of time and space defined by a celluloid frame, and each one, in a way that she cannot explain to herself, politely but insistently reaches through the years.

When she and Jacob were visiting New York years ago, at a time they were students, he took her to a small nineteenth-century film museum he had stumbled across in the middle of the city. She can see it, suddenly, in her mind, the rows of glass cases, even the buttons or gears connected there so that she and Jacob could set the little scenes into action, tricking the eye with illusions of motion, sending a series of still, brightly colored cardboard figures into animation: a juggling magician with pointy-toed shoes, an antelope leaping through a hoop, or a little Victorian lady strolling down a path, her parasol twirling, the movement eternal as long as the hand turned a crank. Jacob could have spent that entire rainy afternoon, she thinks, making the people and animals move in that converted store on Lexington Avenue. But those allusions to magic also dismantled the illusion, when Jacob grew tired and stopped, exposing the truth behind the mystery of the little figures, dancing or leaping or strolling. There it had been: another mystery, in the stilling of the human hand that turned the crank. As the two of them moved away from their play with the machines, the series of pictures edged to a halt. The single dancing magician fragmented into a dozen static figures, standing still and alone, and the Victorian lady became an entire series of herself, each image unique by a fraction. In another glass case, a circular mirror spun slowly and then stopped, containing a multitude of a sudden single image, an ocean frozen with waves, or a horse suspended over its hurdle. And there, in the musty quiet of the museum, they felt it: the stillness beneath the motion, the vast vacuum behind the breath.

That is the stillness of Winnie now, each frame of her indecision a decision.

Sheridan has a sudden urge to blow up each individual frame of her mother rising and sitting, and in that impulsive moment she feels that she could somehow capture eternal movement for her mother, save her from the stasis of her life.

She wants to catch each minute shift in her mother's facial expression, each rearranging of the wrinkles in her skirt, every flow of the amber light across her face as she rises into a shadow. She scrutinizes each frame as if Winnie has sketched a self-portrait there, a careful code that will divulge some secret if only she can read it. The series ends with a torn segment of film that seems to have been ripped once by her uncle's projector.

She draws out another strip of celluloid and finds herself at age two, an addition to the cast of characters on the couch, sitting between her mother and her aunt. Her legs stick straight out in front of her, and a wisp of hair curls up at each temple. With the pleasure and curiosity of someone unexpectedly presented with a wrapped gift, she draws the celluloid closer to her face, letting her eyes slip from frame to frame, unwrapping, unfolding, discarding, searching.

Winnie, it seems, is wiping her face in several squares, obscuring the camera's view of her. And then, a few frames farther, Sheridan emerges again in the film, and begins to move from the couch. One arm swings up, frame by frame, a leg descends from the couch to the floor, and then she is walking. From some unrecorded space, her aunt's hands brush into the frame to propel her small body on, and then the pair of hands brush back out again, retreating. The figure that is Sheridan at nearly two makes her way from frame to frame, from moment to fraction, from fraction to moment. Like a windup doll, Sheridan thinks. Click. Her hand goes up. Click. Her foot moves forward.

Click. Another figure enters a frame near the bottom of the segment Sheridan holds. She unwinds more film from the celluloid curls nested in the canister and holds the frames to the light. Click. A leg enters the frame. Click. A face. Her father waves at the camera.

Sheridan's mouth moves into the shape of a circle. "Oh." The sound is more a breath than a word. The corners of her mouth lift as she closes her eyes and presses the strip of celluloid to the center of her forehead. "Oh." She lowers the film again.

She is approaching her father, step by step, the bow in the back of her romper suit rising slightly as she stretches up her hands, fraction by fraction, to reach for him. Click. Fred's face dissolves in horror. A bowl leaves his hand. Click. Along with a cloud of white particles, it makes its way downward through three frames. In the fourth it crashes on the floor, and the cloud becomes a pool spreading, frame by frame, across the floor. Her father is bending, then kneeling, his arms stretching out.

A pair of hands descends into the frame and catches her under her arms. In the next frames, she begins to disappear, rising up toward the upper edge of each square of celluloid, her mouth wide, her feet dangling until only her shoes are in the frame, and then nothing at all.

Her father begins slowly to fill the frames as he nears the camera. His face looms clearer as Sheridan stretches out the last of the celluloid. Click. Click. His mouth moves in some silent echo from eternity; his eyes narrow. And then the palm of his hand fills the last four frames until they darken into blackness.

Click.

Sheridan stares at the last segment of film, holding it at the edge as if it might be burning and the sudden tingling she feels in her fingertips might come from a fire that has smoldered for over thirty years in those gray frames. Then she drops it into the canister, feeling like an interloper, the very trespasser that her father protested.

SIXTEEN

A CHESS GAME
1987

On a stage in an old auditorium, Sheridan twirls and gestures in a desperate dance, hearing the calls of the audience, invisible beyond the stage lights. People are calling out instructions to her about new dance steps, disapproving of what she is performing, but she cannot quite understand what they want her to do. Then the stage stretches downward into one long ramp, and she can see that every member of the audience is dancing alone too, each enclosed in a spotlight like the one that surrounds her, each hearing his or her own invisible audience. The music and the circle of blinding light around her seem to twist together in a faster flashing rhythm, merging into one, swallowing her up, suffocating her.

She wakes in a sweat. Jacob lies snoring gently beside her, one arm flung off the bed. What was it, she thinks, this dream? And wasn't there another, before this? Something about Winnie sweeping up ashes that lifted like feathers and fell again, in the same spot, over and over. She closes her eyes and tries to see the dream again, to bring it back. Only the dusting of white ashes returns, nothing more. And then sleep returns.

Sheridan sits alone on the sun porch, staring at a chessboard. On it are scattered a few remaining pieces. She frowns at both the Sunday-morning sun and the vulnerability of her queen. She started the game with Jacob the night before, and she suggested that they quit when she grew irritable over her losses, over the cache of black pawns Jacob had collected.

Now, as morning shadows stretch westward, dappling the tile floor of the sun porch, her mood has not improved much.

"What's taking you so long? Can't decide how to lose her?" Jacob sets down two cups of coffee and perches on the arm of her chair. "Death," he says, pointing first to his knight, then to a bishop. "No way out, kid. She's a goner."

"You're making me nervous." Sheridan waves a hand at him. "Don't look over my shoulder."

"Everything makes you nervous since the play closed." Jacob sips his coffee. "It's postpartum blues."

She studies the game. The morning sunlight hits a prism she has hung in one of the sun-porch windows and splashes rainbows across the chessboard. From the ceiling, a Japanese wind sock flutters its blue and yellow and purple strips, making another rainbow that moves with the rhythms of a Pacific breeze.

"It's not the play." She shrugs. "It was a good run. I'm not bluesy over that." She moves the queen diagonally two spaces away, stares at it, then slides her back quickly. "I take it back. I didn't want her there."

"That's illegal, you know. But go ahead." Jacob settles back into a chaise longue and pulls the film pages from the Sunday paper. "So if it's not the play, then what is it? I know it's not this interminable chess game. I wish you'd give it up. Is it the reunion next week?"

Sheridan sighs and stares off at a rainbow on the wall. "All Mama talks about on the phone is the movies. She says everybody's talking about them, trying to remember what's there. Every time she calls it's to ask about some movie—and I have to either tell her it's not there or that she remembers it wrong. It's awful."

Jacob studies her. "You feel guilty."

The remark falls into her psyche like a fishhook.

"I don't know about that," she bristles, sliding a pawn forward, then back. "Oh hell. Maybe I *do* feel like it's my fault. I can't give my mother movies of the life she wishes she'd had." She laughs. "I'm just nervous, that's all. Sometimes I don't even want to go anymore."

"After all our work on those things?" Jacob folds the newspaper back into a roll and frowns at her. "Are you kidding?"

"It's too sad, those movies. Even Uncle Chester's Hawaiian shirt is sad."

A breeze flutters the newspaper, and Jacob sets it down to smooth Sheridan's hair. "C'mon. Chester had a damn good time in that shirt. Don't go feeling sorry for him. Hell. He probably felt sorry for *you* when you married a weirdo like me. Of course you're going to the reunion."

"Oh, I won't miss it. You know that. But it still doesn't mean I don't have any doubts about going." Sheridan pushes her queen forward three squares, sighs, and then moves it back again, in a chess game where the queen is indecisive, the knight makes a clean sweep.

SEVENTEEN

REUNION
1987

In the late Mississippi spring of 1987, Jacob Stern circulates among the guests at the Bloomer family reunion, watching the people around him and hearing their voices. He is trying to be attentive to them, to remember all their names and be pleasant. Yet he feels distant from the conversations around him. Even the sound merges into a swarming cadence, broken by an occasional burst of laughter. At one of the picnic tables, he picks up a piece of pound cake that Virginia has made from Grandmother Bloomer's recipe and bites into its buttery crust. Then he holds the cake out and looks at it as he chews, trying to figure out the secret ingredient in that famous recipe. Bourbon, he guesses, and bites into the cake again.

There is a larger crowd at the reunion this year. Chester has told him that five states are represented, counting his and Sheridan's California and Amanda and Paul's Illinois. That is a record, he has said: five states. Once again, they have all gathered at a park at the Libertyburg duck pond. A lake, they used to call it, Virginia tells Jacob, as she slices several more pieces of pound cake. Or so a neighbor named Ralph Cole once told her, a couple of years before he passed on. Seems like the whole world is getting smaller, she adds, and Jacob does not notice that her cheeks redden beneath her rouge as she mentions Ralph's name. She lifts her chin as if that would wash the blush from her face.

"That's right," says Winnie, overhearing. "Why, who knows? The world is getting so small we just might be having terrorists right here in Libertyburg soon." She deftly slices a thin strip of pound cake for herself.

But Jacob's mind wanders from such conversations, even when they are about the upcoming screening of the old family movies he has restored, spliced together, and transferred to videotape for the occasion. Everyone is excited about it. They want to ask him who is in the movie, how far back it goes, how he restored those old things anyway.

Virginia's older brother, Harold, corners him at the picnic table, doctoring a hot dog with squeeze-on mustard. He wants to know if there are any pictures of him with his veterans' association. Didn't Chester take movies of a meeting back in '47, one where he gave a speech, he asks. Seems like he remembers a time when Chester showed up in Millsdale with that big old bulky camera . . .

But Jacob does not remember seeing a film of it. He brushes cake crumbs from his hands, wads his paper napkin into a ball, and shrugs apologetically. It is hard for him to carry on conversations with Harold. Or, for that matter, with any of Sheridan's relatives today.

Instead, he sees ghosts everywhere, faces older than those of the actors and actresses in the home movies, now neatly condensed into the single video cassette that he has brought to this reunion, tucked into a pocket of his backpack. It is an eerie feeling, seeing these ghosts. He shivers slightly at the memories, the movies, he feels he is walking among.

A line of dogwood trees at the far edge of the park floats like pink and white clouds against the horizon. Jacob imagines that he could watch them float away into the sky, as changeable as these faces at the reunion, as ephemeral as the films of how they once wanted to be remembered.

It is a time tunnel, he decides, but he is unsure whether he has traveled backward or forward. A light wind stirs the wisteria vine that is climbing a blighted oak tree and sends its sweet fragrance across the fields. The oak leaves are unseasonably brown, as if two seasons are present.

Time itself is out of focus.

Amanda's oldest son, Nathan, saunters up and removes the Walkman earphones from his head, where they have circled his baseball cap. The tinny sound of his favorite punk band, So Cool You're Dead, wafts out of the earphones while he tries to pump Jacob casually about what it's like to be a film editor in Hollywood. Does he know anyone famous out there, he asks, any movie stars? Or, better yet, any rock musicians?

Jacob smiles and begins to tell Nathan about working on a video project of Jonathan Demme, a fairly well known movie director.

Nathan stares at him with a blank look, and Jacob pauses. "Well, I guess not," he says.

For years, Jacob had been looking forward to having a long talk with Nathan's father, Paul. He has had only passing conversations with him at these family reunions. Paul usually rounds up teams and then spends the entire time on the softball diamond or the volleyball court, trying to escape the family, or so Jacob suspects. Paul is the only other northerner in the family, and he had felt that he would have an instant source of camaraderie in him. But now he feels a stronger bond to the faces suddenly animated from the old movies than he thinks he could possibly feel to Paul.

Across the lawn, he sees Virginia chattering to Rudy Murphy, her hands clasped behind her back. Rudy is "part of the family," Chester insists, and he always invites him to the yearly gatherings. Now Virginia pats her hair with one hand and gestures with the other, looking up at Rudy with her chin tilted down. Rudy's beer is halfway to his mouth, and he is trying to say something in return, trying to catch a space between her words to respond. Finally he just nods and takes a deep sip of his beer without once taking his eyes from her face.

At the picnic table, Winnie balances Amanda and Paul's younger son, Matthew, on one hip while she talks to Lucille Murphy. Lucille is ripping open a bag of barbecued potato chips and spilling the contents into a Tupperware bowl. She tears the corner with such a quick jerk that the chips scatter across the table. She cups her hands and scoops them up, trying to ignore the animated conversation that Virginia is having with her husband several feet away. Yes, she nods to Winnie, this is a lovely day for a picnic. They couldn't have asked for finer weather.

Winnie glances over at Virginia and tries to keep a frown from wrinkling her face. She turns back to Lucille with a comment on the dogwoods. How lovely they are, all white and pink. And look at this little great-nephew of hers, she says, setting the little boy down so he can explore a bit. What a nice surprise he was, she smiles, two years ago. Now if only Sheridan and Jacob would decide to have . . .

From a distance, Jacob catches Winnie's eye and smiles at her. "Hi, Ma," he mouths soundlessly. He gives her a wave and then strolls on.

But Winnie is calling to him, and he turns back, skirting a circle of children playing tag.

She and Lucille are beaming at him. "Everybody's talking about the movies," she tells Jacob. "I said it last night, but I just want to say it again. I'm mighty proud of you, Jacob, for putting these movies together." She turns to Lucille. "I sure didn't know what to think when Sheridan brought him home from California so many years ago, a New York boy she wanted to marry. To tell you the truth, it kind of scared me then. I didn't think she'd come back home." Now her eyes sparkle at Jacob. "But I couldn't have had a better son-in-law."

The ball from a volleyball game bounces toward them and hits Lucille's foot. Jacob bends down to scoop it up with his free hand and tosses it back over. On the volleyball court, Sheridan catches it and waves to him. He shakes his head when Paul beckons to him to come join the game.

"C'mon! We need somebody on this side." Paul is still waving.

Jacob salutes with his beer can, gives Winnie's shoulders a quick squeeze, and keeps walking.

He has spotted Ruby Ann across the lawn. Her grandmother, Chester's mother, is leaning on her arm, her cane in her other hand. Ruby Ann is easy to spot: her hair has been frizzed so that it stands out from her head like an orbit of curls, lightened to red now. It looks good, Ruby Ann told Sheridan teasingly, above her black-and-white priest's collar. The priesthood was the best rebellion her cousin could possibly have found, Sheridan told Jacob four years ago, when Ruby Ann had made her decision. Almost every other avenue of escape had been explored by her and Amanda years before. New York, Chicago, San Francisco—but, good heavens, the priesthood! How utterly brilliant, Sheridan said to him after Winnie had grimly told her the news. ("Becoming an Episcopalian wasn't bad enough!" Winnie had complained. "She had to go and be a priest!") It was as far from the suburbs of Mississippi, certainly, as she herself had traveled by going to acting school, and as far as even Amanda had gone by marrying a civil-rights worker from Boston. And besides, Sheridan had said, meditating, Ruby Ann had always had her quiet compassion, a strong enough sense of herself to care about other people. She'd be happy, Sheridan had said, and then sighed. At least she hoped she would be.

Now Ruby Ann is smiling politely at something her Grandmother Bloomer has just said. The older woman is holding out one of her Baptist Bible-study booklets, trying to get Ruby Ann to take it.

Before Jacob can reach her, Chester begins waving the group in to the community center. Inside, he has set up a rented video recorder and lines of folding chairs.

"C'mon inside, here, everybody." He claps his hands. "It's movie time, folks."

People begin filing in, leaving their games and conversations and food. Amanda stands at the door, handing out paper sacks of popcorn she and Virginia bagged that morning. As Grandmother Bloomer enters, she hands Amanda her half-filled cola can to toss in the trash behind her. "Co'cola!" She shakes her head. "It just doesn't pick you up like it used to. Are you too young to remember that, Virginia? Back when I was a girl, it really used to give you a lift."

Amanda gives her a knowing smile. "It had *cocaine* in it back then, that's why . . ."

Noisily rattling a sack of popcorn, Virginia slips it into her mother-in-law's hand. "There's a place right in front for you, where you can hear," she says and shoots Amanda a dark, silencing look.

Jacob joins the line, following along in the crowd, trying to be as anonymous as he can. Sheridan appears at his side and slips her hand into his. She brushes off dust from the volleyball court with her other hand.

"It'll be great," she says. "They'll love it"—as much to herself as to Jacob.

But that is not what concerns him. It is the face of Fred, still, that haunts him. He dreads seeing that face he has been restoring on video. He remembers the angle at which Fred approached Chester's camera, the way his face grew twisted and distorted as it neared the lens. His own father-in-law! It seems to Jacob now that Sheridan may have been right when she said that Fred was protecting his own privacy. Now it seems like a warning to them against violating that privacy. Jacob glances around at the crowd. What will they think about that scene? he wonders. Sheridan has told Winnie that it will be there, the face of her dead husband, but will that be enough caution? he worries. Winnie has seemed glad that Fred is there, but who knows how she will feel . . .

Inside, Chester is busily shuffling a few chairs, making sure there are enough to go around. He counts the people as they file in, pointing his middle finger at each one so that his hand has a rhythm of its own, like a metronome or the hand of a clock. Counting heads, he calls it.

Nathan strolls in beside his father and snickers when he sees the way his grandfather is aiming his finger. "Check out Grandpa," he says to Paul. "He's shooting the bird at everybody."

"Shape up, son. That's just how he's counting." Paul reaches over, removes Nathan's earphones from his head and hands them to him. "Watch your manners."

Chester has begun to count the chairs now. He is nervous. What will they think of his movies? he wonders. Will they be glad that he filmed them, all those years ago? Virginia's brother, Harold Moody, had thought his camera was a "damn fool idea" when he'd come home from the war back in '45, until he began to enjoy watching the movies. Will he still enjoy them so many years later? And what will the videotape look like, anyway? He wishes that Sheridan and Jacob had flown in yesterday in time for him to preview the darn thing. But so be it. He smiles politely at his son-in-law, Paul, remembering the wedding film that Rudy Murphy took. It's probably blurred as hell, he thinks, remembering. He poises the tip of his middle finger over the buttons on the machine, searching for the right one, confused.

But then Jacob is there to rescue him, working the proper buttons, making the picture jump onto the screen, and then freezing the image when Chester begins to talk to the crowd, telling them about the movies he began taking in 1942.

"Welcome, everybody," he says, shuffling his feet a bit, smiling. He has rehearsed this talk in the shower for the past three days, but the words still don't come easily. "You all know by now that we've got a special treat in store for you this evening. These are home movies I started taking in 1942. We had the first movie camera on the block, a big army camera I bought up in Memphis for Virginia's birthday—I won't say how old she was. But you can ask

Virginia." He smiles and nods at Virginia, sitting in the third row, an empty seat beside her that she has reserved with her purse for Chester.

Rudy Murphy calls out, a voice from the rear of the rows of chairs. "Why, she was just a child, right, Virginia? Back in '42?"

Virginia turns and laughs, acknowledging the humor, her small role in it. But she makes a mental note to remind Chester that he bought that first movie camera for his own birthday, not hers.

Chester continues. "Well, you might be here, yourself. My niece's husband, Jacob Stern"—Chester stretches out his arm to Jacob—"restored these for us for this occasion, and put them onto television. So we have him to thank. He's made it all possible."

Applause tinkles through the center, and Jacob's face dissolves into a smile at Chester.

"Stand up, Jake." Chester claps his hands together harder.

Jacob rises briefly and holds his beer can up in a salute to the crowd.

"So we have him to thank." Chester repeats himself when the applause fades. He looks down at the floor. Then he looks back at the crowd and folds his arms across his chest. "Well, there's nothing more to say except we're all stars tonight." He shoves his hands into the back pockets of his khaki shorts, revealing a dark circle of dampness beneath each sleeve of his polo shirt.

Oblivious to the chair that Virginia has saved for him two rows back, he takes a seat directly in front of the video screen. It is the biggest television that Chester has ever seen, and his heart leaps at the images that suddenly appear when Jacob rises from his chair to push the pause button again, unfreezing the frame.

In the second row, Sheridan's hand tightens in Jacob's when he returns. On her other side is Winnie, and she bends to her mother to whisper that these first movies are positively ancient, some old World War II parade scenes.

On the television screen, it is 1945. Amanda's little face is looking up to Virginia's, her mouth opening with some silent words, but Virginia gazes off, her attention held by something off the screen.

Laughter, punctuated by someone clapping her hands, rises from the back of the room.

"You look like a zombie, Mama." Amanda has stopped clapping her hands, and she leans forward, propping an arm against the back of Rudy Murphy's chair.

"Totally spaced." It is Nathan, leaning against the back wall.

"She looks like she's receiving divine inspiration." Ruby Ann laughs at her own joke.

But Virginia is not listening to the teasing of her two daughters and grandson. She is listening instead to the images on the television a few feet away from her. The look on her face now bears a remarkable resemblance to her expression on the screen, of more than forty years ago. On the screen, her older daughter's mouth moves again in silence, and her arm waves in a grainy, jerky movement. There is a tiny American flag in her hand.

"That's you, Mom?" Nathan has forgotten to chew his gum.

"Goodness gracious," Winnie's hand goes to her mouth. "I remember this."

Sheridan puts her hand on her mother's knee. "Were you there, Mama? I didn't see you in the footage."

Winnie just shakes her head, her eyes wide.

In a jerking movement, the scene shifts to a close-up of Virginia's face, and it pauses on her eyes. A glisten can still be seen there, even through the grainy texture of the television screen.

"Whoa, Chester! Look at that close-up. You were getting artsy on us there, huh?" Virginia's brother Harold calls out from a seat somewhere along the side.

But the picture jerks to another scene so fast that Chester cannot reply to his brother-in-law. It pulls him back to 1945 again, to a scene he has forgotten.

"Oh, this one's a riot," calls Sheridan. "There's some joker marching in this parade with a Confederate flag over his head."

"I betcha it was the Klan," Nathan cries from the back.

Marching across the screen are rows of soldiers, orderly and silent. There is an ominous presence to them, Chester thinks, in the graininess of the black-and-white street that unfolds before them. In the back row of marching men is the bold striped cross of a Confederate flag, moving as if a live presence. Then the camera seems to spin, and the orderliness is gone, lost in a confusion. A scuffle breaks out, and then the picture blurs.

Sheridan is watching her mother, not the screen. "Mama, what was it? Jacob and I couldn't tell."

Winnie takes her hand from her mouth, and a tiny smile nudges at her lips. "He looked just like Gregory Peck," she whispers. She is still looking at the screen.

"What?" Sheridan wrinkles her nose and laughs. "What are you talking about?"

But the screen has taken over again, absorbing Winnie's face, and then Sheridan's.

"Whoo-ee!" Harold howls at the sight of Virginia in her grass skirt. He nudges his wife and, in a loud whisper, says something about his sister's famous legs.

The tapping of Winnie's high heels echo through the building when she rises abruptly and bustles over to the air-conditioner in the window. She pulls down the hinged flap over the controls and efficiently fiddles with the knobs. The flap bangs shut when she taps back to her seat.

In the couple of seconds that the audience has glanced over to Winnie at the air-conditioner, the movie shifts from Virginia's legs to Chester and Virginia dancing. They whirl together, cheek to cheek, then spin out again. Then the television monitor flickers into rolling gray bars and another scene leaps into focus and then steadies. It is Virginia and Winnie together on a sofa. A Christmas tree is visible in the room.

"Christmas tree!" Matthew calls out from the rear of the room "Santa Claus!" He is standing up in Paul's lap, pointing a finger at the screen.

Chester clears his throat and calls out "Christmas. Must've been the early fifties."

On the screen, Winnie rises, sits again, and then rises again.

"Make up your mind, Winnie!" Rudy Murphy calls out.

Then the image changes so abruptly that Rudy's words still seem to hang in the air, like an inappropriately dubbed scene in a foreign movie.

Sheridan's hand reaches for her mother's.

In black and white, a swinging door brushes open. A leg emerges through it, and, almost beneath it, moves the tiny figure of Sheridan.

Then it is Fred. His body seems to ripple as Sheridan approaches him, and a bowl of popcorn explodes on the floor, sending kernels through the air like a cloud.

The light of the television is the only brightness in the darkening room. The shadows and the sudden silence of the audience have blended into one in the room, and the glow of the video screen is a bud of light. In the bud is Fred's face, growing. His eyes grow until they fill the screen, and then the palm of his hand swells toward the camera. Blackness closes in.

Someone in the back of the room coughs.

The darkness made by Fred's hand is longer than Sheridan remembers. She squeezes Winnie's hand.

Then Chester's mother shakes her head. She fans herself with a folded booklet. "That Fred." Her voice scrapes the words. "That Fred, bless his heart. You just never knew what he was a-goin to do next. But he was a brave boy, all dressed in his uniform."

"What's that, Mother Bloomer?" Virginia half turns, not taking her eyes from the screen. "I'm sorry, I couldn't hear you."

"I say, you never knew what Fred was a-going to do next." She lifts her neck to make the words louder. "Bless his heart."

From the back of the room, Rudy Murphy's voice rises again. "I'll tell you one thing. He sure did know how to make a joke. Yessir. Didn't he, though?"

Chester clears his throat and laughs. In the dim light he wipes beneath his eye with his thumb. "He could be a prankster, all right, when he wanted to be. But he sure didn't like my movie camera. That was no joke."

Winnie recrosses her legs, smooths her skirt across her lap, and raises her voice. "Well, Fred never was one to have his picture taken—not by anybody. He was just funny that way."

"But he sure did know how to make us laugh, didn't he?" It is Rudy Murphy again.

But the picture has moved on, and Fred is gone. A picture of a baseball game fills the screen, and applause rises from the audience.

"Chester, is that you pitching?" someone calls out from the back. A relief of laughter floods the room. "Somebody got a home run off you!"

Sheridan presses Winnie's hand again, and she edges a nervous look at her mother, afraid there will be tears in her eyes.

"Sheridan, honey, you're hurting my hand." Winnie pulls her hand away and shakes it, tilting her face up at the scenes of the game. "Dizzy Dean," she smiles. "The pride of Rinkin." The glow of the screen shines on her face. The flickering images absorb her, speeding by, demanding that the previous movies be forgotten in the rush of the new.

The noise of popcorn being crunched fills the silence, and to Sheridan it is the troubling sound of her family feasting on the movies themselves, digesting the images that hang briefly before them on the screen.

Sheridan shifts slightly in her seat and lets her eyes travel over the group. She suddenly feels isolated from them, at the artificiality of their laughter when her father's face appeared on the screen. They are the movie, she thinks, and what is on the screen is real. Are they even seeing the same images she and Jacob have been studying for five months now? she wonders. And if they do, maybe they are smarter than she is, she thinks. We are, after all, illusions not only to each other but to ourselves, acting out endless scripts, each of us at once the star, the author, and the audience—each in a separate play. So who knows? Maybe they are smart enough to laugh, to instantly rewrite the history here in these pictures so that there is continuity and happiness, so that they believe in themselves and in who they were. So that they believe in who they are, sitting here in this building, here in the spring of 1987.

The light outside slants through the window with the dusty pink of sunset. Since she has already virtually memorized the movies in front of her, Sheridan slips past Winnie and finds the door.

Outside, the air smells softly of magnolia and honeysuckle. She walks aimlessly, breathing the spring, feeling the grass beneath her feet. She reaches down to pull a dandelion from the ground, thinking about her family's laughter, about the home movies. Is that all we are anyway? she wonders, twirling the dandelion stem so that its pods float off into the air like feathery umbrellas. Is that all we are, fragments of light, of gesture and memory, thrown briefly on a screen? The dandelion stem slides from her fingers, and she clasps her hands behind her back. Wasn't there more?

There is something comforting here, outside, even in the fresh smell of the late spring. She strolls over to lean against a pine tree and watch the sun slide behind the far trees. From one of the tree branches hangs a tire swing that has grown still from the touch of the children who have just played there a few minutes before.

It is the permanence here that is comforting, a permanence that is almost palpable, she decides. It is all around her, even in that changing pink cloud, in that vanishing glint of gold in the sunset, in that blooming rose, that returning duck dipping in the pond. Fireflies have just begun to flash in the semidarkness around the swing, making a series of shifting constellations. There is a permanence here, she thinks again, even in the transience, like those ephemeral silent movies inside. They are the stories we tell ourselves, she thinks, that we keep telling ourselves and each other until what really happened is lost, tangled in that web of tenuous tissue, of joy and pain, of endurance and endings, that is all that we will know . . . until the stories themselves—the stories that are told and retold—become what really happened and they are all we have left. It is as if the events have fallen away to reveal the timeless gesture and the enduring words, the continual making and remaking of their lives. And, most important of all, the enduring love they all had for each other, the force that propelled their stories. Yes, she thinks, of course there was more.

Sheridan closes her eyes and feels a cool spring breeze on her face. Behind a pine etched against the pink sky to the west, the sun is slipping down.

She opens her eyes when something brushes her cheek. It is Jacob's hand.

"Hi, hon," he says and bends down to kiss her hair, then draws her closer with his arm. "Are you okay?"

"Yeah, sure. I'm just enjoying the sunset."

They lean against each other, a part of the silence, breathing the smells on the wind.

Throughout the audience inside, bags of popcorn are being emptied and crumpled. Ruby Ann stretches out her sack to Grandmother Bloomer, who shakes her own half-full bag in response. Nathan digs into his sack, tossing entire handfuls of the white kernels into his mouth. His gum is stuck in a green wad beneath Amanda's chair. They feast there, through the films, in a celebration that consumes the images along with the corn.

When the last footage has rolled by in the blur that Amanda and Paul's wedding has become, the crowd mills in small groups that begin to spill out the door.

Sheridan glances up when she hears Virginia's voice calling them. She turns and sees her aunt silhouetted against the light in the door. She is waving to them.

"What are you two doing out there? Come on back in. You can do that sparking later. Chester's got a big surprise!"

Jacob wraps his arm around her shoulders and together they walk toward the yellow rectangle of the entrance hall. "It hasn't been so hard," says Sheridan, "coming back here. I'm glad they liked the movies." She smiles to herself in the dark. "And I don't feel so confused about myself this time . . . it's funny."

He squeezes her shoulders gently and glances down at her. "Yeah? How's that?"

"I'm the sum of my parts," she grins.

They rejoin the group, and Jacob is greeted like a celebrity. Some of them congratulate him and Chester, and Sheridan again has the feeling that her husband and uncle might have cooked a perfect meal together, turning the past into a repast.

Chester disappears into a back room, and Sheridan thinks he is too moved by the scene to stay around and socialize.

Instead, he emerges in a few seconds with a video camera. He pans it over the crowd, catching Rudy Murphy scratching at himself, recording Ruby Ann adjusting her sandal, casting his lens from wall to wall, looking like a fisherman swinging his net. Winnie chases Matthew as he toddles straight toward the camera, and Chester flaps his hand at her to wave them both back into the picture. Holding Matthew on one hip, Winnie eases back slowly until she is standing beside Virginia. Virginia stretches over and pulls at Harold's shirt sleeve, tugging him away from Lucille Murphy, into Chester's new movie. Harold folds his arms across his shirt and sways back and forth, nodding and smiling at the camera as he would treat a new acquaintance. Unknown to Harold, Chester instead is zooming in on Amanda and Paul as they wander up to join the group. Behind them is Nathan, who scowls at the camera and puts his earphones on his head, so that his private music will seal him off from silly adults.

Then Chester focuses on his mother as Ruby Ann helps her sit down and props her cane against the chair. The old woman points an arthritic finger at her son's camera. "You let me fiddle with that contraption next," she tells him. "Don't you go to hogging it."

Behind the camera, Chester nods. "Let me get you first, then you can have it." Grandmother Bloomer lifts her chin in a quiet dignity at the camera, recognizing that it is honoring her, now in her ninety-third year.

"Good, Mama," he says. He waves at Sheridan and Jacob, who are making faces at Amanda from their station against the wall. "Now y'all get in there too. Too bad you don't have your fire baton, Sheridan. And that sparkly majorette costume."

Sheridan laughs and picks up her grandmother's cane. "I outgrew that a long time ago, Uncle Chester. I have a new act now." She marches before the camera and flings the cane into the air, as if to toss it away forever. Just before it would have hit Virginia's head, she snatches it from the air and begins to dance a soft-shoe around it. Virginia ducks and reaches over to tug at Jacob's sleeve, pulling him into the film.

But Jacob feels trapped, suddenly. With the whirring of Chester's camera, he has become a character in someone else's movie, powerless to move a prop or rewrite the script. His fate, it seems to him in that moment, will be told in the tattered squares of celluloid or the blurred videotapes he has been editing. A feeling of near-panic pours through his glands, and he almost turns and walks away.

Then he notices Chester carefully rotating the lens for a long shot, sees the rings of perspiration beneath his armpits, watches him frown and smile simultaneously, worrying about his focus, delighting in his subjects. He sees Chester glancing briefly at the group of admiring relatives clustered over to one side, making sure they are still watching him: Chester the moviemaker, Chester the family historian, Chester the star.

Even the director is an actor. The thought percolates into Jacob's mind, growing until his panic is gone. The feeling of being trapped is all in his head anyway, he decides. Everyone, after all, will see something different when they watch him here later. They will find either answers or questions here, and it will have little to do with him at all.

Beside him, Sheridan dances lightly around the cane, her fingertip at the top of the crook. She salutes the camera before she presents the cane to Grandmother Bloomer with the flourish of a mime.

Then she curls her fingers into a circle before one eye and squints through it at her uncle, making her hand into an imaginary camera lens. With the other hand, she makes a cranking motion, pretending she is aiming an old-fashioned movie camera at Chester.

In an instant, the thought comes to Jacob: the power that they all have, the power of being the observer, the rememberer, that

Sheridan is showing her uncle now. He too, cups a hand to his eye like a lens and aims it at Chester. Then he opens his mouth in a silent call. It is for the camera, for the faces who will watch the video at future reunions.

Decades from now, Nathan's and Matthew's children will see two people—cousin Sheridan and her husband, they will be told, a funny guy, a film editor who worked out in Hollywood back in the 1980's—who are trying to remind them they are all making their own movies, inventing their own lives, even inventing their own interpretations of other people's lives. Even, Sheridan and Jacob are trying to say, those strange people they are watching on videotape. Like the two of them.

Matthew will tell his daughter that Jacob must have been demonstrating the kind of work he did in Hollywood. Nathan's two sons will be told that Sheridan was probably warning her great-grandfather that something was going wrong with his video camera.

But now, Jacob enjoys the soundlessness of his own voice on Chester's video, as if he has sent a call into a chasm, waiting for an uncertain echo.

"Oh, that's good. That's real good," Chester says, moving in for a close-up.